About the Author

JOHN BINGHAM—aka Lord Clanmorris, aka Michael Ward—was born in 1908 near York, England. The only son of the sixth Baron Clanmorris, he began his writing career as a journalist. Shortly before the outbreak of World War II, Bingham joined the Royal Engineers, and it was during a train ride through the countryside that he overheard a conversation in German between two people in his car. The couple were observing and taking notes on the location of military installations and possible munitions factories. Pretending to be German, Bingham spoke with them, obtaining their names and whereabouts they were staying, which he passed on to a friend in intelligence. He was soon recruited by MI5, where he worked with famed undercover agent Maxwell Knight, as well as David Cornwell (also known as author John Le Carré), and remained with MI5 in various capacities well into the 1970s.

John Bingham's first novel was *My Name Is Michael Sibley,* published in 1952; *Five Roundabouts to Heaven* followed in 1953. In the span of thirty years, while with MI5, Bingham wrote seventeen crime novels and thrillers, including *The Third Skin, Night's Black Agent, A Fragment of Fear,* and *I Love, I Kill.* Bingham died in 1988.

Also by John Bingham

John Bingham

My Name Is Michael Sibley

with an introduction by
John le Carré

SIMON & SCHUSTER PAPERBACKS
NEW YORK   LONDON   TORONTO   SYDNEY

Simon & Schuster Paperbacks
Rockefeller Center
1230 Avenue of the Americas
New York, NY 10020

First Simon & Schuster trade paperback edition July 2007
SIMON & SCHUSTER PAPERBACKS and colophon are registered trademarks
of Simon & Schuster, Inc.

For information about special discounts for bulk purchases,
please contact Simon & Schuster Special Sales at 1-800-456-6798
or business@simonandschuster.com.

Designed by Davina Mock-Maniscalco

Manufactured in the United States of America

10 9 8 7 6 5 4 3 2 1

Library of Congress Cataloging-in-Publication Data
Bingham, John, 1908–1988.
My name is Michael Sibley / John Bingham; with an introduction
by John Le Carré.—1st Simon & Schuster trade paperback ed.
p. cm.
I. Title.
PR6053.L283M9   2007
823'.914—dc22
2007010084

ISBN-13: 978-1-4165-4047-2
ISBN-10:   1-4165-4047-4

Introduction

BY JOHN LE CARRÉ

This novel comprises some of the best work of an extremely gifted and perhaps under-regarded British crime novelist, now dead, whom I would dearly like to have called my friend. And for a time, John and I were indeed close friends. We came from totally different worlds, worked together in perfect harmony in an operational section of MI5 for two years but parted a few years later, on John's side, on terms of bitter animosity. If John had been able to hate anyone for long, he would have hated me. That we had been friends and colleagues only added spleen. John had been my professional mentor. He had been one of two men who had gone into the making of my character George Smiley. Nobody who knew John and the work he was doing could have missed the description of Smiley in my first novel, *Call for the Dead*. "Short, fat and of a quiet disposition, he appeared to spend a lot of money on really bad clothes . . ."

John had introduced me to his agent, Peter Watt, and his British publisher, Victor Gollancz. John had encouraged me to write, and read the manuscript of my first novel. John, in other words, by every generous means available to him, had set me on course to become a writer. And I would have been happy to credit him with all this—if our service had allowed me to—and probably I would have dedicated a book to him and acknowledged my debt.

But John saw things quite differently. As far as he was concerned, I had repaid him by betraying everything outside his family that he held most dear in the world: his country, his Service, his colleagues, the bond he shared with his agents in the field, and by extension his own humanity. The fond apprentice had turned wrecker. In an angry foreword to his novel *The Double Agent* written three years after the publication of *The Spy Who Came in from the Cold,* John wrote as follows: "There are two schools of thought about our Intelligence Services. One school is convinced they are staffed by murderous, powerful, double-crossing cynics, the other that the taxpayer is supporting a collection of bumbling, broken-down layabouts. It is possible to think that both extremes of thought are the result of a mixture of unclear reasoning, ignorance and possibly political or temperamental wishful thinking."

No insider doubted that John was writing about me. Or that he was expressing an opinion widely shared by his contemporaries in the Service. He might of course have added that there was a third school of thought about our Intelligence Services, and that it was his own, and my crime was that I subscribed not merely to the two he mentions, but to the third also—his. John, if pressed, might also have conceded that, just as there was an anti-authoritarian rebel in *his* nature, so was there a patriotic civil servant in mine. And that the problem with secret services was the same problem that people have: they can be an awful lot of things at once, good and bad, competent, incompetent, one day indispensable, the next a hole in the head. I might also have pointed out to him that my experience of Cold War intelligence work had extended into fields of which he was fortunate to know nothing, since John had long been stuck in the groove of domestic counter-subversion, whereas I had been fortunate enough to obtain a glimpse of our foreign operations. John was sweetly unaware of the disastrous influence of James Jesus Angleton's spy mania upon the international intelligence community. He knew nothing of black operations at home or overseas. He knew nothing of the training and infiltration and deaths of uncounted armies of small spies against the communist menace. He knew precious little of conspiracy and even less of cock-up. He ran a perfected system all his own. He cherished his agents without the smallest thought of ever betraying them or exposing them to dangers they couldn't handle. But even if John *had* conceded all this, he would never have wanted to read, let alone write, about it.

As far as he was concerned, I was a literary defector who had dragged the good name of the Service through the mud. I had supped at King Arthur's table, then sawn its legs off. In those days I had to listen to a lot of that stuff, and read it in planted reviews. But when it came from John it never failed to hurt. No good my protesting I was engaged in a literary conceit. Or that anyone who knew the secret world as we did would be the first to recognize that I had invented a completely different one. Or that I had used the secret world as a theater to describe the overt world it affected to protect. As far as John—and many others too—was concerned claims of good intent were guff. I was a shit, consigned to the ranks of other shits like Compton McKenzie, Malcolm Muggeridge and J. C. Masterman, all of whom had betrayed the Service by writing about it. Thank God Bingham never lived to see David Shayler on television. On the other hand, I wish dearly that we could have had a conversation about him.

The irreconcilable differences between Bingham and myself may tell you a bit about the conflict of generations within the Service, and a bit about John. But I would not want you for a second to imagine that he was some kind of chauvinistic fuddy-duddy. Indeed, the older I get, the more often I wonder whether he was right and I was wrong. I mean by this that, ever since some PR whiz-kid sold the secret services the notion that they should present an image of openness, they have lost more and more credibility with the public. A secret service that sets out to be loved is off its head. And if my novels in the '60s and '70s in some way invited the opening of that door, then I wish somebody could have slammed it shut.

$$\sim\!\!\!\sim\!\!\!\sim$$

John was a quarter of a century older than I was. He was born into the Anglo-Irish aristocracy and married a Catholic woman of birth, a playwright. He had wandered around pre-war Europe, I expect— though no one says so—for British Intelligence. Certainly I made that assumption when I gave Smiley fragments of John's pre-war past. He spoke French and German though I never heard him do it, so I don't know how well. I know little of his childhood, but imagined that, quite unlike myself, he was born into a world of certainties that time eroded. When I came to write Smiley, I tried to give him the same faint air of loss that John carried around with him. Smiley, like John, I felt, was fighting to preserve a country that survived only in his head, and was clinging to standards long abandoned by the world around him. There was something quixotic as well as shrewd about John. Like Smiley, he was the perfect parish priest of the Old Faith. He was a superb listener. He was profoundly orthodox, but with a nice dash of heresy. He exuded stability and common sense and inspired his agents with his own gentle, old-fashioned zeal. His humanity was never put on. The best of his agents were women. He managed to see some of them almost every day of their operational lives. I could not for one second, then or now, have imagined John caught up in some devious game of bluff and counter-bluff that involved the cynical sacrifice of one of his precious agents. They were his adopted children, his little wives, his creations, his wards, his orphans. John had shared their lives with them, assuring them every day that what they were doing was absolutely vital to the nation's health. He had drunk them into near oblivion when the strains of their double life became intolerable to them. And he was back next morning with the coffee for their hangovers. In this, he was the pupil and stablemate of Maxwell Knight, another Pied Piper extraordinary of men and women looking for an unorthodox way to serve their country.

"Your wife will be spat on in the fish-queue," John told them. "Your kids will be persecuted at school. You'll be hated or at best distrusted by your neighbors as a fire-breathing Red. But the Service will be with you. We'll be walking at your side even when you can't see us." And they believed him—for as long as upstarts like le Carré didn't tell them otherwise.

But le Carré had seen more of the new verities than John had, and far fewer of the old ones. He had not fought John's war, he had never enjoyed the conviction that he was opposing pure evil, a rare privilege conferred by the 1939–45 war, but much harder to sustain in the war between capitalism and socialism, both gone off the rails. Le Carré had emerged not from the aristocracy but from a rootless childhood of chaos and larceny. And le Carré turned Bingham the preacher of certainties into Smiley the disciple of doubt. And I don't think John, if he ever fully decoded the references, would have thanked me one bit for that compliment.

So what on earth has all this to do with the book you are about to read? you ask. It is because in my sadness, and love of John, I wish you to do him justice, not just as a British patriot and supremely able intelligence officer, but as an intuitive scholar of human motive, which is what informed the writer in him. John was not only an intelligence technician but a former journalist. He understood and loved police work. As a dedicated custodian of society he cared passionately about the containment of evil. He wasn't interested in *who*dunnit. But as a master interrogator and explorer of human motive, he wanted to know *why*dunnit and whether justice was going to be served. John's country's enemies were John's enemies, whether they were Germans trying to spy on us, communists trying to undermine the fabric of bourgeois society, or our own criminals upsetting the decent order of Britain as he dreamed and loved it. An interrogator is nothing if he is not a master of many fictions, and John was all of that. Seated before his suspect, listening to the fluctuations of the suspect's voice as well as his words, watching

the body language and the tiny facial inflexions, the good interrogator is subconsciously trying on stories like clothes: would *this*
one fit him, or would that one fit him better? Is he this person or
that person—or another person altogether? All the time he is
plumbing the possibilities of the character before him.

Bingham wrote with the authority of an extraordinarily wide
experience of human beings in bizarre situations. As a novelist he
was held back in part by the sheer scale of the material he disposed
of and could never use, in part by the constraints quite properly
imposed on him by his service; but above all by his own innate
sense of "good form": a notion that died a little before he did.
What drove him was a love of the citadel he was protecting and a
visceral disdain for its enemies. What gave him his magic was something we look for in every writer, too often in vain: an absolute
command of the internal landscape of his characters, acutely ob-
served by a humane but wonderfully corrosive eye.

And John had one other quality that every agent runner
needs: great entertainment value. Now read on.

CHAPTER 1

Sometimes it had been hard work, but I had succeeded, and now indeed I was on top of the world. I had a good job, a market for my spare-time writing, a small private income, and I had Kate. I had her safely now, and she had me, and the future belonged to us to carve as we wished.

Some people can go through life alone, and they do not mind; in fact, they revel in their own self-sufficiency; others need a human refuge to whom they can fly in trouble, or simply somebody to whom they can return at night after the stresses of the day's work. Poor Ackersley, the assistant housemaster, had been like that, and Geoffries, the Lascar seaman, and so was Kate. Kate, so shy and sensitive, was the last person in the world to be by herself.

Yet it had fallen to her to spend a great deal of her life alone. There had been one brief and passionate interlude, I gathered, with a young man in one of the offices in which she had worked, and then there had been nothing; nothing and nobody until I came along, and I, who began by being sorry for her, ended by loving her. It was a story with a happy ending.

I hummed contentedly as I strolled along towards Harrington Gardens that lovely summer evening. I was in one of those moods when you are acutely conscious of the beauty of small, everyday things; I noted how the movement of a small cloud set the sunlight racing from a red chimney pot, down the house wall, and along the road, so that a stunted lilac tree and some laurel bushes suddenly shimmered with a new light, a country green, and the whole grey waste of stucco houses seemed to glow with warmth and friendliness. A ginger cat sat licking its paws on the doorsteps of a house, and looking up at a window I saw a girl on a stepladder hanging up a clean net curtain. As I passed, she looked out into the street and our eyes met, and she smiled; not coquettishly, but as if to show that she knew she looked rather funny perched on that ladder, but didn't care because it was such a lovely evening and so good to be alive. I continued on my way, and let myself into my digs with my key.

I intended staying in, that evening, to finish a short story, and had never felt better in my life or in finer trim for writing. As a professional writer, I knew that to wait for the right mood before beginning work means long periods of idleness and brief periods of writing; nevertheless, there are times when you have more zest for it than others, and I felt I was going to do well that evening. A few seconds after I had gone to my room, Ethel, the maid, who must have been listening for my return, knocked on the door.

She told me that two men who had not given their names had called during the afternoon and asked for me. On being told that I was not in, they said they would return about eight o'clock in the evening.

"Did they say what it was about?"

"No; they just said they hoped you would be in, as it was rather important."

"What did they look like?"

She shrugged her shoulders. "Just ordinary. One was middle-aged, and the other youngish."

I knew a couple of French correspondents with whom I some-times spent an evening, but I thought it unlikely that they would expect to find me in during the afternoon.

"Were they English, do you think?"

"Oh, yes; there was nothing funny about them."

"Well, I'll be in all this evening. Show them straight in when they arrive, eh?"

Upon reflection, I guessed that they were police officers. They would possibly want a few details about Prosset. More likely, the main purpose of their visit would be to tell me that I might have to appear as a witness at the inquest. I did not mind. Inquests held no terrors for me; I had attended hundreds as a newspaper reporter.

I shall never forget the shock I received when I opened the paper and read about the way Prosset had died.

There was not very much to read. Just a small paragraph say-ing that the body of a man identified as John Prosset, of Oxford Terrace, London, had been found in the burnt-out wreckage of a cottage at Ockleton, Sussex. The discovery had been made by a woman from the village who went three times a week to clean the cottage.

I put our local correspondent on the job within the hour, and by midday he was on the telephone to me. But he said that there was little he could add at the moment. According to the local po-lice, an empty whisky bottle and two or three beer bottles had been found near the body; and an inquest would be held. It was believed that he had been dead since about midnight.

"Did you go to the cottage yourself?" I asked.

"No, I didn't. I had another job on hand. It didn't seem worth it. He'd spent the weekend alone, and obviously got tight and set the house on fire. There's nothing in it, but I can go down there, if you like."

I told him not to go. Bitterly I regretted it later. Had he gone, things might have been so different. But the fact is, once the shock of Prosset's death was over, I saw nothing surprising in the corre-spondent's report. I knew he liked whisky.

I had seen the small heap of bottles by the back door as re-cently as Saturday, the day before Prosset was to die in the flames and smoke. I had gone down to stay with him on the Saturday. Previously, I had cancelled the visit; but then, in the end, I had gone all the same, and stayed until early Sunday morning, when I had driven back.

Had I stayed on, I reflected, the thing would probably never have happened. Prosset would still be alive and well.

I looked at them curiously when they arrived.

The Chief Detective Inspector was a broad-shouldered man, well above average height. I should say he was in his late forties. He had a round head, with closely cropped fair hair, receding slightly at the temples, and a brick-red face so keenly shaven that it seemed to radiate hygiene and good health. His features were regular, the nose and jaw clean-cut, but the lips were thin and the general impression you had was of a hard character in which sympathy, or indeed any of the more human emotions, had long since died. His eyes were not large, but were of a curious light brown, tawny colour, and he very rarely seemed to blink; it was as though he were afraid to allow his eyes to shut for even a fraction of a second, in case he missed something.

He did not impress me as the sort of man who would have a single one of those endearing little habits or whimsical sayings which are so often attributed to police officers. He wore a reasonably well-cut black pinstripe suit, a white shirt and hard collar, a dark-grey tie, black Homburg hat, and carried dark-brown gloves and a black briefcase.

The Detective Sergeant was a very different type.

He was slim and dark, aged about thirty-two, and when he spoke I noted that his voice still retained a slight Welsh lilt. His face was naturally sallow, the nose rather pronounced. His eyes were large and dark, and he wore a clipped military-style moustache. To offset his grey flannel suit he wore a green tie with a thin white stripe, which might have been the tie of some cricket club or school, and brown shoes; he, too, carried gloves.

I summed them up as a first-class working team: the Inspector, a competent, ruthless, police machine, thorough, well versed in the routine methods of crime detection, highly experienced. And the Sergeant, more mentally elastic, more subtle, helped by the imaginative strain in his Celtic blood.

When I had closed the door, the elder man said, "We are police officers." He introduced himself and his colleague, and as he did so he dipped his right hand into his jacket pocket, flashed a warrant card in a leather holder, and replaced it. The movement was slick and smooth, synchronizing with his words. You had the impression of a man who had spent so many years of his life doing the same thing that it had become second nature. You could see him, day after day, saying, "We are police officers," and following the words with that quick movement with the warrant card.

Probably nobody had ever had the courage to demand to examine it more closely. It occurred to me that for all practical purposes it might just as well have been a golf scorecard or a laundry list.

The Inspector said, "It's about the death of Mr. Prosset, sir."

"Sit down. What about a drink?"

The Inspector lowered himself carefully into my smaller armchair, placing his hat on the floor beside him. The Sergeant went and sat on the bed-settee by the wall. I thought they might refuse my offer, but they didn't.

"Thank you," said the Inspector. "Don't suppose a drop would do us any harm."

He looked across at the Sergeant, who said he didn't suppose it would either. The Sergeant smiled, showing good white teeth. I went across to a corner cupboard, and poured out three whiskies and sodas. While I did so, the Inspector opened his briefcase and brought out a buff-coloured folder containing papers. I handed them their drinks.

"Cheerio," I said.

"Good health, sir," said the Inspector.

"Cheers," murmured the Sergeant.

"It's just a routine call," went on the Inspector. "As I said, it's about the death of Mr. Prosset. You've seen it in the papers, I expect."

"Yes, I have. I thought you'd call."

"Why, sir?" The Inspector looked at me with his hard, pebble eyes.

"Because I knew him very well. Besides, I'm a newspaper reporter. I know a certain amount about police methods."

"Well, that's an interesting job, I expect, sir. Better paid than ours, too." He smiled ruefully, and looked across at the Sergeant.

"I don't suppose my pension will be as big as yours, even supposing I get one," I replied. We discussed our different jobs for a few moments. Police officers are easy to get on with. They meet all sorts and classes of people, and are good conversationalists.

"Well, Mr. Sibley," said the Inspector at length, "I don't suppose we'll keep you very long. I would just like you to tell us what you know of Mr. Prosset. I'd be very grateful, sir."

He spoke now in a polite, almost wheedling tone, in striking contrast to the natural harshness of his voice when he was not asking a favour.

"I'll tell you all I can."

I was on the point of adding that as a matter of fact I had seen Prosset the day before he died, and had been at Ockleton with him. In fact, I was looking forward in a mild sort of way to the look of interest on the Inspector's face when I should tell him. But although the words were on the tip of my tongue, the Inspector spoke again before I could get them out. I didn't mind. I thought they would sound even more dramatic a little later.

He said, "I don't suppose you mind if the Sergeant takes a few notes?"

"Of course not." I smiled at them. They smiled back.

"Well, let's start right at the beginning. That's always the easiest way, sir. What are your full names, Mr. Sibley?"

"Michael Sibley."

"And you are a journalist? What paper, if I may ask, just so we can give you a tinkle about anything during the daytime?"

I gave him my office address and a few more personal particulars.

"And how long have you known Mr. Prosset, sir?"

"About fifteen years, off and on. We were at school together."

"Were you, indeed? Well, we're in luck. I expect you know all about him."

"I know him fairly well," I said.

"Only fairly well? I see, sir. I thought you said when we came in that you knew him very well."

"Well, I did, in a way. I knew him very well at school. But I haven't seen an awful lot of him since then. Not an awful lot."

The Inspector nodded.

"Well, it's a pity in a way," he said.

"Why?"

"Well, sir, no offence of course, but you're a newspaper man—" He paused and looked at me hesitantly.

"You can talk off the record."

"Have I your word for that, sir?"

"You have. Definitely."

He looked at me again carefully. He seemed reassured by my promise.

"Well, then, between ourselves, sir, it's not quite as straightforward as people think."

"What do you mean? What isn't straightforward?"

"Well, Mr. Prosset had head injuries, for one thing."

"From falling beams or something?"

"No, sir. He was found in rather a protected position, as a matter of fact, with his head under the kitchen table. He hadn't been injured by beams or falling masonry. And there were traces of petrol. See what I mean? What's more, although the whisky bottle contained the remains of pure whisky, there was a good percentage of water in the remains in the beer bottles, sir. You might almost think they had been brought in from the pile at the back of the house to give the wrong idea."

I stared at him. "You mean he was killed? Murdered?"

"I didn't say that, sir. I just pointed out there were one or two odd features. That's all. I didn't say anything about murder, did I, Sergeant?"

The Sergeant looked up. "I didn't hear you, sir."

The Inspector thought for a moment. "Well, anyway, Mr. Sibley, that's neither here nor there. Let's get back. As I understand it, you didn't keep up the association much lately, is that it?"

"Not much," I said. "He went into a bank, and I went up to Palesby on the *Gazette*. We drifted apart a good deal, though we kept in touch by letter from time to time. Of course, after I came down to London, last year, I saw a bit more of him. In recent months, that is. Now and again."

In spite of the careful official attitude of the Inspector, I saw clearly that this was a murder case. Though he might pretend formally that there were only one or two odd features which might easily be cleared up, it was obvious that he thought quite differently. I felt overwhelmed by the news, and inevitably found myself groping in my mind for some pointer as to who could have done it. I found none. It seemed that it could only have been some tramp or burglar in search of easy money; and I cursed myself for not sending the correspondent down to Ockleton itself. On the spot, he might well have picked up some hint that more was afoot than a mere inquiry into an accidental death. Now, after giving my word in the matter, I could do nothing further, at any rate for the time being. I was tied hand and foot.

I heard the Sergeant's pencil travelling over the paper, and presumed he was taking a shorthand note. The Inspector said nothing. He seemed to be waiting for me to continue.

"He left the bank, of course. I think he was disappointed at not being sent out East. He had always set his heart on it. I think that is why he left. He went into business with a man called Herbert Day, as I expect you know, Inspector. Something to do with buying up bankrupt stock and stuff, and I believe they also did some importing from abroad."

The Inspector sat with his tawny eyes fixed on my face; he had a habit, which I found disconcerting, of sitting perfectly still and saying nothing, not even "I see," or "Yes." It was as though he was hardly listening to my words. I have never been a fluent talker, and if I find that my audience is not friendly or receptive I am not at my best.

I continued, rather lamely, with a few more details about

Prosset, floundered once or twice and corrected myself; this annoyed me, because I was telling the truth as far as I knew it.

The Inspector turned over one or two pages in his file. Once again, it was on the tip of my tongue to tell him I had been down at Ockleton, but now a new picture was developing in my mind, and I wasn't at all sure I would enjoy the look of suspicious interest which would inevitably flash across his face when I told him I had been with Prosset so shortly before his death. Moreover, I was trying to sort something out, to think quickly between questions, while still talking, and that is not so easy in practice.

The Inspector looked up from his file and said, "What about this Mr. Herbert Day, sir? His partner, I mean. Know anything of him?"

"I only met him twice. Once, many years ago, before I went to Palesby. We had some drinks one evening. He, Prosset and I, and a few others. I believe he was something to do with the Stock Exchange at that time. The other time was a few weeks ago, when I saw him for a few seconds only in Prosset's car."

The Inspector made no comment. After a moment, he put a few questions about Prosset's family in Ireland, which I answered as best I could. Then, after referring once more briefly to his file, he suddenly said, "I would like to ask you one rather confidential question, sir, just between ourselves, since you were Mr. Prosset's pal. What impression did you form of this Mr. Day?"

"I didn't much care for him personally."

"Why not, Mr. Sibley?"

"There's no particular reason. Some people one likes instinctively, and others one doesn't. That's all, really. But I shouldn't say he was the type to have the courage to do a murder, if that's what's on your mind."

The Inspector looked at me reflectively. He said, "There's nothing on my mind at all, sir. I was just asking, that's all. Do you know any other friends of his in London—or anywhere else, if it comes to that?"

I shook my head. "I'm afraid not."

"Nobody at all?"

I thought then of the party in the public house before I went to Palesby. "Well, I once met a girl he was quite keen on, called Margaret Dawson."

The Sergeant raised his head. "Did you say Dawson, sir, or Lawson?"

"Dawson. But she's married now, to some theatrical producer. I don't know his name."

"And you never saw him with anybody else—recently, I mean?"

"No. At least—"

"Yes?" The Inspector paused in the act of lighting his pipe.

"Well, I once saw him with a man in a public house in Chelsea, but I don't know who he was. He looked like a foreigner, but I may be mistaken. And I know he knew one or two people near Ockleton, where his cottage was, but I never met them. He said they had interests in the import side of the business. He used to go over and visit them. He never invited them to the cottage when I was there, because he said they were bores."

"When did you last see Mr. Prosset, sir?" asked the Sergeant. I looked across at him. He was absent-mindedly tapping his teeth with the end of his pencil. It is difficult to explain why I replied as I did.

Perhaps it was due to my upbringing, which was hardly calculated to encourage that toughness of character which enables a person to face boldly a challenge when it arises and take the straight, if difficult, path. I had largely overcome certain weaknesses since I left my Aunt Edith, but now and again, in some sudden and unfortunate predicament, they would reassert themselves; it is not easy to eradicate the blemishes of early youth, especially such as may be bred into the blood and nurtured in favourable soil. Possibly thrown off my balance by the revelation that Prosset's death had not been accidental, I tossed aside the cool, analytical training learnt in the previous ten years, and lied like a sneak thief caught in compromising circumstances. The struggle satisfactorily to solve the problem I knew would present itself, to solve it between questions and answers, had been lost, and the Sergeant's question found me still undecided.

But now I had to decide in a split second. I had a quick mental picture of driving down to Ockleton, on the Sussex coast, arriving through deserted lanes in the evening, staying with Prosset, driving back, again through deserted lanes, early the following morning. I recalled the local correspondent's words: "He spent the weekend alone." I took the easy way out. The temptation to have done with the whole thing presented itself, and I fell. In the flash of time in which I had to decide, I decided not to face up to matters. It was perhaps moral inertia more than weakness.

"When did I last see him?" I replied, and was surprised at the smoothness of my tone. "About ten days ago. The weekend before last. I stayed with him at the cottage with my fiancée."

The Sergeant nodded and made a note. "You're engaged, are you, sir?"

I told him I hoped to be married in two months' time. The Inspector made some joke about marriage. We all laughed. I felt relieved. The crisis was over. It had been easy.

"What's your fiancée's name, sir?" asked the Inspector in his strong, hard voice.

"Kate Marsden," I replied. "Why?"

"Did she know Mr. Prosset?"

"Very slightly, that's all."

"I was just wondering if she would know anything; any other friends of Mr. Prosset, for instance. That's all."

I gave him her address, though I assured him that she knew no more than I did. I felt pretty certain that was true.

"Just one more question. Have you any ideas at all, Mr. Sibley, about this case? Any theory, perhaps, which you think we might look into? It's not often we ask a question like that, but your position is rather a special one."

"How do you mean?" I asked.

"Well, after all, he was your friend, wasn't he?"

"He was, yes. He was a very good friend of mine, but at the moment I don't know what to suggest."

The Inspector swallowed the rest of his whisky, put the file back in the briefcase, and stood up.

"All right, Mr. Sibley," he said. "Let's leave it at that for the moment. I'm very much obliged to you."

The Sergeant shut his notebook and stood up as well. We shook hands, and I saw them to the front door. On the steps the Inspector said: "If you think of anything else about Mr. Prosset, perhaps you'll be good enough to give us a buzz on the phone?"

"With pleasure," I said.

I could not help smiling as I watched them walk away. There was so much more, in actual fact, which I could have told him. But I could not have told him then, in the course of that short talk, and indeed I doubted if he would ever really understand. On second thought, I decided he certainly would not; not the Inspector, with his hard eyes, so strong and down to earth and unimaginative.

It would have needed a better talker than I to have been able to explain the position to the Inspector that evening. Even I myself sometimes find it hard to understand the story of John Prosset and Michael Sibley.

CHAPTER 2

I cannot say accurately at which particular point I should have broken off our acquaintanceship, or even whether it was possible for me, or for any normally polite individual, to have done so.

You have to have a good cause, a terrible row about something, before you can abruptly terminate an association with a man whom you have known for years; and Prosset had a devastating ability for preventing a row from properly developing. The way he did it was to assume an attitude of amused tolerance directly he saw that you were becoming annoyed. He would look at you with his slightly mocking blue eyes, and stroke his raven-black hair, and his cigarette used to bob up and down between his lips as he spoke, and before you realized it you would find yourself in a position where if you became angry you would, compared to Prosset, merely look silly and ineffectual. You can't have a row with a man who at the critical moment just laughs at you, however jeeringly he may do it.

I tried it once or twice at school, but soon gave up.

There were three of us who did everything together at school: John Prosset, David Trevelyan, and myself. When our schooldays were finished, Trevelyan went and buried himself on his father's farm in Cornwall; he rarely answered letters. But somehow, over the years, Prosset and I kept in touch. It was due to no wish of mine.

It was through David that I got to know Prosset. At our particular school the boarders lived in half a dozen Houses, widely scattered around the main college buildings. There were about fifty or sixty boys in each House. But sometimes, if a House was full, they would lodge a boy out in what they called a "waiting house," which was little more than a large private house run by one of the masters, where six or seven boys, or more, would spend anything from one term to a year until they could transfer to the regular House for which their names had been put down.

David Trevelyan and I were in Bailey's Waiting House; in fact, David had been there one term already when I arrived as a new boy. Unlike Prosset, who was perfectly proportioned, David Trevelyan was a comfortably chubby, medium-sized boy; he, too, had very black hair; and big lustrous brown eyes, rather thick red lips, and fine white teeth. I can see him now, practising with his flute, his eyes fixed on the horizon as he went up and down the scale, his thick lips moulded over the instrument. Nobody ever knew why he learnt to play the flute. When asked, he simply said, well, because he liked it; which is a good enough reason.

I deliberately cultivated David's friendship. Firstly, because apart from myself he was the most junior boy in the House, so that I naturally went to him for advice about the incredibly numerous complications which beset the life of every new boy at a public school; and secondly, because I liked the look of him. I think the attraction was at first somewhat one-sided. I was not very much to look at; I was very ordinary indeed, and still am, if it comes to that. I had mouse-coloured hair, wore spectacles, and had a rather pasty complexion. But I was of medium build, and although not outstandingly strong I was certainly no weakling in a tussle.

David was on what they called the Languages and Maths side of the school, and I was on the Classical. Prosset was in David's form, and that was how they became friendly. They used to eat their buns together in the morning break, and help each other with last-minute adjustments to their "prep." We were all three destined for Buckley's House, but Prosset had already gone there direct.

Thus the position was that both Prosset and I were friendly with David, but beyond a casual meeting here and there we did not yet know each other. Later, when David and I went to Buckley's, we three linked up.

Long after, when we had become thoroughly familiar, they both told me how Prosset used to ask David Trevelyan why he walked to and from college with "that awful tick, Sibley." It was regarded as a good joke, which I was supposed to find very amusing. I was always one to laugh when people were expected to laugh, so I would join in the mirth then.

So there we were, John Prosset, David Trevelyan, and I.

That is how it began, and that is how it stayed for nearly four long years: Prosset, Trevelyan, and Sibley. We were not so much individuals, at first, as a unit. We walked up to college together, and we walked back together. We went up to the tuck shop together, and ate poached eggs on toast together. We lent each other sixpences and shillings, shared the contents of our tuck boxes, schemed to avoid the little troubles which lie in store for small boys at public schools. If one got into a fight, the other two would come to the rescue. As term followed term, and we came to be regarded by other boys as identities rather than as just three small nondescript boys, our unity remained and indeed became famous.

We were secretly rather envied. Many people would have liked to have been in my shoes, bound by the ties of friendship to Trevelyan and Prosset, for Prosset, with his rather pronounced nose and chin and his challenging eyes, was well liked and respected, not only by other boys, but by masters, especially games masters. At first he was tried out for the Colts Fifteen, and played for them and did well; and in the end he played for the college side, not brilliantly, but boldly and with intelligence and tenacity. David Trevelyan and I basked in reflected limelight.

Life was good, on the whole. We had made a niche, and we were not lonely as other boys were sometimes lonely who had no close friends. We were a small, compact gang, and if Prosset was the acknowledged leader, we fell in with his plans readily enough. We had security in the jungle of school life, and that is a very important thing indeed.

Even in the light of what later happened, I must confess that looking back on the first year or two of the Prosset–Trevelyan–Sibley combine we had many good times together.

Whitsun was the great time of the year for us, for on the Tuesday after Whitsun the school was virtually set free to do exactly what it liked. It was started as a bold experiment, and it worked. All bounds were abolished. We could roam over the whole county, on foot, on bicycles, even by train if we wished. So long as we did nothing illegal and were back by 9 p.m., we could regard ourselves as adults.

We three used to hire bicycles and cycle through the countryside, exploring, turning off where we wished, stopping by the Avon for a bathe, going into pubs for a glass of cider, for as yet we disliked the taste of beer, and eating stupendously. It is inevitable that all those Whitsun outings are in retrospect bathed in sunshine.

Once, in a lonely country lane, we passed a beautiful girl cycling in the opposite direction. She was coolly dressed, and blonde and serene; she made our day for us. We goggled openly as she went by, a girl of about twenty-two who to this day does not know that three young fellows aged sixteen, in grey flannels and blazers, fell deeply in love with her after only seeing her for about ten seconds.

For the rest of the day we discussed her off and on, and I for one wove stories around her. She was obviously the daughter of a retired Indian colonel, living a quiet life in some old-world manor, tending her fowls and pigeons and arranging flowers in the house. I imagined her getting into some sort of danger on a horse. Gallant Michael Sibley would leap at its head as it thundered by, bring it to a halt and catch the fainting angel in his arms; to be rewarded with a warm and lingering kiss, two soft arms around his neck, and vows of eternal gratitude. Later, of course, we would get married.

I was rather inclined to indulge in these romantic fantasies, and from the way we occasionally talked I see no reason to suppose that the others did not have similar dreams. These dreams were always delightfully pure, terminating in soft arms and kisses, and nothing more.

We graduated from the Junior Common Room to the Senior Common Room, and from the Senior Common, after agonies of waiting and calculating when it would be our turn, we were allotted each his own study. A crude enough affair, little bigger than a closet, but a place where you could have a table, a chair, a divan, usually made of wooden boxes covered with cushions and a bedcover, a bookshelf and cupboard, and a patch of carpet.

But it was your own place, where you could read or work by yourself, or play the gramophone, or brew hot drinks. When you had a study you felt you had arrived. You were treated with gravest respect by the members of the Junior and Senior Common Rooms; you were even treated in a dignified manner by the House prefects and, highly important, it was an unwritten rule that no study-holder should be beaten by the prefects.

You were a bit of a dog when you were a study-owner. If you were any good at all at games, life became even better. I wasn't too bad. I had my House football colours, and was quite good at running, and was likely to end up rowing in the House boat.

I had bought the contents of my study lock, stock and barrel from the previous owner. Prosset, Trevelyan and I were always in and out of each other's studies. The very first time I went into it, eager and filled with a delicious sense of anticipation, I stopped abruptly in the doorway.

Prosset was there, sitting in my chair, thumbing through a book. He immediately asked me why I had bought the contents from the previous owner. The curtains, he considered, were drab, the chair was inclined to sag, the cushions were worn; the whole place looked a bit cheap and tawdry. Why had I not brought stuff from home, like he had done?

Life normally became quite civilized when you had a study: the only trouble was that I had begun to hate Prosset.

Perhaps I should say more accurately that it was about this time that I first realized that I hated him. I suppose the feeling had been gradually growing in my subconscious mind for a long time, because normally you don't suddenly hate somebody whom you have been friendly with for a considerable period; not deeply, as I hated Prosset. Doubtless I had refused to admit that the feeling was there, or had fought it back. After all, it seemed so unreasonable; we three had many good times together, and Prosset was not always dominating.

I think now that one of the incidents which played an important part occurred when on one occasion several of us—Prosset included—were travelling back to school in the same railway compartment. The others were chattering away about the holidays and what they had done and where they had been, the shows they had seen, and the parties and dances they had attended. I wasn't joining in, because it so happened that during those particular holidays I had not done anything very interesting. Among the few virtues I possess—and in view of later events they must be counted few indeed—is an inability to elaborate incidents to show myself in a good light. If I relate some conversation in which I have taken part, I cannot even to this day alter the context to include smart replies I would have made had I thought of them in time.

So I sat and listened, and when I was not listening I gazed out of the window into the gathering dusk. Opposite me, Prosset was talking to Collet, the son of a rich Yorkshire mine owner. The train drew into a station, and a man came along the platform wheeling a trolley with newspapers, magazines, chocolates, sweets, and cigarettes on it, for this was only a few years after the First World War and such commodities were common. I let down the window and bought a couple of bars of nut milk chocolate; one or two others followed my example, and we settled back into our seats and waited for the train to start. Then it happened. Prosset and Collet were talking about their tailors.

"My man charged me six and a half for this," said Collet,

brushing some ash off his waistcoat, for we smoked like furnaces going back to school.

"I paid eight," said Prosset, "but that included an extra pair of trousers."

"What about dinner jackets?"

Prosset hesitated. I guessed he hadn't got one.

"Ten," he said briefly. Collet nodded. He looked at me. I could see him looking me up and down. Prosset followed suit. I knew what they were thinking. They had no need to tell me. I saw the words forming themselves in Prosset's mind long before he spoke them, though I didn't expect him to be so accurate.

He said, in the lull in the conversation, in the lazy, arrogant drawl he sometimes adopted:

"What about yours, Mike? Three guineas ready-made?"

I nodded. Somebody sniggered.

"Poor old Mike," said Prosset.

There was an awkward silence. I blushed scarlet and stared out on to the platform. The palms of my hands were damp and I was pressing my nails into them. The rough, hard-wearing tweed was chafing my neck. I could feel the skimped trousers clinging to my legs. The train drew out of the station and gathered speed. I gazed out of the window, ashamed and filled with bitterness against Prosset.

———

Although I had secretly begun to hate Prosset, we still did everything together, Prosset, Trevelyan and I. We were still united, and therefore a force to be reckoned with in the House, though none of us was ever a prefect. I can see why Prosset was so popular and treated with respect. It was not only that he was well built and clean-looking, whereas I was bespectacled and pasty, it was also due to his high spirits; his energy and courage, too. Nobody ever challenged him in vain. Combat was the breath of life to him. Not merely physical combat, though when he was fighting or playing games he did it to the last ounce of his strength, but verbal tussles as well.

We were all three of about the same seniority in the school, so we always sat together at the long dining tables; and if Prosset could find an excuse for an argument he would. He loved it. He would take anybody up on anything, challenge any statement for the sheer pleasure of the fight; and if all else failed he would pick an argument with me. If I declined the challenge, he would taunt me until I was stung to reply. Although he was not a bully physically, he was certainly one verbally. He was not content to get his man down; he had to trample in his face as well. Sometimes he would insist on an apology.

"So you were wrong, weren't you?" he would say.

"Oh, all right, all right, I was wrong, then, if you like."

"Well, apologize, then."

"Why should I?"

"Because you were wrong. Go on, apologize."

"I don't see why I should."

"You made a wrong statement. I have proved it wrong. Well, apologize for making it, go on."

"I'm damned if I will. Bread, please."

"Why should I pass the bread?"

"Why shouldn't you?"

"Why shouldn't you apologize and admit you were wrong?"

"I've admitted I was wrong."

"Well, go on—apologize."

"Oh, all right, all right, I apologize. Bread, please."

He was gay and had humour of a sort, and I think he often domineered, not out of malice, but for the fun of the game. But it made it no easier to bear. He seemed so heartless.

On one occasion only, Prosset and I were united on an emotional issue. It was before we got our studies. Ackersley, the assistant housemaster, was the cause of it, a man clearly destined to be one of the world's failures; he was a gentle, middle-aged man with a passion for fly-fishing which he could not afford to indulge, and he would listen avidly to the accounts boys told of the fine fishing they had had, and sigh, and say such fishing was not meant for poor schoolmasters.

In appearance, he was of medium height and slim. He had a

lean face and a long nose, and was afflicted with one of those blue-black jowls and the very red lips which sometimes go with them. He wore gold-rimmed spectacles, and his voice had that soft, bottled-up quality which you sometimes come across. He had neither a voice nor an appearance to inspire respect in boys, and he got none. It was all rather painful, really, and some of us even pitied him, but not many.

When he took "prep" in the evenings, instead of the deep hush normally required on such occasions, the Common Room buzzed and hummed like the stalls on the first night of a new play; until at least even Ackersley felt he had to do something. He would try to raise his voice above the din to still it, and all would be quiet for about five minutes. Then the murmuring, gradually increasing in volume, would begin all over again. It was hopeless.

When he supervised supper last thing at night the air would be filled with pellets of bread as the boys at the three long tables happily pelted each other. Now and again, for a lark, a group of boys by a combined effort would raise their long table almost above their heads. Ackersley would usually pretend not to see. He would keep his eyes glued to the Bible, as though he were reading the text which preceded the evening prayers. It seemed to me that the House mocked and oppressed him in some such way as Prosset did me; I felt that in a measure we were fellow sufferers; I understood how he felt in the face of such mockery: ineffectual, almost tearfully ineffectual. I guessed from the way he occasionally mentioned Mrs. Ackersley, that when he returned home to his lodgings and his wife he found in her a refuge and a balm which he could find nowhere else.

One evening the Head House Prefect was taking "prep," which meant that there was a very deep hush indeed, and no nonsense at all. It was a beautiful summer's evening, very light and still, so that you could hear the birds twittering outside. I was in one of the back rows of desks, drowsing over a geometry problem, and apart from the birds there was no sound except the occasional noise of a desk being quietly opened and shut, or of the leaves of a book being turned, or of a hand brushing paper clean after rubbing something out.

Suddenly one of the other prefects came into the room and whispered something to the Head Prefect. He got up quickly and left the dais and went out of the room for a minute or two. Whereupon, starting at the front row of desks and working back to me, increasing in volume as it approached, came a swift sound like the hiss of the sea on shingle. Each boy as he received the news turned round and passed it eagerly to the row behind; sometimes their eyes were shining with delight which boys have when they can impart staggering news; sometimes their faces were flushed and startled: "Ackers is dead! Ackers has shot himself! Ackers's wife died! Ackers has committed suicide!"

Then the Head Prefect came back and called for silence. He said nothing. Possibly some of us remembered how Ackersley's life had been made a misery. I can't help thinking now that if we had not tortured him so much, if his school hours had not been such a misery, he might have found strength to carry on. As it was, he had not the strength. He did not know where he could find safety from his thoughts at night. His refuge was gone. Only the cruelties, the frustration, the desperate feeling of being ineffectual, unwanted, a comic-looking failure, remained. There was nothing else, I suppose. I think we killed Ackers, taking a broad view of it all, as surely as if we had ourselves pressed the trigger of the revolver he used, only we were not so humane.

When "prep" was over, the House at once broke up into small groups of wildly chattering boys. The noise, the speculations, the rumours drove me from the Common Room. I walked down the long stone corridor, now growing dark, into the spacious quiet of the gymnasium. I thought I was alone until, in the half-light, I saw Prosset, hands in trouser pockets, looking silently out of one of the long windows. He turned round and looked at me as I crossed the floor, and then went on staring out into the twilight.

I said, "I got fed up with all the excitement."

He nodded. "Morbid lot of swine. They make me sick."

We exchanged one or two further comments in low tones; then the supper bell rang. Years later, when the climax came between Prosset and myself, I remembered this incident, but by then it was too late; there were too many other complications.

Thinking back along the trail of the years, I do not think he actively liked me at school, but rather that he liked having me around. I was a good butt for his boisterous humour, in addition to providing an outlet for his mental vigour. He would come tiptoeing into my study, where I sat with my back to the door, and suddenly sweep three or four books off my desk on to the floor, and laugh, and when I bent down to pick them up he would jerk the chair away from under me; or if I was gazing out of the window, dreaming, chin in hand, he would suddenly knock my elbow away; or creep up behind and aim a blow with his hand, directed so that it just skimmed the top of my head. Sometimes he would start a friendly tussle with me, and when I took my spectacles off as I had to, he would grab them and dash off and hide them. And, of course, he criticized me unmercifully whenever the chance occurred.

His relationship with David Trevelyan was different. The Cornishman had an agile brain and quick tongue. Prosset never clashed with David and David never provoked him. There was a tacit understanding that they should respect each other, and sharpen their wits when necessary on me. As a result, David rarely sided with me; he was on the side of the big battalions.

I was the mascot of the team; not even that: I was the tame buffoon; and like the court fool I was well fed, had my just share of everything, and was duly protected against unfair aggression. Like the king's jester, too, unsuspected by everybody I was often extremely unhappy.

It got to the stage where I used to look forward to the occasional days when Prosset might be away from the dining-room table playing an away match for the Second Fifteen, and later, for the First Fifteen. Once, when he was in bed for a week with a touch of influenza, the lightening of the oppressive atmosphere which pressed down so heavily upon me was like a glimpse of sunshine on a heavy day. Although I did not wish him to die, at that stage in our relationship, I was certainly sorry that he recovered so quickly.

But nobody knew of all this. Everybody thought I was very lucky to be able to go about with Prosset and Trevelyan.

Perhaps I should have broken away from them at this point; I say them, because David would certainly have stayed with Prosset. I suppose I could have found some other chap to go around with. There was the studious Willet, a little thing who looked like a white slug; and Banks, red-headed and so temperamental that he rarely kept friends for long; or Wilson, known as "Oiler" Wilson, because he had a greasy, fawning smile; and several others of the rag, tag and bobtail, the residue, the boys who were not popular, the floating population, the friendless and the outcasts.

But on what grounds?

Having gone through three-quarters of our school career together, what reason could I give for suddenly wishing to split the partnership? I couldn't just say: "Because I want to." Prosset would not take that for an answer. I imagined the way the conversation would go:

"Next term I think I'll walk with Wilson or somebody, Prosset. No offence or anything."

A blank silence while he gazed at me amazed.

"But why, old man? What's up with you?"

"Nothing's up with me. I just want to, that's all."

"But why? There must be some reason."

"No; there isn't."

"You can't break up the gang in our last year without some reason, man. Go on, tell me, old man."

"Well, you two rag me such a lot."

"Rag you?"

"Yes. You know, arguing and making jokes about me, and hiding my glasses and all the rest of it. I get fed up with it."

He would give me one of his rather contemptuous looks. Probably he would go and fetch David Trevelyan. They would roar with laughter.

"If you don't want us to take any notice of you, we won't," David would say.

"Oh, let him go and walk with Oiler Wilson if he wants to, David. If he prefers Oiler to us."

"It's not that at all. I can't really explain it." Nor could I have done. I never could talk clearly and with conviction.

David Trevelyan and John Prosset would look at each other in exaggerated mystification. Later, Prosset would record it all in his red diary in his study: Old Sibley had gone all queer! What a funny fellow old Sibley was! But old Sibley had come round in the end. Queer fellow, Sibley.

They would make me feel that here was something so inexplicable that only an oddity like myself could act in such a manner; and if there is one thing a boy cannot stand, it is the thought that he is an oddity, something different from others.

I was an ordinary boy with an ordinary boy's reactions. I felt I could never do it. I never tried.

Should I have tried? Looking back now, the answer must be yes; whatever the price in ostracism, in queer looks from others in the House, in humiliation, it would have been worth it. Anything, I see now, would have been worth it.

Then David Trevelyan left to start work on his father's farm. Thus the trio was broken up; and I was alone with Prosset. Strangely enough, that was slightly better. It put me more on a level with him. Instead of being the third in the trio, the one whom the other two so often united to laugh at, and at other times ignored altogether, I now shared all his conversation.

He was destined to go into the United Imperial Bank, largely because his uncle was manager at one of the more important branches. The idea of it filled him with dismay. The role of a humble and humdrum bank clerk with regular hours had no appeal for that adventurous and aggressive nature. However, he was planning that after a year or two he would apply to be transferred to one of their branches in the Far East. His father had been manager of a branch in Shanghai, but was now retired and lived with his mother in Galway. Here the old man could indulge his liking for shooting and fishing, not to mention an occasional day out with the Galway Blazers, at reasonable cost.

The problem of where he should live in London had always been clear in Prosset's mind. He would have what he called, in the language of Victorian novels, "bachelor lodgings." There he would entertain his friends, and generally live the life of a gentleman about town.

"I expect my pater will help me out with an allowance," he told me. He was always an optimist.

My Aunt Edith, with whom I lived after the death of my mother, my father being in India, once suggested that Prosset should be a paying guest in her house in Earl's Court, but I told her he had already got his eye on a place. Quite apart from my own feelings, Prosset's flamboyant character hardly fitted into that dingy house of fringed tablecloths, small potted palms, and stained-glass windows on the landings. As a matter of fact, I never had the courage to introduce him to Aunt Edith. With her widow's weeds, pale, pear-shaped face and jet earrings, she was hardly his type.

Although things were slightly better during Prosset's last term, I looked forward with longing to the end of it. I was to stay on another term, and during that term I would be free, an untrammelled personality of my own; free to engage on equal terms in the dinner-table conversation, without the fear of being set upon by Prosset with one of his tenacious onslaughts; free to suggest some plan without it being greeted with scorn; to laze in my study on a Sunday afternoon if I wished, instead of being forced to play cricket in the yard, or go swimming; I always regarded cold water with some dislike.

I already had my eye on another boy with whom I would go about. He was called Crane, a worthy, dull individual in the Sixth Form; an eminently likeable chap who would always be prepared to adjust his plans to your own; who would meet you halfway in an argument, and even admit defeat if he thought your reasoning sounder than his. A very different proposition from Prosset. Above all, I would not have to smile feebly when all the time I was smarting under some derisive remark from Prosset, pretending that I enjoyed the joke, that I thought him vastly funny and clever and witty, and what have you, when all the time I was hating him.

It was the custom of the school that those boys who lived in Ireland should leave for the holidays a day before the others. Doubtless it was an attempt to ensure that they should have an equal amount of time at home. So the day before the rest of us went home, I watched the House porter carrying Prosset's trunk out to the old horse cab which was to take him to the station. Then I watched Prosset carrying his tuck box, and even helped him by carrying his overcoat for him.

Old Buckley the Housemaster was there to see him off; beaming, with the spring breeze ruffling his scanty white hair, tugging at the lapels of his grey tweed jacket in the way he used to do, and obviously longing to get back into the warmth of his study. Prosset and I had already agreed, of course, to see a lot of each other in the holidays. I could hardly refuse.

Now he turned to old Buckley and shook hands.

"Goodbye, sir," he said. "Expect I'll see you again before long."

"That's right; come and see us," mumbled old Buckley.

"Probably be down for Speech Day, or to watch one of the rugger matches."

"That's right; always welcome," muttered Buckley. "Come and see us, come and see us."

Prosset shook hands with Smith, the porter, and slipped him some money.

"Goodbye, Smith."

"Goodbye, Mr. Prosset. We shall miss you," said Smith, the old hypocrite, holding the cab door open. Prosset turned to me.

"Cheerio, old man. Be seeing you in London."

"Cheerio," I said. "See you in London."

He got into the cab, and Smith slammed the door. The driver touched the horse with his whip, and the vehicle rattled off.

The three of us, Buckley, Smith and myself, stood by the gate watching as it rattled down the road. I have a notion that at the actual moment when it started, as it was gathering way, I experienced a funny little feeling almost of regret. Even a dog is sad when its master goes away. Maybe it was a form of nostalgia, a sensation that a portion of my life was over which could never now be relived. But as the cab rolled down the road this gave way to an upsurge of relief.

He was gone. Prosset was gone and I was free again. I watched without moving, without saying a word, until the cab turned the corner. Then I felt old Buckley linking his arm in mine and leading me back to the House. I heard him speaking in his gruff way.

"Expect you'll feel a bit lonely without young Prosset. Never mind. Cheer up. Holidays tomorrow."

The silly old fool, I thought, the stupid old imbecile! He thought I was standing there watching the cab to the corner because I wanted a last glimpse of my friend. He thought I was silent and still because I was sad. It was laughable.

I went back to the studies. I strolled along to Prosset's old study. He had decorated it with fawn curtains, and with brown cushions on the makeshift divan. There was a dark green patch of carpet on the floor, and two or three cheap prints, and one or two coloured drawings of ladies in scanty attire such as one found in the glossy society magazines. All the contents of the study had been sold by auction to other boys, and would be dispersed next term.

It was funny to stand there looking at the empty study, and think that Prosset would never again inhabit it. No doubt he would come back wearing an old school tie and glance in for a few seconds, but in effect he was gone for good now and the little room was curiously silent.

Crane saw me standing in the doorway.

"Going to be a bit lost without old Prosset, aren't you?" he asked in his good-natured way. I smiled and shrugged, and he passed on.

I stood looking at it all, at the scraps of paper and bits of string on the floor, at the old textbooks flung into the corner, the writing table with its ink stains, its sheet of blotting paper, and old nibs, and dirty, broken inkwell. I looked at all the debris which is always left behind by one who departs, at the air of desolation which hung over the whole place. Already it seemed to be gathering dust.

It was one of the finest sights I have ever seen in my life.

I revelled in the sight of all the litter and disorder. I could hardly tear myself away from it.

CHAPTER 3

I was not telling the truth, therefore, when I told the Chief Detective Inspector and the Detective Sergeant that Prosset was my friend. But Prosset was now dead, and it did not seem to me that any useful purpose would be served by dragging up the past, even supposing that I could have brought myself to do so.

After all, I had not killed him.

They would do better to concentrate their energies elsewhere. Indeed, I persuaded myself into thinking that I had really acted in the public interest by ensuring that the police were not diverted along a false trail, however briefly, at a time when every hour might be of importance. For I had no doubt in my own mind that, since the Sussex police had already enlisted the aid of Scotland Yard, this was a case of murder.

I could feel no sorrow; in fact, grim though it is to record it, I rejoiced from the bottom of my heart that he was no more. Without him, the world was a better place for me. I had planned, and in great detail, to kill him myself, but it had fallen to another to carry out the deed. For all I knew, this unknown assassin had an equally compelling reason to put an end to Prosset's life.

Yet I disapproved. Instinctively I felt drawn to the side of society in the search for his murderer.

It was not hypocrisy which made me feel thus, but, I think, the instinct of self-preservation. Had I killed him, the identity of the killer being to me no mystery, I should have felt no uneasiness; but with an unknown assassin at large, I felt united with the community, for who could tell whether he might not strike again, and who could say whom he might kill next time?

Thus, though I applauded the result, I deplored the method; and I only deplored the method because I myself had not been the one to do the action. Into such strange paths does instinct lead one.

The talk with the Inspector and the Sergeant had been comparatively brief. I had expected it would last longer. When they had gone, I found the mood for work had also departed. I sat in my armchair smoking, and sipping another whisky and soda.

I felt vaguely uneasy, though as I had a clear conscience as far as the actual crime was concerned, there was little reason why I should. True, I had told them lies, but at a pinch that could be put right. I wondered why the interview had been so short. On thinking it over, I had the impression that they knew almost everything I had told them, and that they were primarily interested in me and my manner. I recalled how they had pulled me up once or twice, and that I had not talked fluently. I never talk fluently, but they would not know that.

They had not tried to help me out much. They had listened in blank silence a good deal of the time, the Inspector with his hard eyes on my face, the Sergeant quietly taking his notes.

I went over again in my mind all that I had said about Prosset being my friend; I felt no apprehension on that score, for I had let the world in general go on believing that there were no better friends to be found than Prosset and I. Even Kate did not know the real extent of my hatred. Then I reviewed my drive down to Ockleton and back, the weekend he was killed.

I was certain nobody had seen my car turn off to take the side road to his cottage, or been about when I drove back to London. What is more, if they had seen the car they could not have identified it, for on previous occasions I had travelled down in Prosset's car. Our local correspondent's report had confirmed my belief that everybody thought Prosset had been alone.

Anyway, I could always prove that I was with Kate at the time of the murder. But at this thought I sat up and impatiently threw my cigarette end into the empty grate: what on earth was I doing to start thinking about alibis? It was damned silly.

I considered it likely that they would go round and question Kate. Indeed, they might be on their way now. Time is invaluable in a murder case; every day makes a case more difficult because every day people's recollections of important details grow fainter. You have to act fast. Yes, I thought, they are probably going round there now. I finished the whisky and got up. I would ring Kate and tell her not to be surprised if they called. It would give her a chance to prepare her mind in advance.

In my digs there was always a chance that somebody would overhear what was said, because the telephone stood at the foot of the stairs, in the hall. I did not particularly wish to let other people know of this affair, and as there was a telephone booth at the end of the road, I decided to use that. I walked quickly down the road, fortunately found the booth was empty, and went inside and dialled her number.

The block in which Kate had her room was more modern than the converted house in which I lived, and the telephone on her landing was built into a recess and had a reasonably soundproof door. I heard the telephone ringing, and then old Tom the handyman answered. I asked for Kate, and he told me to hang on while he put me through; they had a sort of code system in the building, and I waited while he buzzed twice for Kate. In a moment or two she came on the line.

"Look, darling," I said, "I've just had a visit from a couple of dicks from Scotland Yard in connection with Prosset's death. It was only a routine call, but I had to let them know I was engaged to you, and they asked for your address. I thought I would let you know because they may call on you."

I heard her laugh.

"What are you laughing at?"

"Well, you're a bit late. They've arrived."

"How long have they been there?"

"They've only just arrived."

"Listen, Kate. This is strictly between you and me. There are one or two odd circumstances in connection with Prosset's death."

"Good God! Darling!"

"Look, Katie, don't read more into it than I've said. It will probably all be cleared up soon. Anyway, as far as we are concerned, it is only routine business, see?"

"Yes, I see."

"There is nothing to be worried about. Understand?"

"Of course not."

"One other thing. I didn't tell them I was with Prosset last weekend. I didn't think it was necessary."

There was a funny long silence. "Hello," I said. "Katie? Still there?"

"Yes. But why didn't you tell them?"

"It would only have led to complications. There was no purpose in doing so. I'll explain when I see you. I know these police boys."

"All right, darling."

"And Katie?"

"Yes."

"They'll ask you what you know about John Prosset, what friends or acquaintances he had. You don't know any that I don't know, do you? Or do you?"

"No, darling, I don't."

"Sure?"

"Absolutely sure."

I felt relieved. I recoiled from the thought that she might be subjected to a close interrogation, and even more from the idea that she might be called as a witness at the inquest. Some people would not have minded, but Kate was so sensitive and still so shy.

"Kate," I said suddenly, "do you think it is necessary to tell them you were with Prosset the last evening before he left London?"

"I don't know. What do you think?"

"It doesn't seem really necessary to me. It won't add anything to their information." I hesitated for a couple of seconds, thinking quickly. "No. Don't tell them, Kate. They might call you as a witness at the inquest, and it is all quite pointless."

"Well, I'll do as you say," she answered uncertainly. "Supposing they ask me?"

"Why should they ask you? Did anybody see you arrive or leave Prosset's place?"

She thought for a moment. "I doubt it. We went through the basement door. If they saw me they could hardly have recognized me. It was dark."

"Good. And one other thing, Kate."

"What?"

"I don't see much point in telling them I've just telephoned you. Just apologize and say it was some office friend. I'm not really supposed to have mentioned the inquiries to anybody."

"All right, then. I'll say that."

"Bye-bye, sweetheart. And don't worry."

"Of course I won't. There's nothing to worry about."

She said goodbye and rang off.

I stood in the telephone booth staring blankly at the official notices on the wall. She was right. There was nothing to worry about. I left the booth and began to walk slowly back along Harrington Gardens.

As I did so, I began to have doubts again. Yet I knew there was nothing seriously wrong. How could there be? I was a perfectly innocent man and could prove it. If the worst came to the worst, I could explain the little subterfuge I had adopted to protect Kate. I might be reprimanded—indeed, I would be—but that was all, and it might not come to that. The odds were against it.

⁓

That night, as I lay in bed thinking about the police visit, I heard two cats screaming outside. Beyond keeping me awake a little while, the noise did not worry me, but there had been a time, as a boy, when such sounds would cause me to lie rigid in bed, listening, afraid. It was during the school holidays, and I had learnt for the first time that the dreary house in Earl's Court was supposed by my Aunt Edith to be haunted by an elderly recluse who had once lived there.

My aunt admitted she had never seen him, but she said she sometimes "felt his presence," and alleged that on one or two occasions she had heard shuffling footsteps descending the creaking stairs.

There were many cats which frequented my aunt's colourless garden at night. You could sometimes see them sneaking along the walls in the moonlight, or observe them, crouched down, watching each other with endless patience.

Their calls would wake me up, and the eerie sound would cause me to think of ghosts. I would lie awake, staring into the darkness, listening for the shuffling feet of the old recluse.

Each time the cats screamed and I lay listening, heart beating faster, I thought of what Prosset would have said, and the way he would have looked at me; he would have been genuinely astonished that anybody could be even momentarily frightened by a cat in a garden at night, or that I should listen for the sound of an elderly gentleman's ghostly steps. I suppose he would have been quite right, too, but Prosset was an exceptional character. He never knew any fear, and I doubt if he knew any in those last moments in the cottage at Ockleton; he would have looked on death with surprise, maybe, but that is about all. I was never in a position to test his nerve in the presence of anything supernatural, but I don't think it would have failed. He would have reacted as usual, magnificently, chin up, his eyes calculating and cool, facing the direction whence the threat would come.

I wasn't made like that. I wished I had had a loaded gun by my bed, but my little single-barrel hammer gun was down in Somerset in Aunt Nell's gunroom. I wished I had had some means of defence; even if it were only a cudgel, and even though I realized you could hardly defend yourself against a spirit with a charge of gunshot or a club.

I remember that those holidays I went off for my week's stay with my Aunt Nell, as always, in high spirits. Aunt Nell was as different from gentle Aunt Edith as anybody could be.

She was the wife of my father's uncle, a sort of great-aunt by marriage. She, too, had lost her husband and she lived alone in a large Georgian mansion with about eight hundred acres of farmland and woodland. She was a remarkable old girl, beak-nosed, imperious and short-tempered, and in her youth she had been a great rider to hounds. Now she bred polo ponies, and knew as much about farming as any man in the neighbourhood. She did not make the place show a profit, but she at least made it pay its way. When I stayed with her, I saw comparatively little of her.

I would be out with my gun all day. At mealtimes we sat at opposite ends of a vast mahogany table, waited on by a butler and footman in livery. In the evenings she attended to her correspondence and I read a book. I was not much interested in her, and I had the impression that she was not much interested in me, at any rate while I was very young; and that she had me to stay because I was one of the family, and she thought I ought to be brought up with some vague idea of how the English gentry lived on their estates. But, in view of later events, I think I did her an injustice, and that in her rough way she tried to put some backbone into me.

Apart from being in the country, I enjoyed the luxury of the great house, the choice of food, and having my clothes laid out for me at the beginning of each day by the footman, while I still lay in bed, drowsy and warm. It was so different from the house in Earl's Court, with its smell of mice, the dank garden, the horrid little leaded windows on the landings, each with a design in red and blue glass.

I have been down there recently. Aunt Nell is long since dead. Death duties made havoc of the property, so that her nephew, who inherited it, was unable to keep it up. It was occupied for a time during the war, but now it is empty. Nobody wants it. It is too big, too isolated. The long drive is covered with weeds, and where the cars used to sweep proudly round with a swish of tyres to deposit their passengers by the great porch there is now a sea of dandelions.

On the south side, velvety lawns and flower beds led down to a big artificial lake, with an island in the middle joined to each bank by two little trellis-work bridges; and in the mornings, when the dew was still on the grass and a faint mist hung in the air, you could see two or three cock pheasants and half a dozen waterhens on the lawns.

Now you can hardly see that there were ever any lawns or flower beds. Grass grows, knee high in summer, from the house to the water's edge, and only a stone sundial, and a Grecian statue, rising above the wilderness, show that once it might have been something different. Across the lake, you can still find traces of tall poles and sagging, rusting wire netting, where the young pheasants were reared, and where the keepers hung the vermin which they shot. The head keeper is dead, and I believe the second keeper is living in two rooms in Bristol, earning his livelihood as a none too expert mechanic in a garage. The horse boxes are in ruins, the glasshouses shattered, and the vegetable garden choked with weeds.

But when I went there during those last school holidays, for what was to prove my last visit, though I could not suspect it, the place was still in its heyday. My aunt had inherited the estate from her father, because she was the eldest daughter. She had had a short matrimonial life of about ten years, which had given her the right to call herself Lady Bankhurst. I never knew her husband. He was an impoverished Oxfordshire baronet, a man who was happier in a town than in the country, and who was generally considered by the locals to be a pretty poor fish. Certainly my Aunt Nell dominated him as she dominated everybody else; and when death separated them, possibly with feelings of slight relief on both sides, she took over once again the undivided ordering of the place with her accustomed vigour.

She was on the steps to greet me when I arrived.

"Well, young man, how are you? Got your rugger cap yet?"

"No. I play for the House, though."

"Not good enough!" she boomed. "Not good enough by a long chalk! What's the trouble? Afraid to tackle 'em low, or something?"

I saw the chauffeur and butler smiling discreetly.

"No," I replied lamely, "not really."

"Going to get into the cricket eleven?"

"Well, no. My eyes are not good enough, really. About the rugger: I'm not heavy enough for the school pack, and not fast enough for a three-quarter."

"Oh," she said without much interest, and led the way into the drawing room, followed by two cocker spaniels, a fox terrier and me.

"Well, are you in the Sixth?" she asked, as she sat down at the teatable.

"No," I said again, blushing crimson. She gave one of her loud, healthy laughs.

"God bless my soul, Michael, what *are* you good at?"

"Well, nothing really. I mean, I am not *particularly* good at anything."

She handed me a dish of scones and began to pour out the tea. She seemed to be trying to think of something upon which to congratulate me. At last she looked up and asked, "Well, are you a prefect?"

I shook my head. She said nothing. She seemed to be bored with the whole conversation, and I don't blame her.

"Unless you get your colours," I said after a pause, "you only become a prefect in order of seniority. If I stayed on after the summer term, I would probably be a prefect in the autumn. Lots of chaps leave in the summer."

But she was trying to make one of the spaniels beg for a bit of scone and made no answer. I felt my toes curling up in my shoes; I felt hot and uncomfortable. I wanted very much to stand well in her eyes, and I never seemed to be able to. I guessed that, with my pale town complexion, short-sighted eyes and inability to ride a horse with much skill, I cut a poor figure in her opinion. The footman came softly into the room and stood by me.

"May I have the keys to your trunk, sir," he said. I handed them to him, and he went out.

I could imagine the snooty look he would give my ready-made suits, my shirts which Aunt Edith darned and darned again, and my thick woollen socks. He would remember from past experience that he was not going to get much of a tip.

I knew from what Prosset, who often stayed at big houses in

Ireland, had said, that it was customary to give the butler a pound, the footman who looked after you ten shillings, and the chauffeur at least five shillings. But of course that was ludicrous in Aunt Edith's eyes. She provided me with seven-and-sixpence for the butler, five shillings for the footman, and said it was absurd for a boy of my age to have to tip the chauffeur at all.

But in spite of it all I was glad to be there. I spent every moment I could out of doors, killing birds and beasts without the slightest compunction or any feeling other than intense satisfaction when my shots went home. If I wounded one I put it out of its pain as quickly as possible. I did not finish if off with my hands, but fired a further shot.

On Sundays, when shooting was forbidden, I used to accompany my aunt on her rounds when she visited the outlying parts of the estate. It was during these walks that latterly she had endeavoured to strengthen the structure of my character, a character which her natural shrewdness had already divined as unheroic, to say the least, over-sensitive and inclined to envy and spiritual meanness. Prosset would have been her ideal. She was always telling me to stand up for myself.

"If I go and bend down in Trafalgar Square," she would say, waving her ash stick belligerently, "anybody will kick my bottom for me."

Once, when I was younger, she said, "Hit a bully in the wind and he'll double up, and then you can sock him on the chin."

I once tried this out at my preparatory school, but the bully was only irritated by my first blow, and gave me a good hiding before I could get in a second.

She always talked good straight English, and once almost blasted a waiter out of a hotel lounge when he asked her at teatime whether she would like some *gateau*. "*Gateau!*" she roared. "It's cake, isn't it? Why call it *gateau*, man? *Gateau*, indeed!"

Another time, making a rare appointment to have her hair done, she lost her temper with the store's telephone operator because he said he would put her through to the "ladies' salon."

"*Salon?*" She stamped her foot. "*Salon!* I want the hairdresser. He's a hairdresser, isn't he? A barber, isn't he? *Salon*, indeed!"

Two days before I came back to London, something occurred which although it was only of a trivial nature left a curiously lasting impression on my mind, though I do not see why it should have done.

I had spent the afternoon walking around with my gun on the lookout for vermin. It was the close season for game, and targets were therefore scarce. Apart from an abortive shot at a stoat, I had not had any sport. Before turning back for tea, I decided as a last hope to try a small coppice which stood on a raised piece of ground on an outlying part of the estate. It was round and isolated, mostly composed of conifers, and I knew from experience that such places were seldom inhabited by game or vermin, at any rate on Aunt Nell's estate; though now and again you might startle a pigeon out of the tree tops, or hear a jay calling in its harsh, rasping tones.

It was a grey day, and a little wind was rising as I walked over and climbed the wooden fence with which the covert was surrounded. It was dark and sombre among the trees, and the pine needles with which the ground was thickly strewn seemed to deaden all noise except the occasional rustle of the wind in the branches. The place was at first sight utterly deserted and seemed to me oppressive and forbidding. I had often passed by on the outside of this little wood, but although I had peered into it, it had never seemed worthwhile to penetrate inside it. It was obviously a hopeless place for game, and I started to walk across it without the slightest hope of seeing anything.

Suddenly, I saw a very large bird with black plumage and black beak sitting on a low branch. It sat perfectly still, about fifteen yards away, apparently listening, its head thrust forward as though about to take flight. I did not know what kind of bird it was, but the thought leaped to my mind that it was a carrion crow. I saw it drop down on to a still lower branch. In a flash my gun was up to my shoulder, and I fired. Yet I recall that before I pressed the trigger I hesitated for a split second, not because I felt unsure of my aim, but because some unformed doubt entered my mind; then I fired. It fell to the ground, but at once began to hop silently away. I fired again and killed it.

Throughout there had been no sound except the crash of the

explosions and the echoes of the noise through the dark trees. There had been no sound when it dropped to a lower bough, no fluttering of wings when it fell, no crackling of twigs or leaves as it hopped away.

I did not go and examine the bird, and I had no desire to carry it back to hang in the gamekeepers' "larder" with the other vermin. I went out of the wood feeling uneasy, though I could not account for the feeling. I had shot hundreds of things as a boy, including large rooks, but I felt that this great black bird, frequenting alone the solitary wood on the hill, had about it something which was malevolent.

I felt I had done something I should not have done. I was sorry I had shot it, and hastened back to the house for tea and human company. Prosset would never have understood this feeling, and neither, of course, would the Chief Detective Inspector who interviewed me about his death.

~⁓~

I shall always remember the last few moments of that stay at Aunt Nell's place. We stood on the steps as the chauffeur and the footman loaded my trunk on to the back of the car.

The two spaniels were chasing each other about the drive. In the parkland opposite a mare was grazing while her foal followed her, now nuzzling at her side, now gazing with ears erect at the new world around it. Outside the coverts, in the distance, little brown humps which looked like newly turned earth showed where rabbits were eating the fresh spring grass.

My Aunt Nell stood there, dressed in her country tweeds, the sunshine falling on her iron-grey hair and healthy, weather-beaten face. For her, I thought, the years stretched placidly ahead; each day bringing the exhilaration of life on a big estate; each night the peacefulness of deep sleep; the sweet air drifting through the open windows and only the sounds of the country, the startled cry of a waterhen on the lake, or of a cock pheasant in the coverts, to disturb the stillness.

I always counted each day in that house. I would say to myself: I've still got two days, I've still got a full day and a night; and even the night before I had to return to the house in Earl's Court I would say: Well, I've still got all tomorrow morning and lunchtime. But for Aunt Nell, I thought, there was no need to count. For her, life is luxurious and unruffled. Only time was to reveal how wrong I was.

Now the trunk was on the car, and my packet of sandwiches and book were on the back seat, and the chauffeur was holding the door open. Aunt Nell and I never kissed each other. I shook hands with her and thanked her for my stay.

"Not a bit, old lad," she said, giving me a pat on the back and then, a thing she had never done before, a friendly squeeze round the shoulders.

"Come and see me next holidays," she added.

"These are my last school holidays," I replied with a smile.

"Bless my soul, so they are! Well, come and see me again soon, eh?"

"I'd love to. And thanks again."

I got into the car. The chauffeur shut the door and went round to the driving seat. There was a glass partition between him and myself. Suddenly my aunt stepped forward, put her foot on the running board, and thrust her head into the back of the car.

"Don't forget to fight 'em," she murmured.

"Fight who?"

"Fight everybody—and everything! Don't worry if you are not brilliant. Just go on fighting. You're never beaten till you're dead, Mike. Never let anything or anybody get you down."

She stepped back from the car and stood smiling and nodding good-humouredly, and pugnaciously hitting the palm of her left hand with her right fist. The car moved off, passed under the stable archway, under the stable clock, and into the south drive. I remember the time exactly, it was 2:35 p.m.

I never saw Aunt Nell again. But the fault for that lay with me.

CHAPTER 4

As I listened to the cats in Harrington Gardens I began to have my first slight doubts as to whether I had really acted in Kate's best interests or my own. My Aunt Nell would have advised me to tell the truth, and to hell with them, and I rather wished that I had done so, and that I had not inveigled Kate into evasions. But I comforted myself with the thought that I had only acted for the best as it had seemed at the moment.

"Nobody can do more than that," I said aloud. Perhaps the finality of the words, spoken aloud, had some psychological effect for I fell asleep shortly afterwards.

But that night I had a strange and troubling dream, from which I awoke bathed in perspiration and fumbling for the bedside lamp. The dream had no relationship to current events, as far as I could tell, and not a great deal, as it turned out, to future events, but it had a curiously depressing effect, and one which remained with me for a long time, and I think it may therefore have contributed in some degree to my later actions.

I dreamed that I was in a large and unidentified house in the country with Kate. There was a fearful feeling of menace from an unseen horror, such as one not infrequently encounters in a dream. At the end, I was standing watching Kate being driven from the house by this unseen influence. As she fled, hands covering her face, she was compelled to run the gauntlet between a double row of black birds, resembling cockatoos, chained to perches. The birds screeched and mocked her, flapping their wings, stretching their necks out at her, crests raised; jeering and rocking backwards and forwards. I remember thinking in the dream that Kate somehow symbolized light being vanquished by darkness. My terror was due to the knowledge that at the end of the row of dark birds lay madness, or death, or both. I tried to link the dream with my experience in the little coppice, as a boy, when I had shot the carrion crow, if it was a crow, but beyond the fact that the birds were black there was no obvious connection.

I woke up the next morning feeling tired and depressed. But I was busier than usual at the office, and as the day went by I had little time to reconsider the events of the previous evening or the dream. Nevertheless, I went about my work without zest, longing for the evening, when I was due to meet Kate again.

After work I hurried home, ate a hasty meal, and took a taxi to Manchester Square. Kate met me on the landing and led me into her room.

I kissed her and noted with relief that she seemed quite cheerful and happy. I sat down in her armchair and pulled her down on to my knee, noting again how thin and frail she was; indeed, although she was thirty, she seemed hardly more than a child. It seemed intolerable that she should have been living alone in London, fending for herself when she was sick, with nobody to comfort her when she was depressed; and, without necessarily being conceited, I realized what it meant to her to love and to be loved by somebody who would henceforth try to bring her so much that she had missed in life.

"How did you find the police?" I asked.

She laughed. "Perfectly charming. Especially the elder one, the Inspector. I thought he was rather an old dear."

It had not occurred to me that the pebble-eyed Inspector could be seen in that light, but I assumed he had put himself out to be charming. I was glad. I told her the sort of questions the Inspector had put to me about Prosset, and it seemed that her own interview had followed similar lines.

"They talked about you, too," she added. "They said what a nice change it was to question somebody who could give concise, factual answers. They said they supposed it was because you are a newspaperman."

"Did they ask you who it was telephoning you last night?"

She nodded. "They asked in a casual sort of way if it was you, and I told them, no, it was a girl I knew at my office."

"And they seemed to believe you?"

"Absolutely. Of course, they asked whether John Prosset had any enemies that I knew of, and I said that as far as I knew he hadn't."

"Did they ask you how well you knew him?"

"Oh, yes, and I said I did not know him very well; and that's true, really, isn't it? I never knew him well, did I, Mike?"

She sat up and looked at me anxiously. I put my arms round her and said, "That's a hundred per cent true, Katie. You never knew him well, never."

She got up and went to the gas ring and put some water and coffee in a saucepan.

"So that was about all, was it?" I said.

"Well, we chatted a bit about the case, of course. I gathered that they have absolutely no clues to go on. They're just groping in thin air, hoping they'll come across something. Herbert Day has given them the names of a number of business acquaintances, and they're going through them one by one, but they don't seem very hopeful. I forgot to tell you one thing they asked. They asked why you hadn't gone down to Ockleton last Saturday as arranged. Because, of course, I let them understand that you had been in London all weekend. That was what you wanted, wasn't it?"

"Yes," I said uncertainly, "but—"

"They said it must have been fate which stopped you, because if you had gone down Prosset would probably be alive now. The Inspector said you must be feeling rotten about it, as Prosset was your friend."

"How the devil did he know about the invitation? How did he know Prosset had invited me?"

Kate looked around. "Prosset must have mentioned it to Herbert Day, and the Inspector must have got it from him."

It sounded a plausible idea. "What did you answer—I mean about my not going down?"

"I just said that as we had both been down so recently, and as I couldn't go because I had to meet a cousin in London, you decided in the end that you'd rather stay in town. Why? There was nothing unusual about his question really, was there?"

"No, of course not."

She turned round from the gas ring and stared at me, frowning slightly.

"I had to make up some excuse, didn't I? It came so suddenly. I did right, didn't I, Mike?"

"Of course you did right, darling. You couldn't have done anything else. You answered absolutely correctly."

She looked relieved. "I thought you sounded a bit doubtful."

"Did I? I didn't intend to."

I told her in some detail about my reasons for withholding information from the police, pointing out that the gamble was well worthwhile in view of what it would save us in the way of further questioning and possible attendance at the inquest. I made out a good case, and almost removed from my own mind any doubts I may have had. Yet the uneasy feeling remained that I might have done better to be frank.

Kate took the coffee off the ring and poured it into two cups. She handed one to me and offered me the sugar. Then she pulled a cushion down on to the floor and sat on it at my side, in the way she so often did. Eventually she said, "Mike, if you like, I wouldn't mind too much about telling them about that evening with Prosset. It's not too late. I could ring them up now or first thing in the morning, and ask them to come round. I'm sure they would."

"I'm sure they would, too."

"You could tell them everything, too. Don't you think it might be better? Then we'd be absolutely clear."

I stroked her hair, and she reached up and caught hold of my hand and laid her thin face against it. She said, "I only want to do what you want me to do. You know best."

For a few seconds I was tempted to agree with her suggestion. Then I had a mental picture of her standing up in public answering questions and parrying innuendoes. I thought of her reading the newspaper accounts and seeing her picture. I imagined the curious looks of other members of the staff at her office, the inquisitive questions of other secretaries, the giggles and whispers which would stop when she entered a room, and the attempts of older members of the staff to be natural in their manner towards her.

It was not hard to imagine some of the things they would say: "My dear, Kate of all people; she's the last person I would have thought of. I always say it's these quiet ones who are the worst. Still waters run deep, dear. It's not as if she was a beauty, dear, even her friends couldn't call her that, dear. Well, it just shows there's hope for us all, dear, doesn't it?"

I couldn't have that, not about little Kate.

I said, "It's not necessary, Kate, but you are sweet to suggest it. It's just like you, dear Kate."

When I left her, I was once more glad that I had acted as I had done. My doubts of the previous night vanished. I was convinced that in the circumstances it was the best thing to do. I drove back to Harrington Gardens with a light heart.

~

Ethel the maid sometimes used to turn my bed down at night, and if I was working she would bring me a cup of tea at about ten thirty. This was not included in the service, of course, but was a custom which had gradually grown up. I was on good terms with Ethel, and I have no doubt that her actions in this respect were prompted as much by kindliness of heart as by the reasonable tips I used to give her. I learnt early in life that it is a good economic policy to tip people well.

When I saw that lights were on in my bedroom I assumed it was Ethel, but I was mistaken. The Chief Detective Inspector and the Sergeant rose to their feet when I opened the door.

"Well, well, don't you boys ever go to bed?" I asked.

"I'm sorry to worry you so late at night," said the Inspector.

"That's all right."

"There are just one or two points which have cropped up."

I went over to the corner cupboard. "Whisky and soda, as before, Inspector?"

"Not tonight, thanks, sir." The Sergeant also declined.

"What about a beer, then?"

"No thanks, sir. We had one on the way, as a matter of fact."

I poured myself out a glass of light ale, and sat down. The Sergeant took up his former position on the sofa and opened his notebook.

"Well, as I say, sir, we're sorry to have to bother you again, but if you could just tell us one or two things it might be helpful. It's not an easy case."

"It is definitely a case, then?"

"Well, we're working on the assumption that there is something a bit fishy, sir. Now first of all, sir, do you happen to know anything about Mr. Prosset's financial position?"

"Well, no, I don't; not very much. He seemed to have enough, though. As a matter of fact, now you come to mention it, he seemed to be a bit better off the last month or two. He exchanged his old car for a better one, and leased his cottage by the sea. Surely Mr. Day could help you there? They were partners."

"As a matter of fact, we've had a sniff around there," said the Inspector after some hesitation. "This is all off the record, of course, sir, as far as newspapers go?"

"Of course."

"As a matter of fact, they don't seem to have been doing very well lately. Nothing startling. But they hoped it was only a temporary setback, according to this chap Day. But he said Mr. Prosset had been lucky with horses recently. Was he fond of gambling?"

"Yes; he was," I answered. "He had a couple of bets or more every day."

"So that might explain his recent financial improvement?"

"It might. But it's funny he didn't mention it to me. Most people like to talk about it when they win a packet on a horse."

The Inspector smiled. He had not brought his file along with him. He just sat watching me without blinking his tawny-coloured eyes. His arms were stretched along the side of the chair, and he looked relaxed, but I knew he wasn't.

"Mr. Prosset was perhaps the sort of person who didn't tell people everything he did?"

"Perhaps," I replied.

"And that wouldn't exactly make him unique, would it, sir?"

"No." It seemed a pointless sort of remark, and I waited for the next question. But he sat looking at me for a few seconds saying nothing.

"No, it wouldn't, Mr. Sibley," he remarked at length.

"Wouldn't what?"

"I said that perhaps Mr. Prosset was the sort of person who did not tell everybody everything he did, and that that did not make him unique. For instance, sir, it would have been a bit more helpful if you yourself had told us that you had cancelled a proposed visit to Mr. Prosset the day before he was killed. There was no need to hush that up, sir. That was silly, sir, if I may say so, and might have caused us a lot of trouble one way and another. Why didn't you tell us, sir? There was nothing to worry about."

I leaned forward and said quickly, "I know there was nothing to worry about, and as a matter of fact I meant to tell you. But we only had a comparatively short talk, and just when I had it on the tip of my tongue to tell you, you asked me some question about his relatives. I told you about his family in Ireland, and then you asked another question, and I forgot about the other thing completely."

"You forgot about it completely?"

"Yes."

"It was a funny thing to forget, wasn't it, sir?"

"Things like that can easily happen."

He took no notice of the remark. "Your friend Mr. Prosset gets killed, sir. You must have thought that if you had been there he would be alive today. You must have regretted not going. Yet you forget to tell us. It was a funny thing to forget, sir, wasn't it?"

"Maybe it was, if you put it like that. Yes, I agree, it was, but it's the truth."

As he said nothing, I added, "You remember asking me about his relatives, don't you?"

"Oh, I remember that all right, Mr. Sibley. But I'm not a thought-reader, you know. I can't tell what was in your mind when, as you say, I interrupted your intentions. I can't tell that, can I, sir? I'm not psychic, you know. I can only go by what you say out loud."

"I know that, but what I've told you now is the truth. I meant to tell you, and I just forgot, that's all. It's natural, isn't it? I mean, in a way."

But he wasn't finished with the point. He pressed it again.

"But you agree it was a funny sort of thing to forget?"

"Well, in a way yes, and in a way no. One gets a bit keyed up when a couple of police officers come and interrogate you. It's natural."

"Who was interrogating you, sir?" said the Inspector mildly.

"Well, you were."

"I wasn't interrogating you, sir. I was just having a friendly talk about your old friend Mr. Prosset. I wasn't bullying you, was I, sir? I wasn't bullying Mr. Sibley, was I, Sergeant?"

The Sergeant looked up and smiled. "Not as far as I could see, sir."

"Of course you weren't," I said hastily. "I never said you were. I only said—"

"Look, sir," interrupted the Inspector, "here's your pal Mr. Prosset dead as a doornail. Murdered, perhaps. And you were going down to stay the very weekend he was found dead. You didn't go. Well, why should you have gone if you didn't want to? Nobody is going to suggest you should have gone. Nobody is going to blame you for his death because you changed your mind. Everybody can change their mind. It's a free country, isn't it? Of course it is. Well, then? Why didn't you just say, 'As a matter of fact, I was going down to stay with him, but at the last moment I changed my mind. I put him off.' That would have been a natural enough thing to say to me, wouldn't it?"

"I suppose so."

"So you agree it was a funny thing to forget? You now admit that, at last?"

It might have been Prosset talking, fighting, challenging, across the dining-room table at school. Going on and on about some point or other.

"Oh, all right," I said irritably. "I admit it was a funny thing to forget, the way you put it. In fact, I've already admitted it. There's no need to go on and on about it."

"There's no need to get excited, sir."

"I wasn't getting excited."

"Weren't you, sir? I'm sorry. I thought you were. Didn't you think Mr. Sibley was getting excited, Sergeant?"

"I thought he sounded a little annoyed, sir. Perhaps it's natural, if what he says is true."

"Perhaps you're right, Sergeant. Perhaps I was being a little hard. Where were you on the evening and night of May 28th, the night Mr. Prosset was killed, sir?"

The question came so gently and yet so suddenly that for a full second its implications escaped me. Then they struck with the force of a heavy blow in the stomach.

"On the night of May 28th?"

"That's right, sir. That's the question I asked."

"Well, I was here. I was here part of the time. Then I spent the rest of the evening with my fiancée."

"What time did you arrive at Miss Marsden's place, and what time did you leave?"

"I got there about 9:15 p.m. and I left at about one o'clock in the morning."

"How did you come home?"

"How did I come home?" I repeated feebly.

"Yes, sir, how did you come home? I suppose you haven't forgotten that, have you, sir?"

"No, of course not. I did not take my car that night. I walked down to Oxford Street looking for a taxi, but I did not find one until I got to Oxford Street itself."

"What was the number of the taxi?"

"The number of the taxi?"

"Yes, sir."

"I don't know. I haven't the faintest idea. Why should I take a note of the number of the taxi? Nobody does."

He ignored my question. "So you don't know the number of the taxi? That's a pity, but it can't be helped, can it?"

There was a question in my mind which I had to put to him, even though I suppose I knew that he would be bound to give the formal reply which he did.

"What's on your mind, Inspector? You surely don't suspect me, do you? You don't think I killed Prosset? He was my friend."

The Inspector raised his eyebrows so that his tawny eyes looked rounder and more pebbly than ever.

"Suspect you, sir? Why should I suspect you? You ought to know as a newspaperman that we have to check up on everybody's movements. It's just a matter of elimination. There's nothing on my mind, sir. I was just asking a few routine questions."

"After all, I was with my fiancée between 9:15 and one o'clock. She can prove that. And Prosset was killed around midnight."

I saw the Sergeant raise his head. He said, "How do you know that, sir?"

"I read it in the papers."

"You noted that, did you, sir?" said the Inspector. "Well, as you say, you were with Miss Marsden around midnight, so that looks as though it lets you out all right, sir."

I took a deep breath and felt relaxed. I was glad I had made that point. I felt that it settled matters. The Inspector examined his fingernails for a moment, then looked up and stared at me full in the face, and said in quite a conversational tone, "You know, what I can't understand is why you didn't tell me a long time ago that, although you cancelled your visit to Mr. Prosset, you did go down there after all. That's what puzzles me, sir. That's the sort of obstruction that might get you into serious trouble, sir. You know that, as a reporter. Why did you hush that up? I gave you every chance to tell me, here, right now, at this talk."

Both he and the Sergeant were staring at me. I felt the blood mounting to my face. I got up and went over to the corner cupboard and poured myself out a whisky and soda. Behind my back, the Inspector added, "Not to mention getting Miss Marsden to support you in your lies."

I came back and sat down, and said, "All right. I'll tell you the truth. I intended to tell you the whole truth in the beginning, but when I suddenly learned that foul play was suspected, well, I lost my head."

"Why?" said the Sergeant. "Why should you lose your head? You were innocent, sir, weren't you?"

"Why *shouldn't* you have gone down and been with him the day before he died? There's nothing wrong in that," said the Inspector.

"I know there isn't."

"It's a coincidence, but that's all," said the Sergeant.

"But first you hush up that you were invited and refused the invitation," said the Inspector, "and when we drag that bit out of you, you don't even then come clean."

"It's not as though there was anything unusual about it," said the Sergeant.

"I know," I said urgently. "I know it sounds silly now. I was stupid. But it came as a shock. It threw me off balance, if you like. And once I had started, I had to go on."

"So it seems, sir," said the Inspector.

"I thought it would make no difference to your inquiries, and I thought it might save me a lot of trouble, including attending the inquest. That's the only reason."

Surprisingly enough, the Inspector seemed more aggrieved than annoyed. All he said was, "Well, it wasn't very clever, was it?"

"No. And I apologize."

"Well, it can't be helped now." He seemed disinclined to pursue the subject any further. I had expected a long tirade and a severe interrogation, and all that had happened was that I had received a mild reproof. The Inspector thought for a moment, glanced at the Sergeant, and reached for his briefcase.

"Now what about putting it all on paper?"

"Do you mean, make a signed statement?"

"That's the kind of thing. They like it at the Yard."

"Makes things sort of look neat and tidy," said the Sergeant jovially. I looked at them both in some dismay. For some reason I recalled that they had both refused a drink, and this now assumed in my mind an importance which was doubtless out of proportion. I told myself that I had obviously nothing to fear, but although I could not have said why, I felt instinctively reluctant to make a statement.

"Is that necessary?"

"I wouldn't go so far as to say it was necessary, sir. But it might be in your interests as well as ours to have it all down in black and white, don't you think? So that there can't be any argument about it."

"It might save us having to trouble you again," pointed out the Sergeant.

"But you've got a shorthand note," I said.

"Not quite the same thing. Of course, we can't force you, if you've any real objection."

"I've no real objection, but—"

"Well, then," the Inspector laughed, "if you've no real objection, what are we wasting time for? Let's get it over."

He began to unfasten his briefcase.

"I don't want to be difficult, but I really don't see the point of it, Inspector. I'd rather leave it."

The cheerful look left his face. He replaced his briefcase on the floor. I felt awkward, for I could not account for my obstinacy. Probably everybody who is involved in a police investigation is liable to feel that until the guilty person is caught everybody, including himself, is at least mildly suspect. Such being the case, he is slightly on the defensive in regard to the police; they are not so much opponents as intruders into his normal routine of life; they are unknown quantities, and he is reluctant to commit himself in any way.

"So you do object, sir," said the Inspector. "Mind you, I have no authority to press you in any way. Quite the contrary, in fact. A voluntary statement is a voluntary statement, and, as I would have pointed out to you, may at any time be used in evidence. But may I ask your reasons, sir? An innocent man like you has nothing to be afraid of; you know that, sir."

But that was the trouble. I couldn't tell him my reasons. I did not even know them myself. I only felt that it was not in my interests to put anything on paper. It was a purely instinctive reaction, and was almost certainly partly due to the obvious desire of the police that I should do so. All I could find to say was, "Well, I know what signed statements can mean."

He feigned surprise. "And what can they mean, sir?"

"Well, you write some facts down, and sign the thing as true, and later, if you find you have made a mistake it can be twisted to look as though you have written a deliberate lie. It looks bad. You don't need me to tell you that, Inspector."

"Who'd want to twist anything you say, sir?"

"I don't know."

I felt uncomfortable. The Inspector thought the matter over for a few seconds. Finally, he made as if to pick up his hat preparatory to departing.

"All right, sir," he said gently, "just as you like, of course. I'll tell them at the Yard that you refused to make a statement. You'll pardon me if I've pressed the idea more than I should have done. I just thought it might save us both some trouble, that's all, sir. You're quite within your rights, of course. Absolutely."

"Well, but I didn't refuse," I said wearily. "I said I would just rather not. That's all."

"Well, if you'd rather not, it means in the case of a voluntary statement that you won't, sir, doesn't it? Or is my understanding of the English language wrong? And if you won't, it means you have refused to do so. But don't think I'm pressing you. I'm not pressing Mr. Sibley, Sergeant. You're a witness to that. I'm just pointing out a few facts."

"Using a bit of logical reasoning," added the Sergeant. "Miss Marsden made no objections."

Kate had not told me that. Probably she thought it was only a formality. Although my instincts were still against it, I began to weaken. The Inspector pretended to busy himself with the lock of his briefcase. I sighed, took a sip of whisky.

"All right. Get the paper out, Inspector."

"That's the spirit!" said the Inspector loudly and cheerfully. "That's what we like, a bit of co-operation. That's what we expect, too, from intelligent people like you, if I may say so, sir. Not all these evasions and fiddling about. It's silly."

He took out some sheets of foolscap paper and his fountain pen.

"You can write it down yourself, or if you like, I'll write it down, then you can read it over, alter anything, add to anything, cross anything out, and then sign it."

I told him he could write it down. A statement of the kind made to the police is not a literary work of art. Its one aim is to say as much as possible in as few words as possible and as simply as possible. It is a hodgepodge of short, disjointed sentences, a jerky, unlovely thing. The Inspector and I hacked out the statement together. He was perfectly fair about it. He suggested points which I ought to cover, and he tentatively suggested the terse language I should use, but he never put answers into my mind. After a while we had produced the following statement:

> My name is Michael Sibley, of 354 Harrington Gardens, London, SW7. I make this statement voluntarily. I have been cautioned, and realize that it may be used in evidence. To show that I have understood the nature of this caution, I now append my signature:
>
> Michael Sibley.

> I am a journalist. I have known the deceased, John Prosset, since I was nearly fifteen. I am now thirty-one. Prosset and I were at school together. After leaving school I went to Palesby, where I worked on the *Palesby Gazette* until last August. Prosset was then working in a bank. We corresponded now and again. My relations with Prosset were always very friendly. When I came to London I renewed my friendship with him. He was then

engaged in business with a man called Herbert Day, having left the bank.

I visited him three times at his cottage at Ockleton, Sussex, twice with my fiancée, Miss Kate Marsden, of 238 Manchester Square, London, W1. I was invited to spend the weekend beginning May 27th with Prosset at his cottage, but on May 26th telephoned to say I would not be coming.

However, as it was hot weather, I again changed my mind, and drove down and stayed the Saturday night. I did not mention this earlier to the police because I had heard that suspicions were felt concerning Prosset's death, and I did not wish to be involved in inquiries which might cause me trouble and publicity. I know nothing about his death. He was in good health when I left him. He sometimes drank more than was good for him, but did not show any tendency to do so that weekend up to the time when I left him.

I returned to London on the Sunday morning and worked all day in my room. Between 8:30 and 9 p.m. I called on Miss Marsden, and stayed with her until about one o'clock in the morning of May 28th.

I have read the above statement over and it is true.

Michael Sibley.

The Inspector added his own signature as witness, folded the statement and put it in his briefcase.

"There's nothing in that to cause you a sleepless night, I think," he said.

"I don't suppose so."

I smiled. I was glad I had made the statement now, and regretted the earlier hesitations. I felt that having made a clean breast of almost everything, I had little more to hide and had cleared myself in the eyes of the Inspector. I was aware of a lightening of my spirits. The Inspector and the Sergeant went to the door. Just before they went out, the Inspector turned round.

"Just one other point, Mr. Sibley. Do you happen to remember if Mr. Prosset carried much money about with him as a rule?"

"I don't know. I don't think he did."

"He still had a pound or two in his pocket when he was found. Nothing appeared to have been stolen in the house. So it looks as though we'll have to look for some other motive. If it had been a case of robbery with violence, it would have been so much easier. Pity, really."

"Makes it so much more difficult," explained the tall Sergeant in his musical voice with the pleasant Welsh lilt.

I nodded. "Yes, I suppose it does, really."

The Inspector stood by the door looking at me in a thoughtful manner.

"Did you have a quarrel with him, sir, about anything? Don't jump to the wrong conclusions from the question, sir. I just wanted to know."

I felt my heart beginning to pound in my chest. I licked my lips.

"Quarrel with him?"

"Yes, sir. Those were my words."

"Why should I quarrel with him? He was my friend."

"Friends quarrel now and again, sir," said the Sergeant.

"You're beginning to make things up, Inspector." I endeavoured to speak lightly.

"I wouldn't be the first to do that in this case, sir, it seems to me. No offence meant, of course."

"Well, I didn't quarrel with him," I said loudly.

"That's all right then, sir. Only he said you did, see?"

"That's why the Inspector asked," explained the Sergeant.

"He said I did? He's dead! Or was he alive when he was found?"

"No, sir, he was dead. Only he said it in his diary, sir. That's why I asked."

We three stood looking at each other. Overhead I heard one of the other lodgers tuning in the radio, and down below the voice of Ethel arguing with the cook. My mind went back to my schooldays. I could see Prosset sitting in his little study writing in his small red diary, and wondered quite irrelevantly whether the diary at Ockleton had also been red, and whether he always used red diaries.

"There were two entries, sir. One for the Friday before he died, which said, if I remember rightly, 'K came to my place and stayed late. Funny little thing. Not as cold as she looks.' "

I moistened my lips again. I wanted my voice to sound normal, but in spite of all my efforts I could not keep a tremor out of it.

"There are thousands of people in London whose names begin with K."

"Yes, sir."

"Well, then, it may mean nothing at all."

"No, sir. Only his entry for Saturday, the night before he died, was: 'Had a frightful row with M. Was never more surprised. Case of worm turning at last.' "

I said the first, the only thing that came into my mind.

"I didn't have a row. I never had a row. We had a political discussion, that's all. It was really perfectly friendly. And that's that, Inspector."

He looked at me with a faint smile in his eyes.

"There's no need to get angry, sir."

"I wasn't getting angry. You're always accusing me of getting angry or excited or something. I wasn't getting angry."

"Weren't you, sir? All right then, I believe you."

"Why do you try and make me lose my temper?"

"All right, all right, all right, sir. Nobody's trying to do that. You weren't getting angry, and that's that. We believe him, don't we, Sergeant?"

"I never had a row with him. He was my friend."

"Very well, sir. After all, it's only his word against yours, and he's dead, isn't he? Anyway, your relations with him were always friendly. You said so in your statement, sir. You wouldn't put your name to a statement that wasn't true, would you?"

"The Inspector just thought he'd mention it, that's all," said the Sergeant soothingly. "How many suits have you got, sir?"

"Suits?" The question startled me.

"Yes, suits. The things you wear, you know, sir."

"Four," I replied.

"Four?"

"Yes. Why do you ask?"

"No particular reason, sir."

They nodded to me, and went out. When they had gone, I sat thinking and smoking. All my old uneasiness had now returned. It had increased, indeed, and was no longer even mere uneasiness. I was beginning to be afraid.

I now understood how he had learned about my stay at Ockleton, even about the idea I had had of cancelling the visit. It was no miracle of detective work or of slow, painstaking deduction; it was written down plainly for him to see in Prosset's diary. I wondered uneasily what else was written in it.

CHAPTER 5

When they had gone, I began to think again of Prosset and school, and all that had happened since, and of the implications behind some of the Inspector's words.

I remembered how strange and delightful it was to go about at school with the dull but amenable Crane, instead of the high-spirited and bossy Prosset. He never provoked me and we both seemed to find it easy to give way to the other without loss of dignity or ill-feeling. He was a tall, fair youth with small, pig-like eyes and lashes which were almost invisible, but he had a delightful character, and I was sorry that when we left school our paths separated.

I was very happy during those last few months. Collet, witness of the unhappy incident in the train with Prosset, was Head House Prefect, and he and I and all of us of the same age, though technically divided into prefects and non-prefects, formed a happy and

good-natured band. I used to get out of bed sometimes, when the
rest of the dormitory was asleep, and go to the big window at the
end of the long rows of cubicles, and stand gazing out at the House
playing yard when it was soft and white in the moonlight. The
sight of it and of the school buildings in the distance, and the feeling of being surrounded by friends who liked me and whom I liked
filled me with a delightful melancholy.

I knew the end of the stage was approaching and that nothing
could stop it, and I began to count the days, almost with dread,
until the end of term, savouring each moment to the full. Perhaps
subconsciously I loved the security of it all and was loath to leave
the pleasant harbour. It may well be that if I had not had a rather
curious home background, if I had had the absolute security which
parents and a real home can give, I would not have felt that way.

I hardly gave Prosset a thought. The sight of his curtains in one
boy's study, his cushions in another, his patch of carpet in a third
aroused no emotion in me at all, except an occasional feeling of distaste and of appreciation of my new freedom. Only at Whitsun did
it seem a little strange to be going out for the annual jaunt with the
stolid Crane. All my memories of Whitsun had been gay amusing
ones; at Whitsun, Prosset, Trevelyan and I had invariably been
bound together with bonds of good humour, good fellowship and
laughter. Yet it was on a Whitsun weekend, curiously enough, that
in the fullness of time I thought of killing Prosset.

Crane and I decided that on the Whitsun holiday, a Tuesday,
we would cycle in leisurely fashion into Avonham, arrive there in
time for lunch at the Swan, go to a cinema in the afternoon, have
tea, and cycle back again in equally leisurely fashion. It was all a
bit different from former years; there were no wild plans to see how
many miles we could cover, no dashes into pubs for cider, or quick
dips in the river, but it was pleasant enough.

We'd drank sherry, sitting sedately in the garden of the Swan,
had our lunch, saw the film, and after tea strolled around the town
for half an hour peering into shop windows.

One shop in particular fascinated us. It was a kind of general
emporium for lethal weapons. It had guns and air pistols in the
window; also fishing rods, hooks, artificial minnows and flies, rab-

bit traps, mousetraps, and even a swordstick and walking-stick gun. There were one or two wicked-looking coshes, presumably for nightwatchmen or gamekeepers, and right in the corner of the window I saw a pair of aluminium knuckledusters. Some of the air pistols, Belgian made, were quite cheap in those days, and there was one model with a price tag showing only 12s 6d.

Crane, who was always very well off for pocket money, said, "I've a good mind to buy one."

"What for?"

"We could shoot sparrows and things out of the study window."

"Well, but you'll never be allowed to keep it at the House."

"Why not?"

"We're not even allowed to have blank-cartridge pistols."

"But this is an air pistol. That's different."

I shook my head. "You'll have to hand it in. You'll get six from old Buckley if you're caught with it."

"Well, anyway, let's go and have a look inside."

We went in and looked around. Crane examined one of the pistols. Perhaps it did not look so good at close quarters, as indeed he maintained, or perhaps he had thought over what I had said. He decided not to buy one.

But I bought a knuckleduster for 2s.

I remember thinking in the shop about how I had lain in bed, not really believing in ghosts, but nevertheless half listening for footsteps in the passage, wishing I had some weapon of defence to bolster up my courage, however ineffective such a weapon might have proved against an astral visitor. But I bought the knuckleduster chiefly because I thought it would be nice to carry something about with which one could defend oneself if one were ever in a tight corner. Life lay before me, and one never could tell. I knew that it would not only give me a feeling of security on black nights in dark lanes, but that the mere fact of carrying it about would provide a pleasant inward feeling of drama. I would be going about armed, even if not armed exactly to the teeth.

Nevertheless, I felt a bit sheepish about the whole thing. So much so that I waited until Crane had wandered off to the far end of the shop before I picked a knuckleduster out of a box on the

counter and silently handed the shop assistant the money. I don't
know what he thought. Probably he thought nothing; he was a
sluggish-looking, red-faced yokel. I slipped the knuckleduster into
my right-hand trouser pocket, and carried it there without telling a
soul for some thirteen years. Sometimes, as I felt it against my
thigh, I was glad I had it. I never needed it, but it was comforting.

I received a letter from Prosset in the course of the term. He
was, it seemed, having a very good time in Ireland, fishing and riding, and was in no great hurry to start work in London in the bank.

I replied. I need not have answered, of course, but I imagine he
would have written again. Perhaps I could have answered in less cor-
dial terms, though it is doubtful if that would have had any effect on
him, except to cause him a little passing bewilderment. Anyway,
now that he was no longer overshadowing me I saw no necessity to
be boorish. I did not even wish to hurt his feelings. He was, I
thought, a figure of the past. I wrote approximately as follows:

> My Dear J. P.
>   Thanks very much indeed for your letter. You
> seem to be having a very good time, and I envy you
> your fishing. I went down to Somerset during the
> holidays and got a little shooting, but otherwise have
> not done very much. Things are just the same here. I
> go around with Crane. We cycled to Avonham and
> back for the Whitsun free day, but it wasn't like the
> old days. We miss you at the House. Looking forward
> to seeing you in London before long.
>   Yours ever,
>   Mike

Could I have left the letter unanswered, and broken with him
at that point? I submit the answer must be no, and that common
politeness compelled me to reply.

It was my intention to go into the Sudan Civil Service. Well, I failed at the personal interview. I was not altogether surprised.

Directly I entered the interview room, and saw the interviewer impeccably dressed in a well-tailored suit looking me up and down and noting my cheap, skimped clothes, I suspected he would give me an adverse report. Nowadays I can easily imagine what he wrote: "This candidate did not make a good impression. He is very ordinary in appearance, appeared ill at ease and embarrassed, and to lack the necessary personality. His academic qualifications, if they may be described as such, are undistinguished. I understood from the talk I had with him that in the absence of parents domiciled in Britain, he has been largely brought up by his aunts. He wears spectacles. I feel, in short, that other candidates are more suitably endowed for the vacancies which are to be filled. Not recommended."

It was Aunt Nell who came to the rescue.

My Aunt Edith wrote to her to see if she knew anybody who would "give Michael a start," as she put it.

Aunt Nell wrote back a cold little note saying she would see what could be done. She and Aunt Edith had never been warmly disposed to each other since my Aunt Edith had paid a visit to Aunt Nell many years before, and had announced within ten minutes of her arrival that the house had an "atmosphere" which she viewed with misgiving.

Asked what she meant exactly, she said she felt the dead around her, and very close at that. Aunt Nell never invited her again.

A month later, a letter arrived from Somerset. It was addressed to me. A certain Lord Betterton, it seemed, owned a string of provincial newspapers. Lord Betterton, through a mutual friend, had let it be known that if in the intervening period I would care to learn some shorthand and typing, then in three months' time he would instruct the London office in charge of his provincial offices to find me a post on one of his newspapers as a reporter.

"This job will make a man of you," said Aunt Nell in a postscript. I did not consider the inference complimentary.

It was during those three months that I first met Kate Marsden. We sat at adjoining desks in the typewriting room of the commercial school where I was trying to learn as much shorthand and typing as I could in the time.

We were not allowed to rub out typing errors, and there was in the room an individual who made her way around the desks keeping an eye on the toilers, exhorting here, reprimanding there, and in general acting like a more humane overseer in a Roman galley.

But Kate Marsden had a secret rubber.

Working with furtive speed, it was possible to rub out an occasional typing error without the slave-driver seeing, thus saving yourself the trouble of having to type out the whole exercise again.

So I was really attracted to Kate through her India rubber, and in those days there was certainly little else about her to attract a young fellow with romantic ideas about rescuing beautiful women from runaway horses. She was about eighteen then, a thin, bony girl with lank hair of the type that is blond on top but grows rapidly darker towards the roots. Her complexion was sallow, none too clear, and when she typed or did shorthand she was inclined to peer closely with grey eyes which I guessed would one day be fitted with spectacles. Her mouth, though wide, was perhaps her best feature, for when she smiled you caught a glimpse of a generous nature; it was far too broad a smile for classical beauty, but there was something rather attractive about it. Anyway, it was silly to think of Kate in terms of classical beauty.

One afternoon, because my aunt was going to be out in the evening, I asked Kate Marsden if she would care to come to a cinema with me. She hesitated, and I am not surprised; for if she was no Venus, I was certainly no Greek godling. She said she would have to ring up her parents, and it appeared that she lived near Sevenoaks and travelled up and down to London each day.

When she had done so, we went to the Dominion Cinema, saw some Wild West film or other, and afterwards had a snack at Lyons Corner House in Oxford Street. It wasn't much of an evening out, but it was all I could afford.

It was the first time in her life she had been invited out. She was desperately anxious to show how much she was enjoying it, but apart from that she was no conversationalist. She was shy and sensitive and would colour up for little or no reason. I knew what an agony it was to feel the crimson wave mounting in your cheeks, and to know that nothing could stop it. I sympathized. I suppose Kate and I were somewhat similar types in those early days.

It is pleasant for a young man who is not sure of himself to feel that his efforts are appreciated, so I too enjoyed the outing. Thereafter, until I left London, I used to take her out to the cinema and to Lyons regularly once a week. My Aunt Edith, always generous even though her tipping standards were outmoded, would give me the necessary money with a coy joke every Friday morning.

The last three times I took Kate out we held hands in the cinema, and when I saw her off at the station we kissed each other good night. There was no warmth in our kisses. That was all there was between Kate and me, before I left London. We were hardly sweethearts. We were just a naive young couple experimenting diffidently with flirtation. Testing our wings.

But before I left, I saw Prosset again.

The telephone rang, and my heart gave a funny sort of jump at the sound of his voice. He said he had already been in London some weeks, but had been very busy fitting up his flat; I suppose the man actually assumed that I would be disappointed because he had not rung up before.

"You've got a flat, have you?" I said. "Sounds fine."

"Well, it's not exactly a flat in the proper sense of the word. Why not come round this evening for a snack and a glass of beer?"

I did not want to go, of course, but I had no excuse ready. Anyway, if I hadn't gone then, he would have pinned me down for some other evening.

"There's nothing I should like better," I said.

He gave me his address in Oxford Terrace, near Paddington, and I agreed to go round about 6:30.

I can see now that it was in reality a pretty dreary sort of dump; but it was his first independent dwelling, and he was naturally proud of it. I thought it was quite nice, too, at the time, and rather envied him living in it. It was a large basement room in a terrace of houses lying back from the thoroughfare. It had a stone floor covered with a square of cheap carpet, and a divan bed set against the wall opposite the windows. There was a grate for a coal fire, and a small gas fire and a gas ring on the shilling-in-the-meter principle. Two brown upholstered armchairs, a square table and two hard chairs bought from some mass-production furniture store completed the main furnishings. The walls had been distempered a pale-cream colour, but by now there were patches where it was flaking off. For some reason, there were bars on the windows, and in daytime the room was none too bright. Next door was a small bathroom, hand basin and lavatory.

Prosset looked a little less suntanned than usual, as a result of working all day in a bank, but otherwise fit. He greeted me warmly enough, and as he showed me his flat pointed out with satisfaction that although he paid no more than other lodgers in the house, he had a private bathroom; probably this was thrown in as an added inducement to somebody to come and live in this basement. Lodgers were choosy in those days, and landlords were glad to get them. But the place certainly had one advantage, in that it had its own outside door at the foot of the area steps, so that you could go in and out and usually be unobserved.

He had bought a couple of bookcases, a wireless set, a table lamp, two or three cheap prints showing people hunting foxes, and a couple of extra cushions for the divan. After chatting for a while, he produced a pork pie, bread, butter, cheese, and a bottle of beer, and we fell to. He was, it seemed, getting on very well at the bank.

"Only doing unimportant routine stuff, of course, but I think the manager likes me all right. He hasn't said anything, of course."

"But you can tell by his manner?"

Prosset nodded. "He's keen on rowing, too. Thank God I did rowing at school instead of cricket. I've joined the bank rowing club. They're not too hot, frankly. I think he's glad to have some-body from his own branch with a few guts, if you ask me."

"What about going abroad?"

Prosset looked a bit rueful. "I don't suppose they'll let me go until I've done a couple of years, at least, in London. There are a lot of chaps keen on going East, of course, but I think my manager's fairly influential. If I get to know him well, down at the rowing club, he'll probably wangle something."

"As long as he wangles it in the right direction," I said.

"How do you mean?"

"He may like to keep you, if you row too well."

Prosset's chin went up defiantly in the old way. His eyes darkened. "If he did, I'd leave."

"What would you do?"

He shrugged his shoulders and took a pull at his beer. "I reckon I could turn my hand to most things."

I thought he probably could, too, and I wished I felt so confident about myself. He lit a pipe. I think he smoked a pipe largely because he thought it suited his face; he also smoked cigarettes, but later I noticed that when women were present he stuck to his briar. He smoked a short, squat pipe with a round bowl and a silver band; more often than not it was unlit and he sucked at dead ashes.

"What about you?" he asked at length, filling my glass. "What about the Sudan Civil?"

"That's all washed out. They won't have me."

"Won't have you? What on earth happened?"

"I don't know. They just turned me down."

"Good heavens!" He pondered for a few seconds. "I suppose they just thought you were not the right type." He said it in a tone which indicated that, viewing the matter dispassionately, he reluctantly saw their point of view, unpleasant though it was for me.

"Well, what are you going to do, old man?" he asked.

"I'm going to be a newspaper reporter."

"A reporter? Good Lord!"

"What's wrong with that?"

"Nothing. Only it means you'll be stuck in England. Poor old Mike! When do you start? Which newspaper?"

"I start in a month or so on some provincial paper or other. My aunt knows somebody who knows somebody else—that sort of thing."

He looked at his watch absent-mindedly. "It may be quite fun. You never know." It was clear he thought it a somewhat remote possibility. "You may be investigating murders before long, like on the films," he added.

"And I may not. What do you do with yourself every evening?" I asked, to change the subject.

"Muck about, you know. Go and have a beer in some pub, or poke about in Soho, or go to a flick."

"Alone?"

"Sometimes. Sometimes I go with some chap from the bank. And I've met a girl I'm quite keen on. As a matter of fact, I told her I'd probably bring you along to the Mitre, off Dean Street, about 8:30, if you'd care to come. Do you know the Mitre?"

I said I did not. Prosset smiled, brushed some ash off the lapel of his coat, and stood up. "It's about time you began to see a bit of life. Care to come along? She'll be pleased to meet you. I've often spoken about you."

It was obvious he was rather proud of this girl and wanted to show her to me. I agreed readily enough, and in due course we set out.

"Yes, this girl's a bit of all right, old man," said Prosset as we sat on top of a bus.

"How did you meet her?"

He smiled in what seemed to me a rather embarrassed way. "I met her when we were all having some beer one evening after a practice row. As a matter of fact, she used to go around with one of the chaps in the rowing club; he wasn't in my branch, though."

"And now she goes round with you?"

"He was rather peeved about it, I believe, but she said she was fed up with him, anyway."

"That must have been a consolation to him."

Prosset said nothing. He looked at me sideways, cigarette in mouth. He appeared faintly surprised, and I felt I had scored a delicate hit.

The Mitre was like many public houses which have been patronized at one time or another by theatrical people. There were a number of signed photographs of actors and actresses on the walls, and various cartoons. There was a long counter which curved round to the right, with a reasonable cold buffet at one end. There were high stools at the bar, upholstered in green leather, and half a dozen small tables, with modern metal chairs upholstered in leather of the same colour. The walls were panelled with some sort of light-coloured wood; the place was brightly lit, and the barmen wore white jackets.

A girl stood at the bar at the far end, one of a group of five people. Prosset spotted her as we entered, and said, "Oh, my God, the whole gang's here."

The girl looked round as we approached and said, "Hello, John, you've just come at the right moment. It's Herbert's round." She glanced briefly at me.

The man who appeared to be Herbert said, "What are you having, John?"

After a slight hesitation, he looked at me and asked me what I would have. Prosset ordered a whisky and soda; I said I would like a mild and bitter.

Prosset turned to the girl, and said, "Margaret, meet Mike Sibley. Mike—Margaret Dawson. We were at school together. You remember, he's the chap David and I did everything with."

She was about nineteen, I suppose, slightly built, and wore a wine-coloured jumper under a coat and skirt of light grey. Her hair was bobbed close to her head, and was light brown. But the things I remembered mostly about her were her eyes and her complexion. Her eyes were not very large, but they were a very dark, unusual grey, so dark that they seemed to be streaked liberally with black and her skin was of that curiously pallid, almost mottled colour which reminds you of an orchid. It is rare, and the texture is uncommonly soft. She wore no rouge, and only a touch of lipstick, and she applied the tweezers to her eyebrows with restraint. She smoked a great deal, almost continuously, out of a plain, black, unpretentious holder. When she offered me her hand, it was soft and limp; she did not so much shake hands as place her hand in yours, and allow you to do the shaking.

She said "Hello, Mike" without much enthusiasm, and left it at that.

I must confess I looked at her with interest. She made Kate look like an unsophisticated country bumpkin.

John Prosset and Margaret Dawson, one aged twenty-one, the other nineteen or so. Two kids. Life seemed full of promise to them then.

Herbert Day I disliked at sight, and I have had no reason to alter my opinion. He was of medium height, thinly built, with a pale, dark face. He was dressed in a black pinstripe suit, a white shirt, and a grey tie in which he wore a pearl pin. He had a habit of passing his tongue quickly over his lips which made one think of a snake. He seemed to speak partly through his nose. Prosset introduced him as, "Mr. Day. He's on the Stock Exchange." He smoked Cyprus cigarettes, which gave off a peculiar, slightly acrid smell.

A nondescript married couple, aged about thirty, were introduced more informally as "Ada and Ronnie Mason." They had with them a red-haired youth in his twenties whose only name seemed to be Fred. They were all drinking spirits except me.

After a few moments, Margaret spoke to me. "You're the one who's going to be an engineer or something in Africa, aren't you? Or are you the one whose father has a farm in Cornwall? I always get mixed."

"I was, once upon a time, the one who was going to Africa. They won't have me, though. They don't like my face."

Prosset said, "Never mind, Mike. You can become a theatre critic and give Margaret some good reviews. Mike's going to be a reporter, Margaret."

Margaret looked at me for a moment with interest.

"How exciting. Which paper?"

"It's not settled yet. Somewhere out in the wilds. Are you on the stage?"

"Only in amateurs at present. I've got a job as a librarian. I hate books."

Prosset bought the next round and I switched to gin and lime. Then the Masons went through some rigmarole of tossing to see who should pay for the next, husband or wife. Then Fred bought a round.

I have never had a very good head for spirits, and by this time my brain was not as clear as it could have been. I was aware that common courtesy required me to stand the next round of drinks.

There were seven of us. When I had accepted Prosset's invitation I had not reckoned on going out on a drinking bout. I had 5s. 10d.

I thought that seven whiskies and gins would be 4s. 1d. If one or two of them had lime or orange or lemon, it might cost a few pence more. I would just have enough.

It was Herbert Day who upset everything by saying, "Do you mind if I change and have a brandy, old man?"

The barman brought the drinks. He said, "Six and three altogether, please."

I stood looking at the change I had dragged out of my pocket. Out of the corner of my eye I could see Margaret Dawson watching me curiously. I was trying without much success to think of what to say. I put all the change clumsily on the counter while the barman waited. In those days I had a tendency to blush and now, already flushed with drinks, I felt the colour mounting to my cheeks. I pulled out my wallet and pretended to look for some money. Prosset had his eye on me. I felt they were all watching this funny-looking youth who lavishly ordered drinks for which he had not the money to pay.

Suddenly Prosset said in his calm, self-assured way, "Are you short? Here's ten bob I borrowed from you."

He handed it to me without a smile, quite smoothly and naturally. It was beautifully done. The timing was so perfect that everybody would know that I had not lent him 10s, yet they would admire his exquisite tact for the way he had stepped forward to help me out. Just for a second his eye caught mine. "Poor old Mike!" he seemed to be saying, just as he had said it the day when he and Collet had been discussing tailors in the train.

Closing time was not the end. I found myself in the back of Herbert Day's car. Ada Mason was sitting with her husband in front; Day was snuffling through his nose, saying something about keeping clear of the gear lever. I was at the back with red-haired Fred on my knee. Prosset was at the back, too, with Margaret between us. Inevitably her firm thigh was pressed against mine, and I liked it.

But her head was on Prosset's shoulder, and his arm was around her.

I remember later picking at a greasy fried egg and a rasher of bacon which Ada Mason had cooked in her flat. Some of us were sitting in chairs or on the sofa, and some on the floor, and I was dimly aware that since the evening had begun the party had somehow grown in numbers, and there were two or three other people whom I did not know. Prosset's voice, sounding a long way off, said, "Old Mike's looking a bit green."

Somebody gave me a cup of coffee, which improved matters a little, but only temporarily. The smell of fried food in the room, the cigarette and tobacco smoke, especially the smell of Herbert Day's cigarettes, were too much. I rose unsteadily to my feet. Bill Mason, who was more sober than the rest and was doubtless watching for this moment, led me from the room.

When I came back, I had some more coffee and a piece of bread and cheese and felt better. I just felt tired and cold and could hardly keep my eyes open. I wanted to go home, but did not wish to be the first to make a move. Some of them were drinking more beer. I saw Prosset and Margaret and Herbert Day sitting on the sofa. Day was talking ten to the dozen. I watched his tongue flickering in and out.

Suddenly Fred, who had been sitting quietly in a chair, burst into violent life. He began to hum music; then he rose to his feet, pirouetted on his toes, flung his arms out, stood on one leg with the other stretched out behind him, and gradually swung into an energetic ballet dance. Nobody took much notice.

Herbert Day said, "Now he's off. There he goes."

Prosset said, "Fred always does that when he is tight."

"Why?" I asked.

Prosset shrugged his shoulders. "God knows. Sometimes he starts in a pub. Then we have to restrain him."

At about one o'clock we left.

Herbert Day drove with Fred in front beside him. Margaret, Prosset and I were behind as before. But now Margaret was sitting on Prosset's knees; she had her arms about his neck. From time to time Prosset leaned forward and kissed her; they were long kisses, lasting twenty or thirty seconds. They put Fred off somewhere in South Kensington and then drove me to Earl's Court.

On the pavement, I turned round to thank Herbert Day once more for the lift and to say a final good night. He was leaning over the driver's seat looking at Prosset and Margaret. He said, "What about you two? Oxford Terrace for you, Margaret, too, I suppose?"

He sniggered in his nasal, muffled kind of way.

I envied Prosset, with Margaret, in his own basement flat. Fundamentally, I suppose envy and jealousy, and their evil progeny called malice, were at the root of most of my trouble with Prosset.

Two days later I left to take up my job on the *Palesby Gazette.*

As I brooded over the police visit, I was aware that something, some small, forgotten incident, had occurred while I was a reporter at Palesby which I would prefer the police not to know. It was nothing that I had done, nothing illegal, but I felt that in the present circumstances, though it was trivial in itself, it might have some significance to the Inspector. I thought it was something I had said, or something which somebody had said to me, but what it was I could not for the life of me recall.

I mixed myself another drink. As I sat in my chair I kept worrying about Palesby, and about Cynthia Harrison, who lived there.

CHAPTER 6

Although I am a southerner, not merely by birth, but by preference, I must confess that I never encountered in the south such warm-heartedness among townspeople or such comradeship among newspapermen as I met with on the *Palesby Gazette*.

The town is a fishing port on the east coast, and is itself unattractive, though the country just outside it is lovely. There are smoking factories in Palesby, a number of industries connected with the fish trade, and docks where the little trawlers berth side by side in the intervals between their long trips to northern waters. There is not much else.

There is one broad street where the smarter shops are situated, and two or three fairly important long streets served by rattling trams. There are three cinemas, a music hall and a repertory theatre; and there is the City Centre, as they call it, dominated by the Guildhall with its police courts, council chamber and numerous rooms for committee meetings. The rest of the town consists of a great number of small side streets composed of little red-brick houses.

In retrospect, it seems to have rained a great deal, so that the streets were always covered with a thin, watery mud.

There is also the Central Park. I must not forget that, because it played a not unimportant part in my life.

Palesby is not inspiring, then, but it has an *esprit de corps* second to none in the whole of Britain. Its citizens, brought up within sombre confines, regard people who live elsewhere with a sort of restrained pity. Its aldermen and councillors when opening bazaars or making any kind of speech at all will hardly ever sit down without somehow dragging in the name of Palesby in a complimentary manner.

If the occasion should be the presentation of prizes at the police sports, the speaker will point out, amid a seemly round of applause, that Palesby has a police force which is second to none in the country; if it is the annual Guest Night at the Society of Protestant Vigilantes, it will be pointed out that there is no more vigilant, protesting set of defenders of the Church of England than the citizenry of Palesby; on the other hand, if it is a Catenian dinner, it will transpire that nowhere on this side of the Channel is there a more devout body of Roman Catholics than in Palesby. It would not surprise me to learn that the Governor of the local prison stoutly maintained that though crime might be unfortunately increasing, at least the convicts in Palesby were as skilful and yet as peaceful as any in the land.

Even when the local football team was defeated, as it often was, it was heartening to note that this was clearly no reflection upon the skill of the players, who indeed played as cleverly as any in the league; only a mysterious concatenation of cosmic circumstances could account for their ill-luck.

They were, and I suppose still are, a forthright people, like so many in the north and Midlands; but though outspoken they were not offensive unless you were looking for offence.

The *Gazette* offices were in a modern building in St. Mark's Street, which is the main thoroughfare. The reporters worked in a

large room on the first floor; the Chief Reporter, a man called
Grimshaw, had a small room to himself leading off from the main
reporters' room, the connecting door being always open. He was a
tall, heavily built man with a red face, thinning hair and very thick
spectacles. Almost his first words were: "How did you get this job,
lad? Influence?"

This was too near the truth for my liking. I said, "No. I applied
for it in London. Why?"

"I just wondered, lad. Reporters' jobs are a bit difficult to get
these days." He had not believed me, of course, and I knew it, and
he knew I did. He went on looking at some newspaper cuttings for
a moment. He and I were the only people in the room. The other reporters were all out on jobs.

After a while he looked up and said, "Got any digs to live in,
lad?"

"Not yet. I've left my luggage at the station."

"What's your salary?"

"Two pounds a week."

"Any experience?"

"No."

"And you didn't get the job through knowing somebody?"

"No."

He said nothing. Eventually he heaved himself up and went out
of the room. I began idly turning over a file of newspapers. In three
or four minutes he was back again.

"About your digs. You might like to try Mrs. Martin's place.
Here's the address. She's the mother of one of our telephonists;
she'll probably make you comfortable. One of the others, Hailey,
the sports man, lives there. Off you go. You needn't come back till
tomorrow. Nine sharp, lad."

The address was No. 2 Oaks Street, about half a mile from the
centre of the town in a district called Summerfields. I walked back
to the station, commissioned a taxi, piled my luggage in, and gave
the driver the address. I do not know why Summerfields has not
long since changed its name. It lies on a tram route, and is composed of the inevitable streets of red houses, shabby and smoke-
begrimed. There are no fields, and when summer comes with its

heat, the place is almost as unpleasant as in winter, when the mud covers the footpaths. Oaks Street, long denuded of any trees at all, let alone oaks, lies about twenty yards from the level-crossing gates. Periodically throughout the day and night trains rumble across. On the corner is a public house called The Greyhound, though inevitably more often known as The Dirty Dog.

I kept the taxi waiting while I negotiated with Mrs. Martin, just so that she could see that I had not made up my mind for certain. The talk took place in the front parlour, a room which in all the years I lived in the house I cannot remember ever sitting in again.

It had a fawn carpet, a sofa, four high-backed chairs in light oak with rush seats, a round polished table and an upright piano. Near the window was a tall pedestal bearing an empty birdcage. The room was ostensibly kept clean and tidy for special occasions, but after my arrival there never seemed to be an occasion considered by Mrs. Martin to be so special as to warrant its use.

She herself was a small, nervy little woman, thin and grey-eyed with regular features which at one time had certainly been attractive. But she was now in her late sixties, her hands were worn, and she had ill-fitting teeth which clicked. I was to discover that she had a keen sense of humour and took a close personal interest in "her gentlemen" and in everybody at the *Gazette* office. Every evening she would closely cross-question her daughter Phyllis on the day's doings and the day's gossip. She certainly took a closer interest in my own activities than my kind but absent-minded Aunt Edith.

After she had shown me my room, she asked if it would suit.

"How much will you charge me if I take it?"

"Well, I charge Mr. Hailey twenty-five shillings a week, Mr. Sibley." She spoke diffidently, watching the effect of the words on me. Maybe I looked surprised, for she added hastily, "That includes everything, Mr. Sibley, three meals a day and a snack before you go to bed, if you like, and lighting and laundry and everything."

If I looked surprised, it was because it was so much cheaper than I expected. I paid the taxi and moved in. The date was October 2nd, 1930.

Behind the best parlour which was never used were the living room and the kitchen. The living room was a shabbily comfortable place, with a big square table covered with a red-tasselled cloth, a large black grate and two well-worn easy chairs stuffed with horse-hair and covered with black leather. These two chairs were at the disposal of Mrs. Martin's "gentlemen," and there was a smaller chair for the daughter Phyllis. Mrs. Martin, on the rare occasions when she was in the living room with us, always sat at the table mending and darning.

Phyllis was a young woman of about thirty-five with brown hair and grey eyes. She was not good-looking, but she was pleasant; she wore good warm jumpers and thick woollen stockings, and in wet weather galoshes. Phyllis had her meals with Hailey and me, but I never once saw Mrs. Martin eat, though I sometimes saw her drinking a cup of tea. She alleged she had "a bit of something" in the kitchen now and then, but though I came in at all hours of the day and evening I never caught her at it.

On the first floor were two bedrooms furnished with small iron beds, a cupboard, a patch of carpet, and a washstand with a basin and water-jug. On the second floor, at the top of the steep, dark staircase, under the sloping roof, were two more bedrooms. One was occupied by Mrs. Martin, Phyllis and the mongrel dog Peter; and in the other Mr. Martin lived and had his being.

When I was taken up to be introduced on my first evening I saw a man of about sixty-eight, completely bald except for some hair round his ears and neck. He sat in a big, old-fashioned brass bedstead, wearing a grey woollen cardigan. He was almost bedridden as a result of heart trouble incurred during the First World War. He would totter out of bed and wash each morning, and then go back to bed again; his hands trembled a little, but otherwise he was alert and bright. Like his wife, he was cockney born, and still retained a trace of a London accent.

If this description gives the impression that he was a gentle, doddering old invalid with a quavering voice and a mild manner, I must correct it by adding that never in my life have I met a man whose conversation was so besprinkled with "damns," "blasts" and "hells." It was as though a forceful character confined to bed through ill-health found in this way some outlet for his natural energy and high spirits. He had a loud voice and rarely slept, so that at almost any hour of the day or night a roar and a string of strong adjectives might send Mrs. Martin or her daughter, or even me, hurrying to his bedroom to see what he wanted. They loved him dearly, and I am not surprised.

He was never morose or bad-tempered; on the contrary, he was a great talker, read the papers avidly, and had decided opinions, which he sometimes scribbled on paper and sent to the Editor of the *Palesby Gazette*. His hobby was knitting and crochet work, and around Christmastime he would order dolls, naked, from a wholesaler, knit clothes for them and dispose of them to shops in the town. At other times he knitted women's bedjackets and children's garments.

Around him in his room, were all the memories of a lifetime. Every inch of shelf and almost all the wall space were covered by ornaments, knick-knacks, pictures, coloured calendars, photographs and other treasures. There was a large picture of the late Lord Kitchener, a large picture, too, of himself with some other soldiers—his war medals hung beneath it; pictures of himself and Mrs. Martin on their wedding day, of Phyllis as a baby and Phyllis as a little girl; a coloured picture, cut from some magazine, of King George V and Queen Mary; a weather barometer, a polished brass shellcase, and much else besides.

In winter a tiny coal fire smouldered in the room all day. In summer, through the window by his bed, he could just see a strip of blue sky above the house opposite, and a section of the star-jewelled night during his long, sleepless hours. Sometimes, for a short while, the moon would be visible, and he had invented a system of weather forecasting by watching the weather when the moon was on the turn. He swore it was "damned accurate," and even if it wasn't, he added, it "helped to pass away part of the blasted night."

My Aunt Nell was right.

The life of a provincial reporter was a hard one. It turned me from an over-sensitive, introspective youth into something resembling a normal, objectively minded young man who could hold his own with anybody, except Prosset; and I still like to think that had he lived I might even have fought clear of that overpowering, blanketing personality. Only I wasn't given time, in the end; and perhaps I never should have done so, anyway.

Perhaps I am not even free now. He has already reached out to me once from beyond the grave—or so it seemed.

We used to get into the office at about ten past nine, and would spend some minutes glancing through the morning papers while Grimshaw marked up the diary for the day. One reporter would be detailed to attend the Stipendiary Magistrate's Court, another the less important Court presided over by JPs.

A third reporter would be responsible for what was known as Calls. He was the emergency stand-by man, too. He would ring the infirmary and the various police stations, and the fire station, and write any snippets of news which he obtained on the telephone as a result of his calls. There was always something: an accident or two—fatal, with any luck; a fire, a burglary, an occasional suicide. If the news merited it, he would go out and visit the scene of the occurrence himself and write a fuller story.

Somebody would be marked in the diary for Inquests; another man, called Fish-Dock Phillip, covered the fish-dock for news and gossip about trawlers. Hailey would be out getting his sports gossip-column material. If conditions required it, a man was detailed to do the Weather Story, gathering news of drought or floods, water shortage or storm damage, as the case might be.

The police courts often finished by 11:15 and several of us would try to forgather for coffee and dominoes in a café, the loser paying the bill.

In the afternoons there would be bazaars, municipal committee meetings, council meetings, charity parties, flower shows, and all the normal activities of a provincial town. Nor was this all. Three or four evenings a week we would get an evening job; a dance organized by some club or society which had to be reported, or a lecture, or a whist drive. Quite often we went to bed at one or two o'clock in the morning, because we had to have our copy ready written for handing in first thing next day.

I had a certain aptitude for writing and a zest for work. I loved my life. I was independent, earning my own living, and in a happy office. Each evening I looked forward to the following day.

Now and again three or four of us would get together and play cards in somebody's house. We played for small stakes, and there was much laughter and joking, and a mid-evening break when steaming cups of tea and great thick sandwiches and cake would be served up. Sometimes we drank a few bottles of beer; and the air would grow thick with tobacco smoke. On the way home we would stop to buy fish and chips, and walk through the streets eating the food from the newspaper wrapping, which is the only really enjoyable way to eat fish and chips, and therefore the only really civilized way. If we had had enough beer, we sang riotous songs.

During the years I was at Palesby I corresponded at irregular intervals with Prosset and to a lesser extent with Kate, but I did not see either of them on the rare and brief visits I paid to London. I replied to Prosset's letters because, as usual, I felt it was the only thing I could do. He was still at the bank, but expecting to go abroad "any time now"; in the end, he died without ever leaving these shores, except to visit his family in Ireland.

Kate's letters were dull, because her life was dull. They were filled with trivialities which were of no interest to me because I had no real sentimental attachment to her. I always intended looking her up the next time I visited London, but I never did, and inevitably we began to write less and less. But Prosset was different; it was as though he could not bring himself to let me escape from him completely.

It was a good, hard life in Palesby, and I had not a care in the world until one Sunday afternoon when I took the mongrel Peter for a walk in Central Park. By then I had been on the *Gazette* some seven or eight years. This dog was half collie and half something else which it was impossible to determine. He was a very friendly dog, and would sometimes go up to complete strangers and make friends with them.

The day in question was one of those watery April days, and there had been a heavy shower or two of rain succeeded by sunshine. There were puddles on the paths, green buds on the trees, and a fair number of people taking advantage of the warm sunshine between the showers.

A girl was sitting on a bench reading a book, eating chocolate. The dog Peter went up to her and had a sniff. I whistled him off, but he was a disobedient brute. The girl raised her hand, holding the chocolate out of his reach, which the dog regarded either as provocation or as an invitation to play. He raised himself on his hind legs, tail wagging, and put a very muddy paw on to the lap of her navy-blue suit.

I hurried over and hauled him off, but the damage was done, if you could call it that, and a large brown paw mark stained the girl's skirt.

"I'm terribly sorry. I'm afraid he has wrecked your skirt."

I took out my handkerchief and offered it to her. She took it and dabbed rather ineffectually at the mud.

She said, "It's all right. It'll come out when it's dry. It'll brush off all right later."

She had a Palesby accent, but also a lilt of some other origin which was not at the moment clear to me. Anyway, I wasn't thinking about her voice. I was thinking that she was very good-looking. She was about twenty-two, and had light-brown hair and blue eyes; her face was very made-up, the cream being laid on so thick that you had an impression of smooth china; her eyelashes were stiff with mascara, and she had plucked her eyebrows into such a shape as to give her a look of continual surprise. She was small and had good legs and neatly shod feet, but was built rather on the square side for classical beauty. Her worst feature was her nose, which was prominent and had a high bridge. Her face was rather broad, and tapered to a little pointed chin. She was no real beauty, but her blue eyes and white teeth, even the very artificiality of her make-up had its attractions. I think her artificiality was attractive because her general turn-out was so neat and clean that it aided the overall impression that here was somebody who took great trouble with every aspect of her appearance. Anyway, I liked the look of her.

I said again, "Well, I'm really sorry. Are you sure it will be all right."

"Quite all right, I'm sure." She smiled, and when she did so, her face came to life, and I could see that on each side of her mouth were creases which defied the make-up and lent character to her features.

I said, "Do you mind if I sit down and smoke a cigarette?"

I took out my case and offered her one; she hesitated a second, then took one, and I gave her a light.

"What kind of dog is he, anyway?"

"Part collie and part something else. Your guess is as good as mine. He's very disobedient, though."

She looked at me for a moment. "You're not a Palesby man, are you?"

"I'm a Londoner. I got a job as a reporter on the *Gazette,* so I came up here."

"That must be fine. Getting around and seeing things and people."

"It's better than being stuck in an office all day. Do you work?"

"Oh, yes. I'm a typist. At Benton's, the soap people."

"Like it?"

She shrugged her shoulders. "I've got to do something. Dad's dead, and Mum and I live together. We share the house with my brother Bill and his wife. He's a mate on a trawler, so Mavis is alone a good deal. I've got a sister, too. She's married and lives on the other side of the town. She's older than me. She's got a couple of kids."

We talked a little longer, and I told her about my early life. It was naturally a carefully edited account, sufficiently truthful to make her laugh, but omitting the dankness of the garden, the smell of mice, the dreariness of the whole street in Earl's Court. I enjoyed talking to her. When she got up and said she must go home, I knew I wanted to see her again. I could not find anything to say, and was thinking furiously as she pulled on her gloves. All I managed to say was, "Perhaps I'll see you again one Sunday."

"I don't come into the park much on Sundays. Still, you never know. Bye-bye."

It was not what one could call encouraging, but at least it wasn't a direct rebuff. Life was making me philosophical, and I was beginning to know my strengths and weaknesses—what I could do, and what I could not. I knew that at first sight few people liked me, but that if I could talk to them for a while their earlier distaste melted, and that over a period I could rub along with most people very well. Given time, I thought I could make this girl, whose name I did not even know, like me. So far I had not had a permanent girl-friend, though I had occasionally made up a party of four for a visit to the cinema or a drive in the country. Somehow I had not had either much time or inclination or money. At first I had saved a portion of my very small salary to buy decent clothes, and then I had been anxious to save a bit to put in the bank, because journalism is a precarious career and you never quite know when you may be out on your ear without a job.

I watched her as she walked away. She had pretty legs, I thought again, and not at all a bad figure, even if it was a little too square. I returned home, had my usual high tea, and settled by the fire to read.

I did not read for long. There was a telephone in the house because, now that I had settled down in my job, the office agreed that it was useful to have both Hailey and myself on the end of a line. They paid the rental, half the local calls up to a certain maximum, and such toll calls, of course, as were made on behalf of the *Gazette,* which were few enough. At ten past six it rang. I heard Grimshaw's heavy voice on the other end.

"That you, Sibley? Get down to Suffolk Street, lad. There's been a murder there. Some tart's been stabbed by a Lascar seaman, or something."

"A murder?"

I could hardly credit it. There hadn't been a single murder in Palesby since I had been there.

"I've got Charlie down there with his camera. Nip along, lad, and find out something about the woman."

"Righto. Anybody else going down?"

"I can't find any other bloody reporter on the whole staff. They're all out or ill or something."

I remember thinking it was not much of a compliment to have been telephoned last, but I did not care. I pictured myself finding vital clues, an overlooked bloodstained matchstick, perhaps, and being complimented by the Superintendent. There might also be a discreet reference in the *Gazette's* gossip feature to the valuable help afforded the police by the *Gazette* reporter's powers of observation. Perhaps even a picture of the vital matchstick. Prosset had predicted some such drama. Grimshaw's next words damped me down a bit.

"He's given himself up to the police, so be careful what you write, lad. A few facts about the woman, and how it was discovered. Then just say: a man later made a statement to the police. Get it?"

"I get it."

"Keep in touch with the police tonight. Find out if he's been charged. If he has, just say so, and give his name. Get the story in sharpish tomorrow morning. They may do a special edition. OK?"

He rang off. On the films reporters dash off in powerful cars, but not in Palesby. If you couldn't get a lift in the photographer's car, you went by tram. Suffolk Street was down in the dock area. It did not look very different from many other streets in the better parts of town, except that it was narrower and meaner.

There were the same squalid little red houses, the same damp pavements, cats on walls, and children playing around lamp standards. Halfway down the street a small crowd was gathered round one of the houses. Two cars were parked outside it, and three uniformed policemen were keeping the pavement clear in front of the house. We were on good terms with the police in that town, and I shouldered my way through the crowd and spoke to one of the constables.

"I'm a *Gazette* reporter. Can I have a word with the Inspector?"

"He's inside. Your photographer chap has been and gone."

I nodded and went into the little hall. Somebody had had fish for tea, and the smell of it hung about. There was a murmur of voices from a room on the left. The door was half open and I put my head round it. Inspector Daley was seated at a little table taking a statement. With him was a sergeant. Opposite Daley was an old, dirty-looking woman, snivelling into a shawl.

The Inspector and I got on well, because I always gave him prominence when he was prosecuting in the police courts, and he thought the publicity was helpful. He got up when he saw me and came into the hall.

"Where is she?" I asked.

"In the mortuary. Her room's upstairs. On the right. You can go up if you want to."

"Thanks. What about the bloke?"

"He's 'inside.' Coloured seaman called Geoffries—James Nelson Geoffries. That's all I know about him at the moment."

"Charged?"

"Not yet. I'll be charging him when I get back."

"Can I have the woman's name?"

He flicked over two or three pages of his notebook.

"Mary O'Brien, aged forty-two, born in Cork. No regular employment. Prostitute, of course. We've had her inside half a dozen times on different charges."

"How did you catch him?"

"We didn't. He walked in and gave himself up. Threw his knife on to the station counter."

"Know why he did it?"

"Jealousy. That's according to this old bitch I'm questioning, anyway. She'd been going around pretty regular with this bloke Geoffries, even though she was a tart. But when he went to sea, she had to live, of course. He heard about it when he came back and did her in."

"When did it happen?"

"Only about an hour or so ago."

I thanked him and went upstairs. There was another constable standing outside the room where the murder had taken place. In the room on the other side of the passage a Negro, a slatternly white woman and an old man who might have been the husband of the hag downstairs were talking in low tones. The constable had heard me talking to the Inspector downstairs. He opened the door of the room, and I went in.

I have never thought there is anything dramatic or exciting about the scene of a murder, especially if it has taken place in a bedroom. There are too many trivial, everyday things lying about; a pair of trousers on a chair, the seat of the trousers well worn and shiny; or a pair of soiled socks on the floor, or a dirty collar.

Murders in bedrooms do not happen at a time of day when the room has been freshly tidied. There is always an element of disorder. The scene is sordid. The only reason why some of these crimes make tolerable reading, if you like that kind of reading, is because all that which is squalid does not appear in the printed page. The imagination of the reader is left to conjure up a scene of strong human emotions, and emotions, if violent enough, are either sublime or devilish, and in either case are awe-inspiring.

But when you come in person to the scene of the crime, the emotions have departed, and all that remains are things that are extremely mundane. And there is nothing more dramatic about the actual corpse of a murdered person than there is about a fat bluebottle which somebody has squashed on a window ledge. It is a nasty mess, that is all.

The room in Suffolk Street was small, papered with blue-flowered wallpaper which in some places was peeling off. There was an iron double bed occupying most of the room, a marble-topped washstand with a basin of dirty water on it; and by the side of the basin a half-full bottle of gin, a chipped cup and a used glass.

The floor was covered with linoleum, ragged at the edges, and there was a strip of carpet on each side of the bed. An inexpensive dressing table with a hairbrush, a few bottles and pots of cheap cosmetics and a beer bottle stood under the window. A pile of woman's underclothes and a pair of corsets were on a hard chair by the side of a small gas fire. A man's cloth cap was on the floor.

The bed was unmade and crumpled, but the police had pulled the blankets up so that only a few smudges of blood on a pillow were visible.

It was very quiet, and the chief impression you had was as if somebody had stopped a clock. When I turned to leave the room, I noticed a small picture, a cheap, coloured reproduction in a wooden frame on the wall to the right of the door. It was a picture of the Madonna and Child. It seemed a strange thing to find in that room.

I should say that she must have been tempted to take it down sometimes. But maybe she thought that to do so would be finally to admit to herself that she was finished. Perhaps that poor prostitute who slept with Lascars and the riff-raff of a seaport continued to make excuses to herself right to the end. Such women often think that one day they may be able to marry and settle down. Perhaps even on the day the knife killed her some faint hopes had stirred that, some time, her luck would change and everything would be all right in the end.

You can't tell for certain.

CHAPTER 7

That, then, was my first murder assignment.

When I returned home at about 8:15 I wrote my story out, had a cup of tea, and related all the details for the benefit of Mrs. Martin and Phyllis. At about ten o'clock I went upstairs to have a word with Mr. Martin. I usually tried to find time for a chat with him in the late evening, and we used to discuss the day's news.

He was knitting a jumper in red wool when I went in, and had naturally heard about the murder. He sat up in his big bed, wearing the old grey woollen cardigan, hard at work under the harsh electric light, and barely looked up when I went in.

"How's it going?"

He put his knitting down. "Can't dam' well grumble. They tell me you've been out on a murder."

"That's right. Not much in it, though. The chap gave himself up."

"No mystery to solve?"

"No. I suppose he'll swing all right."

"Oh, he'll swing all right. Hell! Of course he will."

"Serves him right, the brute."

I was thinking of the picture on the wall by the door, and of the woman who had not known that morning was to be her last. The old man picked up his knitting again and said nothing. He was like that; when he did not agree with you, he would sometimes remain silent.

I said, "Are you one of these people who don't agree with hanging?"

He took a sip at the glass of milk which Mrs. Martin had brought him in accordance with her nightly custom.

"Don't you believe in hanging?" I pressed him.

He looked at me ferociously and said, "No! Hell, no! Except in cases of poisoning."

"Why on earth not?"

"Because it's cruel. That's dam' well why."

I had always thought he was a man of sound common sense, a representative of the middle classes, an upholder of tradition, and a bulwark against political extremism and crankiness in general.

"But what about the poor bloke who's been done in? What about him?"

"He's dead. Nothing is going to bring him to life. Besides you don't only hang the blasted murderer. Have you ever thought what it's like to be the mother or father or wife or children of a murderer who is hanged? Counting the damn days, then the hours, then the blasted minutes. Knowing that somebody you love is getting more and more afraid. Bloody hell, it's awful. And then the anniversaries: they keep thinking, 'It was a week ago today,' or 'It was a month ago,' or a year ago.'"

"The chap ought to think of that before he kills somebody," I said obstinately.

"Maybe he ought to, but he doesn't. And whether he ought to or not makes no difference to his dam' wife or mother. Besides, suppose there's been a mistake? What then?"

"There never is a mistake. Not these days."

"Ever heard of circumstantial evidence?"

"Of course I have."

"It's dangerous. Hell, it's dangerous."

"Oh, pooh," I laughed. "Not these days, it isn't. They never hang the wrong man these days. Anyway, it's a good job you're not Home Secretary."

I attended the police court proceedings when Geoffries appeared in the dock the following day. They only lasted a few minutes. Inspector Daley, in evidence, described how he arrested and charged Geoffries. When charged, Geoffries replied, "Yes, sir."

"And on that evidence," said the prosecuting solicitor, "I ask for a remand for a week."

Everybody looked bored. One of the warders in the dock with Geoffries was picking his teeth with a pin; the other had his elbow on the side of the dock and was leaning his head on his hand.

Geoffries sat staring at the floor of the dock, and did not look up except to say, "Not murder. She made me do it." Asked if he wished for free legal aid, he said, "Yes." For the rest of the time he sat leaning forward, his elbows on his knees, his hands hanging loosely. He wore a chocolate-coloured suit, but no collar or tie. Because he was dark-skinned, he looked very much alone in a white man's court. He also looked quite listless, as though he had now seen enough of this world.

It was strange to think that the ageing and painted prostitute whose ill-used body was lying in the mortuary had meant enough to him to make him lose his life on her account. I suppose that in an alien and unsympathetic port she was his sole anchor, the only person who brought him, or simulated for him, what passed for human warmth and affection. Rather than risk losing her, he killed her. Ackersley, the schoolmaster, had at least made certain of his loss before he killed himself. Though the one was a semi-savage and the other a cultured man, they both broke, in their different ways, under the same strain.

Later, at the Assizes, his counsel based such defence as he could muster on provocation, and made some sort of emotional appeal to the jury to find him guilty of manslaughter. The judge, of course, tore it to shreds, and it was all quite useless. Counsel might as well have saved his breath.

One may doubt, too, whether the Home Secretary found cause for any really lengthy consideration of the affair before dismissing the appeal. May O'Brien had to be avenged and other prostitutes protected.

It was what they call in official circles a nice, straightforward case.

But I was too young to feel any pity, and anyway I was very busy, and soon had something else to occupy my leisure thoughts. On the day when Geoffries was remanded I had an evening job. The Palesby police had organized a dance in aid of the Police Orphanage.

Such dances never give a reporter much trouble. You go along and do a couple of descriptive paragraphs, noting any unusual decorations or events; you give a paragraph to the Mayor's speech, in which he says the town's police force is second to none in the country; and you add the names of the Master of Ceremonies, the band leader, and any local dignitaries who may be there. Then you can either drink beer in the bar, dance, or go home—whichever suits you best. Hardly any of the men wear evening dress, and any young man can go up to any girl and ask her for a dance without the formality of an introduction.

I had never had any dancing lessons as a boy, but once or twice at similar functions in Palesby I had been persuaded to shuffle round the floor, usually with some not very good-looking girl whom somebody had forced upon me. Now, as I stood on the edge of the floor, I had all the details I wanted and was wondering whether to go home, or to go and have some more beer with Inspector Daley, when I saw with great delight that the girl I had met in the park was standing talking to another girl on the far side of the floor.

As I watched, a young man in a sports jacket and grey flannel trousers went up to them, bowed, and took her companion off for a dance. I went over at once. She looked round as I drew near and smiled.

"Hello. How's the mud patch?"

"Oh, that's gone. I was wondering whether by any chance you'd be reporting this dance."

"What about coming and having a drink?" I said, secretly very pleased that she had thought of me at all. "I'm afraid I'm not much good at dancing."

"Well, I've just had one."

"Well, have another to keep it company. Make you grow into a big girl."

"What about Mavis?"

"Who's she?"

"My sister-in-law, the girl I was talking to. She'll wonder where I've got to."

"She won't have far to look. Come on," I coaxed.

"Well, I should like to."

I bought her a gin and lime and ordered a beer, and we went and sat at a small table. Her brother Bill was at sea again, so she and her sister-in-law had come to the dance by themselves.

"After all, as I said to Mavis, it doesn't do Bill any good for you to be sitting moping at home while he is away. I mean, does it?"

She looked at me questioningly. I thought that doubtless Mary O'Brien had said much the same thing. It was only a matter of degree.

"Not a bit," I said. "What about you? Have you got a boyfriend at sea?"

She turned to me with an amused expression in her blue eyes.

"Listen to us! We are getting nosey, aren't we? What if I have or I haven't?"

"Nothing. I just wondered. A chap can ask a question."

"Those who ask no questions get told no lies."

"So I've heard before somewhere."

Her eyes, which had been fixed on my face with the peculiar surprised look brought about by the way she shaped her brows, flickered very slightly. She was, I discovered later, a quick-witted girl, despite her unfortunate tendency to talk in clichés.

"Are you one of the sarcastic kind?" she asked tartly.

"Of course not. Butter wouldn't melt in my mouth."

"That's just as well, then. I don't like sarcastic chaps. If you want to say a thing, I always say, then say it, and don't wrap it up and try to be clever. So you'd better keep your sarcasm for London. We're plain folk up here."

"I don't think you're at all plain—if I may say so."

This miserably crude compliment seemed to mollify her. She smiled, and after a short pause said, "As a matter of fact, if you want to know, I did have a boyfriend, and he's here tonight. But I've chucked him up."

"Why? Mind you, I'm very glad to hear it."

She stamped out her cigarette in an ashtray. "That doesn't mean the situation is vacant, even if you are a reporter and a quick worker. Don't get any funny ideas."

"My ideas are never funny. They're mostly deadly serious."

She gave me a quick look, which I was to recall later, but said nothing.

"Have another gin and lime?"

She shook her head and suggested that I should dance with her.

"But I can't dance. Not properly."

"Then it's high time you learnt. Come on. I'll give you a lesson." I got up rather reluctantly.

"Well, don't say you haven't been warned. I suppose you know I haven't any idea what your name is? Mine's Michael Sibley."

"Mine's Cynthia Harrison," she said.

I followed her out of the refreshment room. She was dressed in a flowered pink frock, with an artificial rose on one shoulder. Round her neck she wore a string of small artificial pearls of the kind which you could buy at that time for about 30s. On her left wrist was a thin engraved bangle made of some light metal resembling platinum, and in her ears were a pair of cheap earrings manufactured in the shape of tiny roses which served to enhance the porcelain-like look of her face. She walked with short, firm little steps, and because her dress was cheap and fitted too closely in the wrong places, her posterior wobbled briskly every time she put her foot down.

We went on to the floor just as the band was beginning a fox-trot, which in the early stages of its development was an ideal dance for beginners who were content just to shuffle around the room.

"You've got a good ear for rhythm," she said after a few moments. "I'll be able to teach you fairly easily, I should think."

"Do you like dancing very much?"

"Love it. So if you want to go out with me at all, you'd better put your mind to it. But do you?"

"I'm a quick learner."

I ventured to press her hand. She neither returned the pressure nor protested. She looked up at me with her wide blue eyes and smiled. I felt happy and excited. I'd got a girl.

The next moment I felt bewildered.

The band had stopped playing, and I was leading her off the floor when a tall, bony youth with red ears which stood out from his head blocked our path. I stepped to one side to pass him, but he moved into my way. I looked at him enquiringly.

He said quite simply, "Hop it."

I looked at him in surprise.

"What's the matter with you?"

"Go on. Hop it, there's a good chap. Hop it off 'ome."

I was vaguely aware that Cynthia had melted away from my side. This was clearly her jilted boyfriend.

I said, "I'm not doing any harm."

He thought this over for a few seconds. I made as if to pass him, but he stopped me with a large red hand.

He said patiently, "Look, ol' man, I don't want to sock you, but hop it off 'ome. Go on."

I took off my glasses with my left hand, folded them up and put them in my pocket. With my right hand, I fumbled for the knuckleduster which I had carried ever since I had bought it with Crane.

He had had a few drinks and spoke rather thickly. I had had a few myself, and was not feeling at all cool and collected, otherwise I should not have been so silly; you don't use a knuckleduster on a drunk in a friendly dance hall, even if he does happen to be bigger and tougher than yourself.

I said, "Don't be unreasonable. Look, I was just—"

"I swear I'll sock you if you don't clear off."

I slipped the knuckleduster on my hand, but I did not even have to take it from my pocket. Strangely enough, in the long run, it would have been better if I had done so, but there was no means of knowing that, that evening. But had I had a few more beers inside me, and acted impulsively, that stupid incident at a dance hall in Palesby might have made all the difference to me. At the time, I was glad I had kept my head, to some extent anyway.

Cynthia returned with Inspector Daley. Daley laid his hand on the young man's arm.

"Now then, now then, what's this?" he said cheerfully. "Trying to break up the happy family gathering, Harry? This is the *Gazette* reporter, Harry. We shall not get any report of the dance in the paper if you go and knock him about, shall we, Harry?"

Daley led him off towards the bar. I heard him saying, "Come on, Harry. Come and have a quick one to pull you together, eh?"

"Don't take any notice of him," said Cynthia. It struck me at the time as rather superfluous advice, now that the incident was over. I smiled and put my spectacles on again.

"Jealous, I suppose?"

"Now you see why I chucked him."

"I suppose you can't blame him really."

She shook her head impatiently. "Well, I do blame him. Too blinking possessive; that's the trouble with him."

"I suppose he is pretty keen on you."

"Well, if he is fond of me, he ought to like me to be happy. But, oh, not at all! He wanted me all to himself. He wanted to get engaged, and get married, and have children. And me still young. I want to have a bit of fun out of life first. I'm still young. Haven't I a right to have a bit of fun out of life?"

"Of course you have," I replied warmly. We sat down, and Cynthia's sister-in-law joined us. After I had been introduced, she said, "Was that Harry making a fuss?"

"He threatened to knock Michael about. That settles it, making a scene in front of all these people. Made me feel a proper fool, I can tell you."

"Harry was always hot-headed," said Mavis. "I could have told you there'd be trouble."

She was a blonde woman of about thirty, with grey eyes, and on the plump side. She was dressed in pink, and inclined to be spotty. She wore a number of cheap bangles, and talked a great deal and very fast, and for the next ten minutes she and Cynthia chattered about the various people present. Sometimes they talked in undertones and giggled, and I assumed they were discussing other women. But I was quite happy. Cynthia had referred to me by my Christian name. Cynthia had been indignant when Harry, the abandoned Romeo, had wanted to knock me about. Cynthia was my girl. Almost, anyway.

We left shortly before the dance ended. I walked back to their home with them. The house was slightly bigger than the one where I had a room, and had a small lawn, hardly larger than a bedsheet, between the little gate and the front door. Otherwise, it had the same atmosphere, and rather similar furnishings.

The Harrisons, however, actually used their front parlour. There were two easy chairs in it, a sofa, a fern in the window, and the usual upright piano squeezed against a wall. In Palesby the first thing you did to establish the fact that you were financially sound, and therefore quite respectable, was to buy an upright piano.

Mrs. Harrison was a widow, and there was a picture of the late Mr. Harrison, a heavy-jowled man with drooping moustaches, on the wall above the fireplace. By the side of it was a small frame containing his Boer War and Great War service medals. Elsewhere on the walls were a wedding group and two large lithographs, heavily framed in black. One showed "The Battle of Balaclava" and the other "Nelson's Last Signal." On the upright piano, under glass cases, were a number of small stuffed birds sitting on twigs.

One, apparently a hummingbird, was not sitting on a twig, but was suspended by a thin wire in mid-air above an exotic tropical flower in wax. Others had their beaks open, as though singing an eternal song of joy and thanksgiving for the privilege of adorning Mrs. Harrison's front parlour in Palesby. Cynthia, bringing in the usual tea and cake without which no social evening in Palesby could end, caught me staring at them.

"I've told my mother time and again to get rid of them, but she won't."

"There's no reason why she should, if she doesn't want to. They were quite fashionable at one time."

"Wedding presents," said Mavis. "Gruesome, I call 'em. Poor little things. I wonder the moth hasn't got at them."

"Mother keeps mothballs inside the glass cases, to make sure," said Cynthia, pouring out the tea. We talked and drank tea for half an hour. I rather hoped Mavis might go to bed, though I doubted if I would have the courage to flirt with Cynthia even if she did. But Mavis stayed obstinately drinking her tea, and in the end I decided I had better leave. Before doing so I asked Cynthia to come to the cinema with me the following day.

"You'd better give me your office telephone number, in case I can't make it at the last moment," I said. "You know, you never can tell on a newspaper."

"I hope you're not going to let me down," she said. "I don't like men who are always letting me down. Harry was a bit unreliable sometimes."

And look what happened to Harry, I thought. It was about one o'clock when I said good night. It took me twenty-five minutes to walk home, but I thought it was worth it. I was feeling pleased with myself, and thought of Prosset. I had a job which, for the moment, anyway, was more interesting than his, and possibly even better paid. I was self-supporting, reasonably dressed, and now I had got myself a girl, and not a bad looker, either. I almost looked forward to meeting him some time in London.

As I walked along the silent streets, I planned an imaginary trip to London with Cynthia some time in the future. We four, Prosset, Margaret Dawson, Cynthia Harrison and I, might make up a foursome one evening. It would be a good test for me, I thought, and warmed to the idea.

I was always rather brave about Prosset when he was a long way away.

In only one respect was he now more of a man of the world than me. I remembered how the obnoxious Herbert Day, with his snuffling voice, had turned to Prosset and Margaret in the back of the car, when I was saying good night, and how he had sniggered and said, "What about you two? Oxford Terrace for you, Margaret, too, I suppose?"

CHAPTER 8

I took Cynthia to the cinema on the following day, as arranged, and thereafter we went out together a couple of times a week. Sometimes I would take her along to a dance with me, sometimes to a lecture, if I thought the subject interesting. She was quite an intelligent girl in her limited way, and anxious to be more so. She was a girl who was determined to get on in the world, either by marriage or through her own efforts; which might well amount to the same thing.

You could tell it, apart from anything else, by the way she walked. If she was not carrying anything, she was inclined to swing her arms across her body rather than backwards and forwards, which gave her a purposeful air. There was little doubt about the reason why she had thrown aside the unfortunate Harry with the big red ears. After going around with him for a while, she decided he was not likely to go much further than the end of the counter in the radio shop where he worked. This did not mean that she would necessarily marry for money; but it did indicate that she would have to be crazily in love before she married without it, or without at least a good prospect of it later in life.

I think that subconsciously I must have been aware of this practical, unromantic strain in her from the first. In any case, to a man of more mature years, a short acquaintanceship with her mother would have provided a pointer.

Mrs. Harrison was a Finn. I gathered that she had been born on a farm in the interior, and like many peasant girls had migrated to Helsinki to work in a hotel. There she had met Mr. Harrison when he was third officer on a ship plying between Palesby and Helsinki. At least one reason why girls moved in from the farms was the hope of making a reasonable marriage in Helsinki.

Mrs. Harrison succeeded. She had made good. Ever since, she had lived contentedly in Palesby. She still corresponded with relatives in Finland, but she never went back. Only at Christmas would she get a little weepy and sentimental, and then not for long. She spoke English perfectly, but with a slight lilt, which Cynthia had caught from her. She still wore in her ears the gold earrings of her youth. Now, in her middle age, there was no mistaking her peasant ancestry. Her face was angular and thin, the cheekbones high, the eyes set rather close together. Her movements were slow, and she was made on the big side, with fine, strong hands and hair only just beginning to turn grey. She was a sensible, practical woman, who knew which side her bread was buttered without being mean.

There was in Palesby a hostel for Scandinavian seamen, and five evenings a week, from seven until ten o'clock, she went down to the hostel to help in the canteen. I should say that within ten minutes of meeting me she had weighed up my likely salary and my prospects in life. As they presumably impressed her more than those of the unfortunate Harry, she was invariably courteous to me. She was prepared to approve of me, at least until somebody better turned up.

Monday being my fortnightly day off, I had a regular date with Cynthia every other week, apart from any evenings which were arranged as and when opportunity occurred. One Monday, about six weeks after we had met, I went round to her house for high tea as usual, at about 6:30.

Mrs. Harrison had gone to the canteen, and Cynthia was preparing the tea. We were to have smoked haddock, bread and butter and cheese, followed by buttered buns and jam, and cake if we felt like it; and tea, in large cups, very sweet and strong, poured out of a great brown pot. The kettle would remain simmering on the stove, ready to refill the teapot if necessary. The kettle was solid, too, a big black one, with a long spout, so that you could direct the flow of water accurately: a kettle that took some time to boil, maybe, but one in which the water stayed hot, a very different affair from these modern tin things with hardly any spouts at all and a whistle plugged into them.

"Where are Bill and Mavis?" I asked, as we settled down to eat.

"They've gone round to Ken and Margot Lockets' for the evening. Ken's one of Bill's trawler pals. They've got a couple of kids."

"Pity Mavis has never had any kids."

Cynthia looked at me briefly, and said, "Maybe. Still, you can't tell. Kids are an awful tie, I always say. I mean, there is no real freedom on your holiday if you've got to look after kids, is there? It's not like being alone with a chap."

"Would you like to be alone with a chap on your holidays?"

"Depends on the chap. It'd have to be all clean and above board, of course, if we weren't married."

"The phrase is—'and no hanky-panky,' I believe."

It had started to rain and I was looking out of the window as I spoke, wondering if she meant what she said. Suddenly I heard her voice, angry and protesting.

"There you go again! Sarcastic! Making a mockery of me! Making fun of me just because I wasn't brought up posh like you. You make me sick, you and your highfalutin' talk. Sick—that's what you make me!"

I looked at her in astonishment, hardly recognizing the bitter, hard tone in her voice.

"I wasn't mocking you at all," I said hurriedly.

"Oh, yes you were, and what's more you're always doing it. You and your sarcasm and sneers."

"Cynthia, please believe me, sweetheart, I promise—"

"Sweetheart! Who said you were my sweetheart? Who said I was yours? There's some people, Michael Sibley, who've got pride, see? Some people don't like being patronized, see?"

"I wasn't patronizing you. It's just that I was trying to be a bit funny. You know, on the music halls you often hear people talking about 'no hanky-panky': and when you—"

"Oh, you needn't apologize, I'm sure!"

She got up and began collecting the plates together, quickly and rather noisily. I helped her to clear the table and carry the things to the sink. Neither of us spoke. Her annoyance had made her eyes sparkle and heightened her complexion. I thought miserably that she looked prettier than ever; moreover, she was wearing the coat and skirt in which I had first met her in the park. I stood silently drying the plates as she handed them to me, and picking up the knives and forks which she threw on to the draining board. It seemed as though the whole evening was spoilt, and worse: there appeared quite a possibility that I was about to suffer the fate of the long-eared Harry.

I can look back on it now and smile, well aware of half a dozen possible reasons for her outburst, none of them remotely connected with what I had said to her.

"Well, I suppose we had better be going if we are not to miss the newsreel," I said when we had finished.

"I don't want to go to the cinema."

"Why not?"

"Because I don't—that's why. You've spoilt the evening."

I pleaded with her for a few moments, but she remained adamant. I followed her out of the kitchen into the front parlour.

"Anyway," she said in a slightly calmer tone, "it's raining and cold."

She lit the gas fire and switched on the radio. I sat down beside her on the sofa and lit my pipe. When I offered her a cigarette she refused it. We sat listening to the music for about ten minutes without speaking. Eventually, noticing that her hand lay on the sofa between us, I placed mine on top of hers. I had kissed her several times on the evenings when I had taken her out. They are a practical people in Palesby, and when you take a girl out and pay for a seat for her at the cinema, you are considered perfectly entitled to try to get a goodnight kiss on the doorstep. You may not get it, but nobody thinks a whit the worse of you for trying. In fact, the young men sedulously hand down from one generation to another a convenient theory that the girls are insulted if you don't try.

I put my arm round her shoulders, but she drew away, and I thought she was sulking. She got to her feet and went over to the windows and drew the curtains.

"I don't see why the whole neighbourhood should see you kissing me, Michael."

I laughed delightedly. "Dear Cynthia!"

She came back and sat herself down without hesitation on my knees. She put her arms round my neck and kissed me long and hard. After a while, she said, "You're a bad boy, Mike. I really don't know why I am fond of you."

I held her closer. "Are you really fond of me?"

"You don't think I'd be sitting on your knees kissing you if I wasn't, do you?"

"I suppose not. But it seems so wonderful."

She kissed me again. "What seems wonderful, Mike?"

"Well, that a pretty girl like you should fall for me."

"Am I pretty? Do you really think so? As pretty as the girls in London?"

"Prettier. Far prettier."

"Sure?"

I assured her with great intensity that she was one of the prettiest girls in England. Thereafter the conversation followed the normal channels peculiar to such situations. Both of us lied freely, I in my descriptions of her beauty, and she when she declared that she knew I must be exaggerating. While I certainly thought her attractive, I did not think her half as lovely as I said; and she herself undoubtedly thought herself twice as pretty as she allowed herself to admit. There is only one word which adequately describes the conversation, and that is a comparatively modern one: corny.

After a while, she said she felt hot; she took off the top half of her blue costume. When she sat down again, she sat down beside me, but leant her head on my shoulder. She was wearing an artificial silk blouse with short sleeves. I slid my arm behind her neck and drew her to me again and kissed her. She gave kiss for kiss, responding with a warmth she had never shown before, kissing with her mouth half open so that I bruised my lips on her teeth.

I noticed with delight how soft was the texture of the skin on her arms. They were fine arms, rounded but slim and blemishless. She asked me if I loved her, and of course, I said I did, and a lot more besides. It is likely that at the moment I almost believed a good deal of what I said. I certainly thought her exciting. We did not talk a great deal after that, and apart from the hissing of the gas fire, the room and the whole house were quiet. The street was quiet, too, for the rain was keeping most people at home. Only now and again the wind grew suddenly gusty, and rattled the panes, and sprayed them with rain.

After a while she said, "I'd risk an awful lot for a man who was fond of me."

This seemed to be the green light all right. As I drew her to me my thoughts flew to Prosset and Margaret Dawson, and I thought: now he hasn't got anything on me at all; now we're level.

Above us the image of Mr. Harrison gazed down upon his daughter with what must be considered unusual stolidity in the circumstances, and the little stuffed birds, as usual, regarded the scene without comment, silent and open-beaked.

Eventually, she made a cup of tea, and we sat happily chatting.

I had no intention of proposing marriage to Cynthia Harrison, and at first she would certainly not have accepted me even had I done so.

The next year or so was a happy period of my life. I felt reasonably secure in my job, and in addition I had started to write short stories. To my great astonishment, the first one I wrote I sold. Thereafter I had many failures, but enough successes to keep me at it. I found plots came readily to my mind, and my experience as a newspaperman rendered my style, if not brilliant, at least lucid and reasonably concise. I would write on average four or five a month, and could generally reckon on selling at least one, and possibly two. It was not a high average, but it was encouraging. They were all rather short, and gave me little or no trouble; quite often I would write them in the law courts during the hearing of some dull case.

I took Cynthia out twice a week regularly, and sometimes three times, and the fact that she never once hinted at an engagement suited me perfectly. I do not think I was ever in love with Cynthia, but there were moments when I felt a deep affection for her. She took a great interest in my work, and was invariably encouraging me to write short stories, and enquiring when I was going to start a novel. But I had no time, what with evening jobs for the paper, short stories, and Cynthia, to embark on a novel. That would have to wait.

I think she had selected me, in her practical way, as a good candidate to groom for stardom; at the back of her mind was the thought that if she could build me into a moderately successful machine she would marry me. I don't suppose it ever occurred to her that I might not ask her. She doubtless thought that because she had given herself to me, and continued to do so from time to time, this implied at least an unspoken understanding that in due course, if she wished, she had the right to a wedding ring.

When I first went to Palesby I had gone back to Earl's Court for a weekend once every few months, but with the passing of time I went less and less.

Once I went so far as to telephone Kate. She was, she told me, employed at a firm of solicitors in Moorgate, and was living in Manchester Square. She had a girlfriend called Marjorie, with whom she went to the cinema once a week and to an occasional concert. Each weekend she went down to Sevenoaks to her parents. I promised to call and see her the next time I came to London, but I never did: she was a reminder of the days when I was broke.

Each Christmas my Aunt Nell sent me a Christmas card, and I sent her one back. That was the only correspondence between us. I never went to stay with her, and she never invited me to do so, though had I asked I have no doubt she would have made me welcome. But I scarcely gave her a thought. She was a remote, aggressive figure of the uneasy past when I wore ill-fitting clothes, couldn't pay for a round of drinks, and blushed; of the days when largely due to Prosset's influence, I had despised myself.

Aunt Edith never heard from her, either. Typical of the coolness between Aunt Nell and my branch of the family was the fact that when she died neither of us knew about it until the funeral had already taken place.

I first learnt of Aunt Nell's death through her solicitors. They wrote and told me she had left me £1,000, unconditionally, in her will.

She had died from the ravages of a malignant growth from which she had been suffering for years. She must have had it, I gathered, when I last visited her. I recalled her display of restrained affection when she had said farewell to me before the car drove away from the great house. Perhaps she had a feeling she would not see me again. In telling me to fight back in life, she was telling me to do no more than she was then doing herself.

I imagined her lying in bed in her high-ceilinged room, alone, looking at Death and bidding him take her if he could. Now she was no more, and the hand was gone from the helm of that estate. I felt it would die with her, and I was right.

I said nothing of my bequest to Cynthia. If anything further were to develop of our relationship, there would be time enough then to tell her. I do not think she would have married me specifically for the sake of £1,000, but I had an instinct that if her thoughts should happen to be running along matrimonial lines the news would at least give them an added impetus.

That summer we planned to spend our two weeks' holiday at a little seaside place about thirty miles from Palesby called Whitney Bay. Her mother had agreed to this, only stipulating that for the sake of Cynthia's reputation we should occupy separate hotels.

The weather was fine and warm, and I think that during those summer days I felt nearer to falling in love with her than ever before or afterwards. I had bought a small second-hand car for £40, the only extravagance I allowed myself on hearing of the bequest, and we piled our suitcases into the back and went by road.

In the mornings we bathed and lazed on the little beach among the sand dunes; in the afternoons we usually went for a run in the car, returning in time for a drink before dinner. After dinner we went to the cinema, or danced at a local dance hall, or strolled along the sea front.

Naturally, when Mrs. Martin heard of my holiday plans she winked at Phyllis and said archly that she had a feeling that before long she would be losing one of her lodgers. Even Mr. Martin, knitting and cursing in bed, put forward the view that before long I'd be "bringing up a family of dam' brats," if all he heard was correct. And it was generally assumed at the office that in due course Cynthia and I would take the plunge.

On the whole, their guesses were not so very far out. As one sunny day followed another, I became very conscious of how much I liked being with Cynthia. It was largely a physical attraction. The sunshine had browned her face and body, and the sea air had made her eyes sparkle. She was gay and passionate, and if I had not had occasionally the feeling of being organized, I might have proposed to her of my own free will. As it was, it turned out somewhat differently.

We had just finished lunch on the eighth day of our stay when the hall porter came into the little dining room and said I was wanted on the telephone.

"The gentleman says it's your office, sir."

I looked at the porter in dismay.

"What on earth do they want?" said Cynthia casually.

"I'll find out," I said. I got up. I had a nasty feeling in the pit of my stomach. The great cloud that hangs over the head of every reporter when he is young is the threat of a libel action, or of perpetrating some inaccuracy which will involve the paper in the payment of damages.

Something had gone seriously wrong, I thought, something that could not wait until I got back from my holidays. I visualized myself driving hurriedly into Palesby to examine the shorthand notes of some court case I had reported. I recalled one or two of the more recent and complicated ones. I wondered if I had somehow mixed up the names of the prosecutor and the defendant, as one unfortunate reporter had done on the *Gazette* and thereby earned a species of immortality.

I picked up the receiver and was not at all reassured to hear Grimshaw, the Chief Reporter, at the other end.

"Is that you, lad?"

"Yes, Sibley speaking. Anything the matter?"

"Did I disturb your lunch?"

"I was having lunch, yes, but it doesn't matter. Anything wrong?"

"London's been on the phone about you, lad."

My heart sank. If London was telephoning Palesby about me, it must be serious. Our head legal department was in London.

"Oh, yes?"

Grimshaw cleared his throat. "Would you like a transfer to the London office, Sibley? They've got a vacancy. As you're a Londoner and have had a bit of experience in the provinces, they've offered you the job."

Through the glass door of the telephone box I could see Cynthia sitting at our table sipping her coffee. My thoughts were confused. When I had come to Palesby I had dreamed of Fleet Street, like most other newspapermen. But with the passing of the years I had settled down, I had made many friends, I was well thought of at the office, I had Cynthia. It would mean uprooting everything, starting all over again in London among strange colleagues. It would mean leaving Cynthia, at least for a while. I suppose I had an instinct that if I left her it would be the end of everything between us. The idea gave me a little feeling of pain. I was trying to think quickly, but I could not sort out my emotions. There was Cynthia, pouring herself another cup of coffee, and at the other end of the line was Grimshaw, waiting for the answer. I temporized.

"It's a big step. Can I think it over?"

I heard him snort with surprise. "Of course you can't think it over, lad. They want an answer right away. If you don't want to go, say so, and they'll have to find somebody else. What do you think I'm wasting the firm's bloody money for on a toll call?"

Beyond Cynthia's head I could see the line of the blue sea. I knew that if I opened the telephone box I would hear the sound of it through the open hall door, and perhaps catch a glimpse of the sunshine glinting on the parchment wings of a gull. Although I was a southerner, I felt the tug of dirty old Palesby, the warm comradeship, the reasonably assured future, Cynthia, and all the social friendliness which you rarely find in London. It was on the tip of my tongue to say that I would rather stay in Palesby.

But I thought of Prosset, still toiling away as a bank clerk. I remembered his sneers and air of superiority. He was still in the ruck. Here was my chance to soar up in my profession, to earn twice, perhaps three times as much as he was earning. Here was a chance to get a bit of my own back next time we met. It was the decisive factor.

"All right, then," I said.

"What the hell does that mean? Do you want to go, or don't you?"

"Yes. I'll go."

"You don't sound any too bloody keen."

"I'm not. I like the *Gazette*. When do I start?"

"Monday, 9:30 in the morning, sharp. You'll have to come back here on Saturday, and travel down on Sunday. They'll bump your salary up, of course. All right, then. I'll say you accept. Having a good holiday?"

"Fine, thanks."

"How's the girl?"

"She's fine."

"She won't be too pleased, I suppose. Well, better make the most of your time. Bye-bye. Don't forget—Monday, 9:30, sharp."

He rang off. Monday. Nine thirty, sharp. I was reminded of my first talk with Grimshaw. He wouldn't want me till next day, he'd said—nine o'clock, sharp; it was always "sharp" with Grimshaw.

I went back to the table. Cynthia looked up as I sat down.

"Well?"

I said nothing for a moment, wondering how I should break it to her, and finally decided it was no use trying to wrap it up.

"They want me to go to London." She did not at once understand the significance of it.

"When?"

"Next Monday. Actually, I'll have to travel down on Sunday. I'll have to leave here on Saturday morning."

"How long are you going for?"

"For good," I said, drawing a deep breath. "I'm going to work in the head London office, which serves all the provincial papers in the group."

She looked at me wide-eyed for about five seconds.

"But what about me? What about us?"

I shrugged. "It's going to be tough. Of course I'll come up at weekends pretty often. And maybe you can come down to London now and again," I went on, feeling her unhappiness. "I could fix a room for you, and all that. We'll still see a lot of each other."

She shook her head slowly and tried to smile.

"We won't see much of each other. You know that as well as I do. I wonder how it is all going to turn out."

I think that she, too, was nearly in love, but not quite.

The evening before we left we walked along the sands after dinner. It was a still, close night, but down by the water's edge there was a little breeze. We did not speak much, but walked arm in arm until we came to the sand dunes at the end of the beach, and here we sat down and lit cigarettes.

I knew that the following day would be one of hustle and confusion, of handing over of work and clearing my desk, drawing such salary as was due to me, making out my current expense sheet, and packing; of farewells and drinks and all the business inseparable from a departure. And just as at school when I had gone to the dormitory windows and gazed out half sadly at the moonlit buildings during the summer nights of the last term, so now I was suddenly loath to leave Palesby, and gazed at the moonlight on the waters of the bay with a strange illogical dejection.

If anybody had told me when I first arrived at Palesby and saw its dreary houses and damp pavements that I should ever be sorry to leave the place, I would have considered him to be joking. But I have heard it said that it is not so much the work you do, or where you do it, which makes for happiness, but rather the people you do it with. There is much truth in this. Palesby, with its blunt but friendly people, who had at once accepted me as a comrade, had in due course become a safe haven, like my school had been. Inside the haven, the waters were sometimes choppy and disturbed, but at least you could fathom their depths. Outside, who could tell?

And once again I thought of Ackersley, who had shot himself because his wife, his refuge from the torments of schoolboys and from the realization of his failure, had sickened and died; and of how Geoffries, the Lascar, faced with the threat real or imagined of the loss of poor, tawdry Mary O'Brien, in a few wild moments of atavistic desperation had hurled the woman to destruction and placed a noose about his own neck.

Or did I have some premonition, as I sat with Cynthia by that calm sea, of the crisis which lay ahead, and was my spirit even then, as perhaps earlier at school, pulling hopelessly against the stream of events which were now to carry me, and Cynthia, and Prosset, and the almost forgotten Kate, to the climactic struggle? It is a tempting enough theory, but I doubt it.

Cynthia had been sitting with her knees drawn up to her chin, her face averted, watching, as I thought, the lighthouse winking in the distance. I put my arm round her shoulders and felt her body quivering. She turned her face to me and I saw she was crying. I tightened my arm round her, and drew her face to mine and kissed her.

I told her not to cry, because I would often write to her and telephone her, and would see her quite frequently, too. I even sketched out an impromptu plan whereby I would come to Palesby, and she would come to London, alternately. This seemed to cheer her and she smiled and wiped her eyes.

But suddenly she said, "You remember that night we met at the dance? You remember what you said?"

"I said a good many things."

"You said one particular thing."

"Well, go on, tell me."

She hesitated for a couple of seconds.

"Well, I said something about you not getting any funny ideas,

Mike, and you replied, 'My ideas are never anything but serious,' or something like that."

"Did I? I don't remember." I did remember, but I wished her to declare herself.

"Well, you did say that. I have never forgotten it. I have often thought about it from time to time. I thought it kind of set you apart from other men. Sort of made me feel I could rely on you."

"I hope you can."

She must have noted the careful wording of the phrase. She looked at me quickly and keenly.

"You haven't been leading me up the garden path, have you, love?"

"Of course I haven't. What on earth do you mean?"

She put her arm round my neck and kissed me full on the mouth, and whispered, "We've been a lot to each other, haven't we, love? I've given you a lot, haven't I, love?"

"Of course, darling. You've been marvellous. You're my sweetheart, Cynthia. You know that."

I pressed her closer, but she pulled herself away.

"Why can't we get married now, Mike? Or in a month or two, anyway?"

To gain time to think, I replied, "Why, darling, I didn't know you wanted to get married. Only a little while ago you were saying you wanted to see life a bit first. That's why you chucked Harry, wasn't it? Because he was too possessive and jealous and wanted to rush things."

She shook her head slightly, impatiently. "Well, I've changed my mind, what with you going away, and everything."

"Look, I'm not earning nearly enough, Cynthia."

"They'll give you a rise when you go to London. They must."

"Living is much more expensive in London."

"We could manage. I know we could."

She watched me intently as I stubbed my cigarette out on a stone. I took another one out of my case and lit it. I remember how thankful I felt that I had never told her about Aunt Nell's bequest to me.

I said, "Look, we've got to be a bit patient, sweetheart. I'm not going to get married until I've got a home for you."

"We could live in a flat, love. And save money to put down a deposit for a house."

"With the salary I'll be getting, we could never afford to save anything for the house. We'd just go on wasting money paying rent for years. I want to start married life with a home and all debts paid. Then when the children come, and have to be educated—"

"Who said there'd be any children?"

"There would. A couple, anyway."

"There might not be. You can't tell."

I said nothing to that. She lay on the soft, dry sand, looking up at the stars, plucking at a tuft of coarse grass. After a while, she put out her arm and drew me down. She put both her arms round my neck again, and pulled me closer. As we had been walking along, I had taken off my jacket because the night was hot. I could feel the soft warmth of her body through my tennis shirt.

"You do really want to marry me, don't you, love?"

I thought of nothing but the warmth of her and the closeness of her.

"Of course I do," I lied.

⁓

Try as I might, I still could not remember what it was that had occurred at Palesby which could cause me worry. Yet the idea grew in my mind until it became a certainty that in the kaleidoscope of events which had occurred during those years something had indeed happened which would interest the police.

I had a notion that it was connected with the stuffed birds on the piano. So far my memory went, but no further. My inability to recall what it was, and my feeling that it would be better if the police did not know about it, increased my uneasiness over the Prosset case. A horrid fear was tapping at the back of my mind that before the affair was over, the whole story was going to come out, of Kate and Prosset and me, since I came to London; and nobody was going to be spared, not even poor little Kate, who had not harmed a soul.

CHAPTER 9

I came to London from Palesby in August, 1938, and stayed for a few days in a hotel near Paddington until I could find myself some lodgings. My Aunt Edith suggested that I should return and live with her in Earl's Court. But I had had enough to last me a lifetime of the dreary house and garden.

Moreover, the necessity of explaining my comings and goings if Cynthia should come to town was in itself a barrier. I therefore told her that, as the life of a newspaperman was one of irregular hours and mealtimes, I felt it would be better for both of us if I took a room elsewhere. She did not press the point, being by now far too busy with her own affairs to care a great deal one way or the other.

I found a room in Harrington Gardens, South Kensington. It was a ground-floor room, barely furnished and cheerless, with a high ceiling, mass-produced furniture, and the inevitable shilling-in-the-slot gas meter. I paid 30s for bed and breakfast, and dinner in the evening was 2s extra. The place was clean, the staff obliging enough, and I was reasonably content with it.

I would have liked a basement flatlet, like Prosset's, and my first instincts were to go along to Oxford Terrace to have a look round; but though I now felt myself every whit capable of holding my own with him, I thought that on the whole it would be as well not to live too near to him or I would have him continually popping into my digs, just as he used to be always popping into my study at school.

Technically, work in the London office was easier than in Palesby, for there was not the overwhelming attention to detail which is required of a reporter on a provincial paper. Our task in London was mainly to follow up stories appearing in the national newspapers with a view to developing some slant on them which would be of interest to the provincial papers we served.

The work was less arduous than in Palesby, the hours easier, the pay better. There was little or no night work, so that for the first time since I started work I found myself with plenty of time on my hands after six o'clock. I devoted two or three evenings a week to short stories, which were now selling more easily, the income they brought in being equivalent, on an average, to some £3 a week.

So the position was that I had about £1,300 in the bank, an income of about £13 a week, and a reasonable and interesting job. It seemed to me then that after a shaky start the course of my life was favourably set. I was aware that a reporter's position is rarely completely secure, and that I might find myself suddenly without a job; but even if this occurred, I reckoned that by devoting myself entirely to fiction I could make enough to keep myself until I could get another newspaper job, even if that should take a long time.

Then, as if to consolidate my finances still further, I had not been in London more than a few weeks when I received a cable stating briefly that my father had died in Delhi after a car accident. The news affected me emotionally but little, for we had known each other so slightly that I felt no more than I would have done had I heard that a friend whom I had known for many years, but seen very little, had suddenly died abroad.

Upon his death I became the recipient, after payment of estate duties, of an annual income from trust investments of £200 a year.

No wonder that at that period my position seemed impregnable. I had a profession, private money and good health. I contemplated writing novels, and if I was as successful with them as with short stories I thought I would retire from the newspaper game. Perhaps I would travel, gathering material for my work, which in turn would improve it, leading to wider sales and further and more ambitious travels. But I would not retire from newspapers until I was sure how my novels would be received. I was going to act sensibly.

Ironically, the access of money which Cynthia Harrison imagined would bring our marriage nearer only served to render its fulfilment less likely. Wider horizons were opening up, and within the picture I saw no figure which resembled a local Palesby girl. There were women in the picture, but now they were women of a more exotic and sophisticated kind; I record this with some shame.

Nevertheless, outside the world of dreams, Cynthia was still there; we were exchanging letters full of endearments, and I had already paid one visit to Palesby, staying at the Station Hotel, and seeing her almost the whole weekend. She herself was to come to London soon for a weekend. And lurking in the wings, unseen but ready to step upon the stage, was Prosett.

I never harmed a hair on his head, but he struck back at me after his death. Nor am I certain now what I could have done to prevent it.

⌒

It was November before I called on Kate Marsden.

Indeed, I only did so because I had nothing better to do. I had spent two evenings in succession at my short stories, and felt like taking an evening off.

I looked down the list of films showing in the West End, and saw nothing that attracted me. Entirely on impulse, I made my way to Manchester Square. Her room was no longer at the top of the house, but it was still small. It was hardly bigger than a normal bathroom. It was distempered in cream, and had the usual bedsettee, one small easy chair, a hard chair, a basin with hot and cold water, and a small folding table which she had bought herself. Against one wall was a bookshelf, and there was a small chest of drawers in one corner. She kept her dresses on hangers behind a cheap curtain which covered a recess in one of the walls.

She was sitting in front of a gas fire reading when I knocked and went in. I noted that she had had to take to using spectacles, and was wearing a blue horn-rimmed pair. This was a pity because her eyes had been her best feature. She quickly put down her book and got up.

"Hello, little stranger," I said, taking her hand, "how are you?"

"This is lovely," she replied. "This is a great evening. Sit down, Mike. I was going to make a cup of coffee, so you've come at a good moment."

I went to fetch the hard chair from the side of the room, but she insisted on me sitting in the easy chair while she made coffee.

I asked her how life had been treating her. She had taken off her spectacles, and now she looked round at me from the basin, where she was putting some water into a saucepan, and smiled.

"Not too badly. Office, and the flicks now and again. The usual thing."

"Still at the same office?"

She nodded, stirring some coffee into the water. "Same old place, same old faces. Still, I suppose there are worse faces around the town."

"Home every weekend?" I asked.

"No; I don't go home much now. Mummy died, and Daddy married again six months ago. It made a bit of a difference. She's a very nice woman, I suppose, but it's not the same. I don't think she likes having me around very much. I expect she thinks I remind Daddy of the past, and all that. You can't blame her, really. It's not what she says. She's always very polite. Rather cool and indifferent, you know. Nothing you could pick on, but I just think they are happier if I don't go down too often."

"That's bad luck."

"Oh, well, it's just one of those things. Really, it is nice to see you. You've been a rotten correspondent, you know."

I offered her a cigarette and a light. I said, "My trouble is, I can never write a short letter. And that means that, as I know I'm going to write a long one, I always keep on putting it off till I've got more time."

"Well, it's a bad habit."

She was sitting on a cushion on the floor by my side, a position of hers which I was to get to know well in time. She peered up at me a trifle shortsightedly and smiled.

"It is," I agreed.

I thought that the intervening years had added depths to her voice. She was also taking much more trouble with her appearance. She was wearing a brown coat and skirt, and her hair, though still rather lank, was neatly done, and her feet were neatly shod. I told her about my transfer to the London office.

"That's fine for you! You're getting on fine, aren't you?"

After a while she got up and brought out half a bottle of tawny port from a little cupboard under the window sill. She poured some into two cheap glasses, and handed me one. She raised her glass and said, "Let's celebrate your return to London."

"The prodigal's return?"

"If you like. Anyway, here's success to you."

It was not very nice port, and I thought it fitted in well with her dreary existence. On the other hand, I assumed in the way men do that she didn't mind living in that horrid little room. I thought she had probably grown accustomed to it and was even content. She told me some more about her life, and about her friend Marjorie, and I outlined a few things about Palesby.

"Do you always go to the cinema with Marjorie?"

"If you mean, have I got any boyfriends, the answer is no."

"What, none?"

"No. One or two people have taken me out now and again,

when they've had nothing better to do, but that's all there is to it."

She added with that devastating ability to face the truth which I was to associate with her later, "I'm not very good-looking, you know."

"You're being a bit modest. You look very nice to me."

"I'm not being modest. I may be shortsighted, but I can still recognize what I see in my mirror."

"Well, I think you look much nicer than when I went away, you're more *soignée* and assured."

"So are you. You would never have noticed that ten years ago, or said it even if you had."

"We've both grown up a good deal."

She smiled at me rather wistfully. "Growing up is a two-edged weapon for a woman. It's different for a man."

"When did you start wearing glasses?"

"About a year ago. We work in an electrically lit office. It's a strain on the eyes. Of course, I only really need them for reading. I can see all right without them, otherwise."

"Can you?"

"Well, fairly well, anyway."

"I think glasses suit some girls. I think they suit you. They enhance the delicacy of some people's faces."

She put her hand on my knee impulsively. "Dear old Mike! Still trying to say what you think people wish to hear?"

"Well, it's true in your case, anyway," I insisted.

She sat staring at the gas fire for a while saying nothing. Suddenly I saw the pathos of her position. I saw her coming home each evening to that room and cooking her meal, and sometimes going to the cinema with her girlfriend. I thought it must be pretty miserable to be a girl who was not wanted by anybody in particular, not even her own parents. A girl who was neither remarkably good-looking, nor very intelligent, nor even very witty. It must have seemed so hopeless.

When finally I got up to go, I said on the spur of the moment, "What are you doing on Sunday, Kate?"

She made no pretence of thinking if she had an engagement.

She said at once that she was doing nothing at all, and that since she had stopped going down to her parents' she very rarely did do anything on Sundays.

"What about driving out to Hampton Court, and then having tea and coming back and going to a cinema?"

"I'd love to, unless you've got anybody better to go with."

"There is nobody I would rather go with," I answered firmly, "nobody at all."

I did not wish her to think that I was taking her for a trip to Hampton Court because I felt sorry for her.

Yet what a dangerous thing pity is! It warps judgments, deflects justice, raises false hopes; it makes men risk worthwhile things for something which may be fundamentally of only transient worth; it will colour a man's whole outlook so that he forgets honour, morality, honesty, even personal safety. Pity is much lauded, yet in excess it can be an insidious poison which can make a man mad and lure him to destruction. But I did not know all that when I invited Kate to Hampton Court the following Sunday.

I only saw a girl who was lonely.

No doubt I should have known that each evening in her room she would be looking forward to Sunday, reckoning it a day when a boy-and-girl romance, interrupted by events, would be renewed, and that when she had almost reconciled herself to a life of work and monotony a chance seemed to be offered her to seize something which she thought had eluded her forever.

I did not understand how far I was committing myself when I extended that casual invitation in her room that evening.

＿＿＿＿＞

So we went to Hampton Court and strolled about the palace and gardens, and afterwards had tea in a hotel opposite the main gates. You could get a good tea out in those days, and we had crumpets thick with butter and sandwiches and cakes, served to us near a big fire as the day was closing in. Afterwards we drove back and went to an early film. I have forgotten what we saw, but I know that later we went to a restaurant in Frith Street, and had dinner.

It was a pleasant enough day, and I found Kate a pleasant enough companion. The shyness and reserve which I had associated with her from earlier days had largely disappeared when she was with me; it had almost gone, together with the ill-arranged stockings, the untidy hair, and the face devoid of make-up. She used a fair amount of make-up now, taking advantage of her natural sallowness rather than seeking to hide it, using a suntan cream and powder, and an orange lipstick. She was certainly not beautiful, with her horn-rimmed spectacles and ungainly walk; and I could well see that her serious manner and deliberate speech might put men off. But she was no longer dowdy, and if she had not Cynthia's rather brittle prettiness, she was a more attractive conversationalist.

Cynthia spoke of practical everyday things. Her talk was full of what she had done, and what she proposed to do later in the day, tomorrow and next week. She related what people had said to her and what she had replied; what she had bought and what she would like to buy.

Kate did not strike me as very practical; having left home soon after she became an adult, she had not the domestic experience and interests of Cynthia. On the other hand, she had read widely and more selectively. She had in her bones a sense of history, a feeling for the past, a love of old things and ways, of traditions and customs. It is a curious yardstick by which to measure them, but I should say that of the two Kate was the more patriotic. Her great interest was in the eighteenth and early nineteenth centuries, and she had read the lives of Nash, Brummel, Sheridan, Parson Woodford, and many others.

She had also developed a pleasant facility for doing pen and wash drawings. They were not great art, but they had a freshness and spontaneity which were attractive. I presumed, and rightly, that she had developed this talent, for such it was in a small way, to give her something to do when she went away on her summer holidays. She usually went alone.

When I paid the bill after dinner, and said I supposed we had better be going home, she agreed readily enough, but I noticed that the sparkle died out of her eyes.

I thought: she is like a child who has come to the end of a party to which she had been looking forward for a long time.

She said frankly, "This has been one of the loveliest days I've had for months."

"Well, maybe we can go out again some other time."

"I'd love to." She hesitated. "What do you do in the evenings? I suppose you are very busy?"

I told her that sometimes I wrote my stories, at other times I had a job for the office, or had to go round and see my aunt. Yes, I said, I was pretty busy on the whole.

I had no desire to leave myself wide open.

"Are you doing anything on Thursday? I was wondering if you would care to come along and meet Marjorie and have something to eat. Nothing much, or course. Just bacon and eggs or something, and a glass of beer. Rather dull, really. Still, if you'd like to come, just drop in. There's no need to decide now. See what you are doing."

"I'd love to come if I can."

But I was pretty sure I wouldn't go. I thought I'd like to see Kate now and again. She was a nice girl, but not wildly exciting like Cynthia under the sand dunes or even on the settee beneath the beady eyes of the little stuffed birds. Cynthia, for all her superficiality, had animal magnetism, and that is a deadly weapon when a girl is dealing with a young man.

I knew now I didn't want to marry Cynthia; I just wanted to see her from time to time. If the price was a few endearing letters, it was well worth paying. It was a dangerous and unscrupulous game, and I knew it, but I didn't care. I thought in the end she would fall for somebody else, that it would all work out somehow. I thought I had the world under control and the skies would always be blue, or if not eternally blue at least only clouded from time to time by occasional swiftly passing showers.

When I returned to my room after taking Kate out that evening, I found awaiting me a letter from Prosset which had been forwarded from Palesby. It was strange to find that the sight of his handwriting still gave me a curious twinge in the pit of the stomach. I thought I had got over that sort of thing. It was as though the ink itself radiated some strange aura of his domineering personality.

I looked at the writing, forward-sloping and regular, the downward strokes thick and determined. I realized then that, despite what I had accomplished, despite my independence, I still stood in awe of John Prosset, the ill-paid bank clerk.

As I took the letter to my room, I felt dismayed not because I was going to meet him again, but because I had not shaken off even now the feeling of inferiority which all those years before had made me rejoice when he went away to play a football match; and had left me, his so-called friend, free to talk and laugh as I wished without the threat of a sneer or a challenge from across the school dining-room table.

But I was wrong in one thing. John Prosset was by now no longer a bank clerk. His letter read as follows:

> My Dear Old Mike
>
> How are you? A bloody fine correspondent, for a journalist, I must say. As you see, I have not gone to the East. All those plans have gone by the board. I waited some years before really pressing the bank for an overseas appointment. At first they held out high hopes of me going. But I believe there was a hell of a lot of wangling by chaps at head office. As you know, they are not a big bank, and there are not an awful lot of replacements needed abroad.
>
> Anyway, in the end I said that if they would not send me out soon I'd leave. They said if that was the way I felt I had better go right away. So I went. Luckily, Herbert Day—you remember him from that boozy party—had just started a small business of his own. I hadn't any money saved up, but he agreed to take me as a partner.
>
> Jolly decent of him, I think, as otherwise I'd have been in a bit of a spot. I get quite a decent screw

really, considering we've only just started. I have to
travel about a good deal and am probably coming up
your way soon, so don't be surprised if I pop in on
you. Let me know your news, you lazy skunk.

Cheerio,

John.

Could I have broken things off at this point? I could have left
his letter unanswered, but nothing would have been gained. It
would never have occurred to Prosset that I did not want to see
him. He would have been told in Palesby about my transfer to London, and when he returned he would have sought me out.

Prosset's letter was written on some cheap business notepaper
bearing an address in Middlesex Street. I put the letter in my
pocket and went to bed. The next morning I telephoned him at his
office. He seemed pleased to hear from me and to learn that I was
now in London permanently.

"What about a bite of lunch together?" he asked.

"Lunchtime is awkward for me. I never know where I'll be."

"Well, what about a drink and a snack this evening?"

"The last time I went drinking with you, you got me tight."

He laughed. "I suppose you know you still owe me ten bob
from that evening?"

"I'll bring it along," I promised.

We arranged to meet at the Six Bells in Chelsea at 6:30 p.m. I
was there a few minutes early and saw him walk in with a middle-
aged man who from the cut of his clothes and his complexion
seemed to be a foreigner. Prosset saw me and waved, but rather to
my surprise did not come up to me; instead he went to the other
end of the bar with his companion and ordered some drinks. When
he had paid for them, he said something to his companion and
came over to me.

"Don't think me rude, old man, but I've just got a couple of
things to settle with this bloke and then I'll be with you. OK by
you?"

"It's OK by me."

I watched him walk back to the other end of the bar. He had

filled out since I had last seen him and his face, instead of the healthy glow it used to have, had turned rather red. But he was still a remarkably handsome young man, his clothes were as well cut as ever, and he wore his pork-pie hat at a jaunty angle. When he walked he swung his arms across his body, in the way Cynthia did, but in a more pronounced manner.

Prosset and the other man talked together for some fifteen minutes. Now and again they seemed to be disagreeing about something. The other man supplemented his words with quick little movements of his hands. Once, across the bar, I heard the stranger mention Herbert Day's name. Prosset smiled and shook his head and did not seem to be much impressed. When they had finished their business, the other man went out and Prosset came over to me.

"Sorry about that, old man. Max will talk such a lot."

"What are you having?" I asked.

"A whisky, if I may."

I noticed that he still had his old habit of talking with his cigarette in his mouth, so that it bobbed up and down as he spoke. I ordered two large whiskies and sodas and we raised our glasses to each other.

"So you've left the bank?"

He nodded. "I don't think I was cut out for a banking career. Not in England, anyway."

"I don't think you were. What sort of business are you in?"

"We buy and sell. Do a little importing, too."

"And they pay you all right?"

"Not too badly. But I have a feeling that Herbert Day will be paying me more soon, or else he and Max will find themselves in—" He broke off.

"Find themselves in what?"

A hint of fire, indicative of excitement or anger, flickered for a moment behind Prosset's eyes and was extinguished.

"Find themselves in—difficulties," he answered lightly. "That's all. Just in difficulties."

"What sort of stuff do you deal in?" I said at length.

He took a deep pull at his whisky. "Anything really. We've got one or two chaps who go round the country buying up bankrupt stocks. Then we sell them again, cheap. I have to travel about a good deal at the moment, as I told you in my letter. But when we get really going, of course, I'll just do the organizing."

I could well believe it. I thought it would just about suit Prosset to sit back and tell other people what to do.

"It must make a change after being stuck in a bank."

"We could do more, if we had a bit more capital. I suppose you haven't got £250 you want to invest in a nice, growing concern? We're going to do big things one day."

"Newspapermen don't have much opportunity to acquire capital. How's Margaret?"

He signed to the waiter to fill our glasses again.

"Margaret's all right, I believe. She got married, you know."

"No, I didn't know," I said in surprise. "I thought she was rather keen on you."

He smiled and shrugged his shoulders. "As far as she could be stuck on anybody, I think she was. But Number One came first for little Margaret, you know."

"Whom did she marry?"

"Some producer chap. You remember how keen she was on the stage. I've no doubt he dangled a few minor parts before her eyes. The funny thing is, from what I hear, I understand that no sooner were they married than he decided that he would like to have a wife who looked after his home and who would give him some children. I believe she more or less had to give up her acting ambitions. You never know what turn life is going to take, do you?"

He thought for a moment.

"Take ourselves, for instance. You imagined you were going out to Africa or somewhere, and I thought I was going to end up in charge of our Shanghai branch or something like that. Now you're a reporter stuck in London, and I'm buying and selling things. Oh, well, I suppose it might be worse."

He gave one of his careful smiles. "Good old Mike. I'm glad to see you again. You bring back some happy memories."

"So do you. Do you ever hear from David?"

He shook his head. "I wrote a few times, but he hardly ever answered, the lazy swine."

We stayed drinking and talking about old times until nine o'clock, and then went to a nearby restaurant and had a meal. I told him about life in Palesby, and how lucky I was to be transferred to London. I think I wanted to show him that all in all I had so far made more of a success of life than he had done. I thought that he would be impressed that I was now a Fleet Street man. But he was not.

I was irritated and disappointed at his attitude. I could tell from the disinterested, patronizing tone with which he greeted my remarks that while he was inclined to regard all journalists as ink-stained and shabby, he saw himself, already, as one of the directors of a large and flourishing business.

He talked about the pleasure one got out of building something up out of small beginnings, about the zest it gave one to be organizing—indeed, to be creating something almost from nothing. And how enjoyable it would be in due course to be able to regard one's creation and find it good.

"You sound rather like God," I remarked.

He looked at me thoughtfully. "You've changed, you know."

"Have I?"

"You've sharpened up, somehow. Frankly, you needed it. I always thought you a bit of a dope at school, you know."

"I dare say I was in some ways."

"A nice dope, of course. David and I used to talk about you. We agreed that it was almost impossible to imagine you in bed with a girl. It seemed ludicrous, somehow."

"I suppose it did."

"You looked so funny. I remember once, when we had been beaten in a House match, I mentioned to some chap that we weren't up to full strength, and I said you weren't playing, for one thing. Do you know what he said?"

"I'll buy it. Go on."

"He said, 'Who's Sibley? Oh, you mean that chap who looks like an influenza germ.' "

"Complimentary sort of chap."

When I got home that evening I looked at myself in the mirror. I saw what he meant. My face was dark, irregular, bespectacled and pale.

I went to bed and lay thinking about Cynthia. I recalled her circle of friends, and her sudden change of mind about wanting to get married when she heard that I had been transferred to London. Doubtless I seemed to be heading at least for a greater measure of success than the lads she already knew in Palesby.

I reflected suddenly, and with some bitterness of heart, that if you were a practical girl like Cynthia it might almost be worth-while to marry an ugly man, provided he could give you a nice, steady home and background. This train of thought led me to think once again how strange it was that although I was better off than Prosset in every way he still contrived to make me think of myself with contempt. I knew for a certainty I had not shaken off the feeling of inferiority to him, which had started at school and which had caused me even in those days to hate him. He was the first person I had ever hated.

I knew, lying in the dark watching the street lamp outside my window, that I still hated him.

I decided not to see him any more. It wasn't worth it. I would have to be firm. It had been easy in Palesby, but here in the same city it would be more difficult. But I would do it. I would break with him. It was absolutely absurd that I should go on seeing a man socially if I did not wish to do so.

It would have to end. It would end. I fell asleep content.

I went to Kate's after all, on the Thursday evening. I knew she would more than half expect me to turn up. It was a pouring wet night and I took a taxi. This was one of the little luxuries which I could now afford without a thought of the cost. I had still not quite got over the pleasure of finding that I had more money than I really required for my immediate needs. After years of counting, if not the pennies, at least the shillings, I got a real kick out of thinking that if I liked the look of a fountain pen in a shop window, or a pipe or a knife, I could go in and buy it for myself without a qualm.

Kate had bought half a bottle of gin and some lime juice, and gave me a drink, and we chatted until Marjorie arrived. She told me again how much she had enjoyed going out on the previous Sunday.

Hardly had I been introduced to Marjorie when she said she had been hearing what a lovely day Kate had had with me the previous Sunday. I was growing tired of these constant references to the matter, until it occurred to me that what had been for me a pleasant but unexceptional day had in truth been something to be remembered and talked over by Kate. Even Marjorie Barnes had obtained a kind of vicarious pleasure from it.

Somebody, and that somebody a man, had taken one of them out. There had been a break in the endless monotony of working days, cheap lunches in drab restaurants, suppers cooked over a gas ring, visits to the cinema together, and weekends spent mending, washing and reading. Somebody had actually considered one of them sufficiently good company to wish to take her out and spend money on her. Wonderful!

Marjorie worked in the same office as Kate. She was short and plump and red-faced, and over-enthusiastic about everything. She adored her boss. She thought the chief clerk "a real old darling," and the office boy absolutely sweet. She considered the gin and lime divine, while the eggs and bacon were in her view a feast fit for a king.

We spent part of the evening chatting and part listening to gramophone records. It seemed that it was Kate's gramophone, but they each bought records for it. Kate bought classical music, Marjorie jazz. We listened to both. Music leaves me cold, but I simulated some sort of enthusiasm, while Marjorie greeted the end of each piece with her loud little cries of ecstasy, and hurried forward obligingly to wind up the machine and put on another record. At 10:30 I left.

Marjorie was going to stay on for a short while. I knew that she would tell Kate what charm I had, what wit; what good looks, in an ugly sort of way, perhaps; and would probably add that she much preferred ugly men to handsome ones. They were much less spoilt, so much steadier, so much more reliable.

It seemed to me that women like Marjorie were like bright, welcoming fires on a cold night. The world was the better for them. One couldn't deny it. They were unselfishness personified, invariably cheerful and helpful, optimistic, generous; they were ready to do anything for anybody at any time except be quiet. They bubbled over with good neighbourliness. It was distressing that they were such bores.

Kate came down to see me out.

She had stopped her pretence of not really needing to wear spectacles. She stood in the hall, under the dreary yellow rays of the hall light, and put out her hand. She thanked me for coming. I told her it had been a delightful evening.

If she hadn't come down and stood under that depressing hall light, looking thin and lonely, I wouldn't have said, as though it were an excuse: "I've got to go up to Palesby this weekend. Maybe I'll see you on Sunday week?"

. I saw the light in her eyes brighten up her whole face. I thought: Oh, blast, hell and damnation. Why the devil did I go and say that?

CHAPTER 10

In human relationships no major effect can be unhesitatingly ascribed to a single cause. The issue is swayed by details, by eddies and cross-currents of emotion, some from the distant past, some of the present, some based upon hopes or fears for the future. All of them are intermingled and confused, some exercising a restraining influence, others urging the subject forward, until, for better or for worse, the matter is decided. Later, it is hard enough for an individual to uncover even to himself the secrets of his own mind, to gauge the relative importance and weight of each of the strands which pulled him onwards or held him back.

Although I am tempted to ascribe my change of relationship towards Kate as stemming directly from an incident which occurred the following spring, it is certain that other factors were at work which played parts equally important though less apparent.

All that winter, I had spent an increasing amount of time with her. At first I had taken her out once a fortnight. I regarded this as a charity which I could well afford, and anyway I found her company quite congenial. Inevitably, I found myself compelled as a matter of courtesy to accept invitations from her to have supper in return in her room, usually on a Thursday, when Marjorie was present.

Ironically, Marjorie must bear some of the responsibility for subsequent events. Twittering enthusiastically, hopping about the room like some cheerful robin, always good-humoured, always over-eager to please, finding everything and everybody nice, she began to get on my nerves to such a degree that I found the evenings at Manchester Square dates to which I looked forward with misgivings. To avoid the ordeal, I began making excuses about being tied up with work for the office on Thursdays. Instead, I would invite Kate to come to the cinema on the Wednesday. I learnt later that Kate considered this to be a move on my part to enable us to spend the evening alone, and although such was basically true it was not for the sentimental reasons she thought.

So we would make some minor excursion every other Sunday, and each Wednesday we would go to the cinema. I still had not told her about Cynthia; I said that every other Sunday I had to spend the day with my Aunt Edith, and if she thought it strange that I never invited her to renew her acquaintanceship with my aunt she made no comment. Only my comparative lack of experience with women prevented me from seeing the increasing significance which Kate attached to these regular meetings.

So matters continued all that winter until the second Sunday in April of the following spring. We had taken our lunch in the form of sandwiches and driven to Whipsnade. Normally on such occasions we had a cheap supper in some restaurant, but on this day we arrived back late and tired, and Kate offered to fry some sausages and bacon in her room. Afterwards I sat in the chair watching her wash the few utensils we had used. I sat smoking my pipe and felt relaxed and contented. When she had finished she came and sat down on a cushion on the floor at my side, and lit the little gas fire. I offered her a cigarette and gave her a light.

After a while I said, "Got any plans for your holidays this year?"

It was a natural sort of question to ask in the spring of the year. Just as in the past I failed to see the significance in her eyes of my repeated invitations to go out with me, so now it was only when it was too late that I realized along what lines her thoughts were running.

"No," she said, "I've no plans at all yet. What are you going to do?" She looked up at me.

"I don't know either," I said. "Will Marjorie be going with you?"

"No; we always go on holiday alone. It's better. We see such a lot of each other during the rest of the year."

"I thought I might go on a two weeks' cruise of the Norwegian fjords," I said. "It's a bit expensive, of course, but I've never been on a cruise and I believe you have quite good fun."

I went on talking about a colleague of mine who always went on cruises and swore by them.

"What about your third week?" she asked.

"I haven't thought about it."

This was a lie. I had thought about it, and I knew that Cynthia had already arranged to go with me to the same hotels at Whitney Bay as we had stayed at the previous year.

I forget what I said to Kate next, but it was some remark entirely unconnected with holidays. Kate made no reply. She turned to stub her cigarette out on an ashtray which lay on the ground by her side. She had her face bent over the ashtray, so that, looking down, I could see only the top of her head. It was quite a well-groomed head nowadays, but I noticed how the blonde, rather lank hair turned dark towards the roots. She was a long time stubbing out the cigarette and when she had finished began to play about with the ash, drawing designs in it with a burnt matchstick.

As I watched I saw a drop of liquid splash on to the back of her hand. She quickly wiped it away. I dropped my hand lightly on to her shoulder and bent down.

"What is the matter, Katie? What is it?"

I tried to turn her face towards me, but she drew herself away and sniffed and groped for her handkerchief. I gave her mine.

"What is it, Katie?" I said again.

By now she was crying silently, her head bent forward into her hands, her shoulders shaking. Sitting on the floor, her legs drawn under her, she looked more like a child than ever. I put my hand on the back of her neck and ran my fingers caressingly up through her hair. I did not know the cause of her tears and felt helpless.

"I'm just being silly," she said at length.

"Tell me what has upset you, Katie dear."

"It's nothing."

She blew her nose, dabbed at her face, and looked at my handkerchief now damp with tears and smeared with lipstick.

"I'll wash it for you," she said.

"Never mind about the damned handkerchief. Tell me why you were crying." But she only shook her head again and said it was nothing important, and that she wouldn't embarrass me again in that way. I slipped down on to the floor beside her, put my arm round her shoulders, and said, "Don't you trust me, Katie?"

"Of course I do."

"Tell me the trouble. I won't laugh at you or anything."

"It's no use me telling you; otherwise I would. I don't want to tell you. I'm angry with myself as it is."

But I was going over in my mind all that we had said just previously. I was beginning to have a shrewd suspicion of the cause of the tears. She got up and went to her handbag and took out her compact and came and sat down on the floor again beside me. I watched her making-up her face afresh.

I felt deeply troubled, for now I knew just where pity had led me.

I had been taking her out partly because I liked doing so, and partly because I knew she was lonely and was sorry for her. To a girl who had received few attentions from men, and none of lasting nature, there was only one conclusion which she could draw from it all.

I do not think that at that period Kate was in love with me, but I think she was desperately in love with the human warmth I brought to her, and such moderate and courteous male attentions as I paid to her. A new vista of the future was opening out before her, and had been slowly taking shape until the moment when I failed to include her in my holiday plans.

The realization of it filled me with a strange mixture of dismay and tenderness. Hitherto I had had nothing to do with the dispensation of power and authority except to adjust myself to it as best I could when it was wielded by others. At school I had spent much time doing the will of masters, prefects and Prosset. At Palesby I was engaged in carrying out the orders of an Editor and Chief Reporter. I had never even kept a dog for whose welfare or otherwise I was responsible.

In a sense, the same considerations had applied to my affair with Cynthia. It had been Cynthia who had been the dispenser of good things and I who had been the recipient, according to her moods. It had been Cynthia, certain of her own power to attract men, practical, clear-sighted and logical, who had decided to marry me, rather than the other way round. And Cynthia, much as she undoubtedly enjoyed it herself, had used our physical union to form the cement in the edifice which she was building for the future. Neat and well ordered though it certainly would be, the cornerstone of that building would be Cynthia.

Now I had power over the happiness and well-being of another suddenly thrust upon me. Unthinkingly, I had built up a responsibility for another's joy or sorrow; somebody, moreover, who could not hit back or defend herself; Kate was not the type to make a late marriage, and even if she were, the circumstances of her life were such as to make it unlikely that she would meet many men. So there she was, to make or break.

These thoughts did not occur to me clearly at that moment. They have been clarified and simplified with the passage of time. But in a confused and unformed state they were agitating within me as I sat beside her. I felt no pleasure, but I sensed a sudden renewed uprush of compassion for her on account of her loneliness, her defencelessness, her miserable, circumscribed ambitions, the little with which she had to be content, and the narrowness of the knife-edge on which even that little was balanced.

I made up my mind as to what I would do, but I had to be careful, for I did not wish her pleasure to be in any way lessened by the thought that I was solely actuated by the sight of her tears. I offered her another cigarette and asked casually if her father was very strict about what she did. She looked surprised at the question.

"No; I don't think he is anything out of the ordinary."

"That's good."

"Why do you ask?"

"Some parents are still pretty strait-laced, even in these days. I was just wondering, Kate."

"He doesn't see much of me, so he can't be very concerned," she said with just a touch of bitterness.

"Is he expecting you to spend some of your holidays with him?"

"I don't know. I hadn't thought about it, Mike."

"What I had in mind," I said after a short pause, "was the third week of my holiday. I was wondering if we could wangle it so we spent it together somewhere. Perhaps you could even come on the two weeks' cruise with me. I could contribute towards your fare. I'd like to do so. I'd like you to come with me, Kate. Would you like that, Katie?"

There are certain supreme moments in a lifetime which you look back upon with joy, whatever the subsequent events. I recall now with thankfulness the happiness I gave Kate during those few moments that evening. I can still see her eyes, half-filled with tears, but with tears of joy now, blazing back at me with such a light as I had never seen in a woman's eyes before. Her lips were half-parted and the blood had rushed into her rather colourless cheeks. A less ingenuous girl might have made some attempt to be casual. I looked at her and smiled. On a sudden impulse I bent down and kissed her.

"Well, what about it? You haven't given me your answer."

"Do you really mean it?"

"Of course I mean it, Katie." I put my arm round her waist and squeezed her affectionately. She said nothing, made no movement, but continued to stare into the gas fire. At length she turned and looked at me and said, "I cannot think of a more heavenly idea. But why did you suggest it, Mike, dear? Tell me the truth."

It was another of those questions which have to be answered smoothly and at once, without the slightest hesitation. I saw her looking at me seriously, anxiously. Somehow the thought of causing her any diminution of her joy was intolerable, and in a flash, the reflex logical reaction to make her happier still overcame me. It was madness and it could have had the most cruel consequences, but I hardly hesitated.

"Why do you think, Katie, dearest?" I said, and kissed her full on the lips.

She clung to me for a long time, returning my kisses with a passion, an abandon even, of which I had not thought her capable.

Kate was slimmer and smaller than Cynthia. I could hold her more easily. Her mouth was larger, her lips softer; her skin amazingly smooth. Cynthia kissed fiercely, with primitive enthusiasm, with her body as well as her mouth, with her basic instincts. Kate was quieter, more feline, more sinuous. Both had fire. But Kate fed the fire with her spiritual emotions.

It is true that when love has turned to pity it has lost its meaning, but it is false to declare, as some do, that love cannot grow out of pity in the first instance. A man may very easily find himself being friendlily disposed to a woman because he is sorry for her, and through his association with her discover qualities and attractions which at first he had not noticed. In the end he may fall in love with her.

I took Kate out at first because her forlornness and her loneliness made me pity her. In a sudden mood of quixotic sentiment, because her tears moved me as they might not have moved a man more experienced with women, and doubtless because I was not really in love with Cynthia, I suggested that Kate and I spend part of our holidays together.

I realized all that that implied concerning Cynthia. I knew I was acting shabbily towards her. It was clear that it would have been kinder to have told Cynthia before leaving Palesby that she should not regard marriage as certain, since either of us might fall in love with somebody else while we were separated. That would have been quite reasonable, too. But I did not have the moral courage to do so. I had acted with her as I had so far acted with Prosset: I had been vacillating and weak.

It was only when I found Kate's feelings were involved, and that either she or Cynthia was going to get hurt, that I was prodded into action. Of the two, I knew that Cynthia could take care of herself in the long run, and Kate could not. I had little by little become for Kate the refuge, the harbour, the warmth in the whole world, representing in some measure that for which Ackersley had shot himself and Geoffries had been hanged.

Had there been other men in Kate's little world, even acquaintances, I might have thought that I was conceited. But there was nobody. I was not much, but I was all she had.

It was strange how she changed, almost from the evening when I first really kissed her, for I do not count the earlier diffident kisses of our extreme youth. It was as though something within her had been unfrozen, so that she suddenly blossomed out into a warm, responsive girl; her movements quickened, she laughed easily, and from a rather serious-minded lover of books about the eighteenth century she became gay and increasingly able to hold her own in badinage. Her looks improved and she spent some of the money she had saved on new clothes, visits to the hairdresser and to the manicurist. She began to buy cut flowers for her room, instead of being content with a dull-looking fern in a pot, and even took to using a cigarette holder because, I suspect, she thought it looked more attractive.

I fell deeply in love with Kate.

We resolved to get married in the following August. You could get little flats easily in London at that time, and we decided that about June we would start looking around for one.

But there was still Cynthia.

I spent the best part of an evening writing to Cynthia, drafting and redrafting the letter. I might just as well have saved myself the trouble and written a short, simple note. However you wrap these things up, they amount to the same in the end, and what they amount to is that you have changed your mind and fallen in love with somebody else. No amount of camouflage can disguise the fact that it is the most terrible slap in the face which a man can give a woman.

For some days I received no reply.

I envisaged the possibility that she was consulting her solicitor with a view to a breach of promise action, for which she certainly had ample evidence.

But I underestimated that practical, common-sense character of hers. I have no doubt that after calm, cool reflection she decided that, as she was still young and good-looking, the amount of damages she would get would hardly compensate her for the humiliation which a court case would bring her. In due course I received an envelope from her. Inside was a thin gold bracelet I had once given her. There was nothing else. No letter, not even a signature.

But in her bitterness Cynthia remained essentially herself: she had registered the letter. It would have been against her nature to risk a valuable thing like a good gold bracelet getting lost in the post.

One early evening, after visiting my Aunt Edith, this time with Kate, I turned the car right at the main road to drive towards Kensington, with some idea of seeing whether there was a good film showing at the Odeon. I heard a car horn sounding two or three times and pulled over further to the left to let the driver pass. I was aware that an old Alvis went by. The driver accelerated until he was a couple of hundred yards ahead of me and pulled in to the kerb. He opened his door and signalled me to stop.

I had seen Prosset three or four times since the evening I had spent with him at the pub in Chelsea, but never with Kate.

There was nothing for it but to stop and have a word with him. I did not wish to do so. I knew that before we parted he would somehow manage to show me in an unfavourable light in front of Kate. It might not even be done deliberately. It might be only a question of competition, a challenge to show himself a better man than me in front of a third person, a woman, and Prosset could never resist a challenge of that kind or any other kind.

I pulled up behind the Alvis, and he walked up and leant over the side of the car.

"Hello, Mike, me boyo!" He shook hands perfunctorily, his eyes on Kate at my side.

"Kate," I said, "let me introduce you to an old school friend of mine, John Prosset. John, this is Kate Marsden, my fiancée. We're getting married in a few weeks' time."

"Married! My God, why didn't you tell me about this? I never gave you permission to go and get married, Mike! Well, well, well! Congratulations, and all that. This calls for a drink."

"Well, as a matter of fact, Kate and I are just going to see what's on at the Odeon."

"I can tell you. A bloody awful film called *Something-or-other Melody*. I've seen it. I advise against it. Don't let him take you there, Kate."

I looked uncertainly at Kate. As usual when Prosset was around I was beginning to lose a grip of the situation.

"There's no need to appeal to her, old man. Look, madame, I put it to you frankly: I spend my best school years looking after this chap and keeping him out of trouble, and he wants to go to some lousy film instead of buying me a drink to celebrate his engagement. Is that civilized conduct? Dammit, I will lend you the money if necessary. Remind me to tell you some time, Kate, of the epic occasion when old Mike ordered a round of drinks and hadn't got any money to pay for them, and stood at the bar blushing to the roots of his hair! That is one of my most prized memories."

"Don't drag me into this," said Kate lightly. "I don't mind what we do." She turned to me. "But if Mr. Prosset feels strongly about it—"

"John," said Prosset, "we might as well start right away with Christian names. I expect we'll be seeing a lot of each other in the future. All I can say is, if you won't have a drink with me to celebrate your engagement, I shall certainly consider you no friends of mine in future, and that's flat."

The mind toys in retrospect with what might have been.

How delicious it would have been, what a triumph, what a recompense for the past, just to slip the gear lever into first gear and say, "That suits me to perfection," and drive off leaving him agape in the roadway! But all I said was, "Well, if that's the way you feel about it, lead on. Where shall we go?"

That was the beginning of it as far as Kate and Prosset and I were concerned. After three or four rounds of drinks we ended up by having dinner together in some restaurant in Dean Street, and when we parted for the night it had somehow been arranged that Kate and I should come down the following weekend to his cottage in Ockleton.

I didn't want to go, of course. But it just happened that way. Prosset had a way of making things happen as he wished. Sometimes I have wondered whether all the time he may not have been instinctively aware of what I really felt about him; whether he knew that I struggled to free myself from his influence, and that I really hated him, and that I hated him because from boyhood he had made me feel a miserable second-rater; and whether perhaps he delighted in keeping me forever on the end of a string.

I did not know for certain.

It presupposes a cat and mouse relationship and a strong streak of sadism in Prosset which it may be unjust to ascribe to him. Yet I do not know. And now I never shall know. To my mind, the barrier between this world and the next is invisible, intangible, and yet as thick and soundproof as the stoutest steel door. You may tear at the grass which grows on the grave. You may upset the headstone and beat on the coffin, but it will avail you nothing.

With bitterness and an aching heart, I could see that Kate liked Prosset just as I had liked him when first I met him with David Trevelyan. I did not blame her. I could not, for he was a type with which she had not come into contact before. There had been nobody at her office with his good looks, his high spirits, his challenging optimism; or if there had been, they had taken no notice of her. Nor did I feel able at that time to explain things to her. It was only later, under the tremendous pressure of events, that I felt myself constrained to do so.

For the moment, I could only watch, despising my own inaction, yet not knowing what course I could follow with any prospect of success. I felt numbed and helpless.

When he first invited us down to Ockleton he approached the subject by a casual question to Kate.

"Do you and Mike do much at the weekends?"

"Not much. Sometimes we go for a run in the car," Kate had answered.

"Where are you going this weekend?"

"Nowhere, as far as I know, are we, Mike?"

"Well——" I began, but Prosset interrupted.

"Why not bring old Mike down and stay at my cottage by the sea? I've bought a sailing dinghy, and it may be warm enough to bathe."

I tried to stamp on the idea at once.

"It's always difficult for me to make a firm date," I said slowly. "I never quite know whether the office will want me for anything. It's one of the disadvantages of being in the newspaper racket."

"You can give me a ring at the last moment if you can't come," said Prosset. "It won't put me out at all."

"It's very unlikely you'll be busy," said Kate innocently. "You haven't had a weekend job for months."

"That doesn't mean I won't get one this weekend. In fact, by the law of averages——"

"Don't come if you don't want to, old man," said Prosset, his cigarette bobbing up and down between his lips. "It's only an idea. I thought a breath of sea air might do you good. You're looking a bit pale and towny. Anyway, you don't need to bathe, if you don't want to. Kate and I can go and have a swim, if the weather's fine, and you can cook our lunch, eh, Kate? Mike never was a great one for cold water, were you, Mike?"

"Oh, I don't know," I replied uneasily. "I quite like a swim."

"Then you must have changed. You were never one for it at school, were you?"

"Well, sometimes."

Prosset laughed good-humouredly. "Rot, old man! Can you tell me of one instance when you suggested to David and me that we should all go for a swim?"

"Of course I can't give you an instance, after all this time."

"It's not a question of how long afterwards. There never was an occasion. If there had been, I'd have remembered it! So would you, I expect, if only with regret."

I saw Kate smiling and obviously enjoying what she considered to be his cheerful badinage.

"Well, it's no good arguing about it," I said.

"I wasn't arguing," returned Prosset, smiling broadly at Kate. "You were doing the arguing, old man. I merely made a statement, and you contradicted it, didn't you?"

"Because it was not correct."

"But you contradicted it, didn't you?"

"Yes, I did."

"Therefore you were doing the arguing. You started it, didn't you? Go on, admit it and apologize. He ought to apologize oughtn't he, Kate?"

It was the school dining room all over again. Prosset showing off, thrusting and parrying, scoring off his opponent, master of the situation and of himself, enjoying every minute of it.

"Well, how about it, old man? How about it, Kate?"

"I should love to go," said Kate.

Prosset took a pull at his beer. "That's fine, then! OK, Mike?"

"So long as the office isn't tiresome at the last moment."

Prosset dismissed the office with a wave of his hand.

"They won't want you. Anyway, I'm on the phone there. I'll pick you up at Kate's place at about 2:30 on Saturday. We can all go down in my car."

"I think we'd better drive down separately. I may have to get back to town in a hurry."

"Oh, I'll drive you back if they want you. What's the point of having two cars? Anyway, Kate'll be much more comfortable in my car."

"Don't you run down Mike's car," protested Kate.

"I wasn't running it down. I just said you would be more comfortable in mine, and you would, wouldn't you?"

"Perhaps I would and perhaps I wouldn't."

"Anyway, it's a much faster car than Mike's. You'll have to buy yourself a proper car one of these days, Mike."

"What's happened to you?" I asked. "Things must be looking up. A different car, and a cottage by the sea."

"Things are looking up. Don't forget I gave you a chance to invest some cash in the firm once, Mike! You'll be sorry you didn't, one day. £250 would have bought you a partnership once. It will cost you more now, and if you wait much longer it'll cost you more still."

I shook my head. "I'm a newspaperman, not a businessman."

Prosset smiled at Kate. His looked seemed to say: "See what I mean? No initiative. A dull, plodding type who will never do anything much because he will never take a risk. A bit different from me, eh?"

That's what his look said, as clearly as if he had spoken the words aloud. Poor old Mike, it seemed to say.

Later that night, when I was alone with Kate, she said, "You don't think it would be a good idea to go in with John Prosset and Day?"

"No, I don't."

"I was only thinking that as a partner you would be more your own master. You would have more time to write books and things. That's all I was thinking."

"I don't trust Herbert Day, for one thing."

"I don't want you to do anything you don't want to do, darling."

I fell back upon the same words I had used to Prosset. I could think of nothing else. "I am a newspaperman, not a businessman."

She sensed something in the tone of my voice. She said, "Is anything the matter?"

"Of course there isn't. What should there be?"

"You do want to go down to the cottage on Saturday, don't you? Because if you don't, we can easily cancel it."

"Nothing is the matter."

"You do want to go down, don't you?" she persisted.

"Yes; I want to go down."

"You do like John Prosset, don't you?"

"Of course I like him. He's my old school friend. We've never had a row in our lives."

I could not humiliate myself in her eyes by telling her the truth. To have done so would have been to reveal myself in her eyes as a poor-spirited, backboneless creature, and I knew that in general that was not true.

I had stood up to many people, held my own in varying circumstances and acquitted myself in a manner of which I had no reason to be ashamed. It was only Prosset against whom I could make no kind of headway whatever. Prosset had only to look at me speculatively with a faint, amused look in his eyes to have me all keyed up and tense, wondering miserably what attack, direct or oblique, he was about to make on me.

Only Prosset could turn me into a rabbit, but who would believe that? If I told the whole story to Kate, I should be playing into Prosset's hands. By comparison with the poor showing I should make, he would rise in stature. Would Kate believe in her heart that only Prosset could have this effect on me? I doubted it.

"Prosset and I are, and always will be, the best of friends," I said doggedly.

Kate came and sat on the arm of my chair.

"I think he likes me, too, you know. I'm glad. I want all your friends to like me. Actually, I like being liked, if you know what I mean. It sounds silly, but I do."

"You haven't made a bad start," I said.

CHAPTER 11

Except in sudden cases of ungovernable rage or when discovered in some criminal act and cornered, one person does not suddenly decide to kill another. It is a thing which grows upon you gradually.

At odd moments you begin to think how nice it would be if somebody were to die suddenly, painlessly, peacefully, from natural causes. Barely have you realized along which lines your thoughts are running than you pull yourself up short. You tell yourself insistently that you hope he or she will live to a ripe old age, but though the words form themselves in your brain they lack conviction, until in the end you reconcile yourself to the idea that if they die peacefully you will not be unduly upset.

In the case of somebody you hate, as I hated Prosset, the next stage comes fairly quickly. You begin to think out, purely for fun, you tell yourself, how you would kill an enemy if you should ever wish to do so. It rapidly becomes clear that in a highly populated and civilized country this problem is by no means easy of solution, but you do not despair. You persevere until you have perfected a plan which, if you wished to kill him—though naturally the idea is unthinkable—could be put into action with the minimum of danger to yourself.

I myself came to the conclusion that the only safe method is to push your victim over a cliff.

Here you are not faced with the troublesome business of disposing of the body nor, if you should be questioned, of explaining away awkward wounds or suggestive grains of arsenic. The body is there for all to see, the wounds are only those which have been incurred as a result of the fall. Providing the timing is right, there need be no signs of struggle on the top of the cliff, and providing the cliff is high enough there need be little fear that the victim will tell the truth before he dies. Suspicion may be heavy, perhaps, particularly if there is a good motive for the crime, but there can be no proof unless luck is badly against you.

You cannot guard against ill luck. There is some risk, as there must always be.

The victim's fall may be broken by some protruding branch, bush or ledge; such miracles do happen, and have happened in cases of accidental falls, and there is no reason to suppose that they could not happen in a case of attempted murder. In which case you would go to jail for a very long stretch.

Or it may chance that a coastguard trains his telescope on that part of the coast for the first time for years and catches you in the act; or some ardent bird-watcher, gathering material for an essay on the breeding habits of a certain species of gull, may be observing you as you walk along the cliff past his hideout with the victim; and curse you for frightening the birds and interfering with his hobby.

If that sort of thing happens you will be hanged, of course.

I went through all these preliminary mental phases towards the end of my association with Prosset, but for long I lacked the final impetus which could induce me to risk my neck. For long I did not contemplate killing him, but merely watched with ever-increasing apprehension as affairs came to a climax.

For two weekends in succession I was engineered into taking Kate down to Ockleton. The cottage had been at one time a coast-guard's station, and stood at the top of a cliff overlooking the sea about a mile from the village. To reach the sea you made your way through a small front garden, out through a side gate, and down a steep path to a sandy cove. This small cove was cut off from beaches on either side by headlands of rugged rock across which it was possible to clamber; but so much labour was involved, and so much time, that few people ever did, so that the beach was almost always deserted.

It was a long climb from the cottage, too, and the path was steep and somewhat unsafe in places; a handrail had formerly af-forded some sort of safeguard at the narrower points, but this had partly rotted away, and nobody had bothered to repair it. It was an ideal place in which to eliminate an enemy by the method which I had planned.

It seemed that when the last coastguard had folded his tele-scope and had been transferred elsewhere, the cottage had for some years remained uninhabited. Then a painter of seascapes, a man of little talent but possessed of private means and great enthusiasm, had bought and furnished the place and lived in it for some eight-een months before moving to the South of France, where the colours are brighter and simpler to put on canvas.

This man had put the cottage in the hands of local agents, and sometimes during the better weather a family would take it, or a writer in search of peace and quiet in which to finish a book would live in it. It was stone-built and sturdy, heavily timbered inside, and consisted of a kitchen and living room on the ground floor and two small bedrooms upstairs. Somebody, presumably the well-to-do painter, had built a little wooden shed from the kitchen and in-stalled an old-fashioned bath and geyser in it.

The furniture was of dark oak. There was a window seat in the living room covered with what once had been bright-flowered chintz; it was now faded and stained with sea water, and the car-pets were threadbare. Behind the cottage was a patch of grass and some trees, stunted and twisted by the sea winds. It was a shabby enough little place, but Prosset made much of it, pointing out the exhilarating quality of the air, the fine view, and the pleasures of early morning bathing for those who cared to clamber down to the sea before breakfast.

Succeeding tenants had left their traces behind them. In an outhouse was a doll's pram with one wheel missing, and a large pile of dusty wine and brandy bottles whose contents had doubtless been swallowed by the artist. There was some manuscript paper and a few torn carbons in a drawer in the writing desk, and some fishing tackle mouldering in a heap in the shed which called itself the bathroom. On the bookshelf in the living room was the usual collection of cheap novels, one or two yellow French love stories, and, for some reason, a set of three volumes on human anatomy.

Such was the cottage which Prosset had rented for a year; you could approach it either along the road which ran through the village, and which served the other cottages along that part of the coast, or you could take a short cut, bypass the village, and use an old twisting road which was now little more than a disused cart track partially overgrown with weeds.

During both the weekends we were fortunate with our weather, and spent the time lazing on the beach or in the garden or walking along the cliffs. In the evenings we went into the village and had drinks at the Anchor. Kate thoroughly enjoyed it all; and there is no doubt that we came back on the Monday mornings looking the better for the change.

Looking back, I think that Prosset acted with considerable subtlety.

For the first afternoon and evening which we spent with him during the first weekend, his attitude was impeccable. To Kate he was friendly and amusing, but the greater part of his attentions were devoted to me. It was as though I were the honoured guest and Kate the very welcome addition to the party. He spoke of our schooldays, recalling various amusing episodes in which he and David and I had been involved. He talked of the House, and speculated about what had happened to the various people who had been with us during those four years. We recalled the tragic affair of Ackersley, the idiosyncrasies of some of the masters, and generally indulged in the sort of talk which old school friends enjoy. It was delightful.

I was a fool to succumb to it all, but I did. I have never been able to harbour bitterness, and have always been a sucker for a warm approach and any suggestion that bygones are best forgotten.

It may be admirable in theory, very Christian and praiseworthy, but in the world as constituted today it is crass stupidity. Today you have to be hard and wary, and unforgetting, otherwise you are riding for a fall, as I was riding for a fall at Coastguard's Cottage with Prosset and Kate.

He looked so open and friendly and frank; so healthy, with his raven-black hair and suntanned face; and when he smiled at me with his eyes and talked nostalgically of the old days I said to myself that whatever he had been in the past, he was changing. He was mellowing, becoming more human.

Perhaps I can make a close friend of him yet, I thought, and for a couple of hours or so on the first Saturday night at Ockleton I was happy. I was glad I had come. There we were, Kate whom I loved, Prosset with whom I seemed to be reconciled, and myself who wanted to be friendly and on good terms with everybody. It was a fine beginning. I felt a glow inside me, and it wasn't all due to the whisky at the Anchor.

So I agreed readily enough when Prosset said he hoped we would come down again the following weekend. "Just to kind of cement firmly the friendship of us three," he said.

I not only agreed, I went further, and said, "If by any chance I have to work, you could always get Marjorie to come down with you, Kate. John wouldn't mind, would you?"

"Certainly not. Let 'em all come. Who is Marjorie?"

"A friend of mine," said Kate. "I haven't seen her as much as I used to do, since Mike came on the scene. Poor Marjorie."

"Is she blonde and is she lovely?" asked Prosset, simulating an evil leer.

"She is not. She is mousy and dumpy on the outside, and on the inside she is angelic."

"She sounds awful," said Prosset cheerfully. "Let her come by all means, if old Mike can't turn up, but I expect he will be able to."

I slept in the room next to Kate upstairs, because Prosset insisted that as the host he must occupy the sofa in the living room. I slept very well indeed, because the air and the talk and the drinks had tired me, and because I was mentally at ease, with no inkling of what lay ahead.

It all changed next day. There was nothing very marked at first. A woman might not have noticed it. But just as a woman can read another woman's mind more easily than a man, so a man is quick to note certain actions in another man which would be undetected by a member of the opposite sex.

What it boiled down to was that I was no longer the honoured guest. It was Kate to whom Prosset mostly turned during the conversation, who was supposed to appreciate the little jokes which he made against me. And she, poor dear, only too anxious to make a good impression on one of my friends, encouraged him in his sallies.

I had to join in the laughter, too, of course. What else could I have done except pretend to take it all in good part? But now I understood the previous evening. He had prepared the ground well. He had established himself in Kate's eyes as a devoted old school friend, a man who held me in great affection. Thereafter anything he said to my detriment, any little barbed reminiscences or disparaging remarks, would be considered devoid of all malice or cruelty. Just fun, that's all. Just an old school friend pulling his pal's leg, that's all.

There was a good deal of it. He was at his best. He performed wonders. And there was little one could do about it. There rarely is. If you laugh with your tormentor, you invite further attack. If you show feeling, you look a fool and may as well pack up and go home. The only thing to do is to counter-attack; for that you require a wit as keen as the other man's, and I was never a good talker or much good at repartee.

The second weekend was even worse. Mid-week I made a half-hearted attempt to avoid going down. I said to Kate, "About this weekend, are you very keen to go?"

She looked at me in surprise. "Well, I thought it was all fixed?"

"So it is. But I suppose we could put it off somehow."

"But why? I thought you enjoyed yourself last weekend!"

"So I did. It's just that I quite like being alone with you. That's the only reason I asked."

I could see she looked disappointed. I gave in.

"Forget it, Kate. It was just a passing thought."

"I think we ought to go, Mike, as we said we would."

"Forget it," I said again. "We'll go."

I could have invented some job for the office, and let Marjorie go with Kate. But it was too late for that sort of thing. Now I could not bear the thought of Kate and Prosset being together without me. My hate was now mixed with jealousy. Perhaps in some degree it always had been, but this was a different sort of jealousy. It was sex jealousy, than which there is nothing more emotionally terrible or tormenting in the world. So I went down with Kate.

He was in excellent form again that weekend. Most witty.

Then Whitsun was almost upon us.

Prosset had invited us down for Whitsun, but we had declined. When he had pressed his invitation, I had compromised by saying that we might drive down for one day, the Sunday, if the weather was fine, but that we would not stay the night. I only agreed to it because I thought Kate would like it.

He knew that every Friday evening I stayed in at my digs to write. At about four o'clock on the Friday afternoon before Whitsun I was at the office going through the London evening papers when the telephone sounded. It was Kate.

She said, "Mike, John Prosset has rung me up. He wants to know if I would care to go dog racing this evening. You remember I told him I had never seen any dog racing."

"Yes, I remember," I answered. I felt suddenly shaky and almost ill. "What did you say, Katie?"

"Well, I said I'd love to, provided you agreed. You don't mind, do you? I mean, you'll be at your digs all the evening, anyway. It'll be something to do."

"I don't mind," I said. "Why should I? Have a good time."

"I knew you wouldn't mind. How are you, darling?"

"I'm very well, thank you."

I could hear old Charlie Baines, who was in charge of the office, talking on the telephone to somebody in the Midlands; somebody else was rattling away on a typewriter in a corner of the room. Above both noises I could hear the rapid thudding of my own heart.

"You sound very stern, Mike. Is anything the matter?"

I made a supreme effort to sound normal. "Why, no; nothing at all. Just a bit busy, that's all, darling. Have a good time. Don't go to bed too late."

"I won't. See you tomorrow?"

"See you tomorrow," I said. "And by the way, tell John we shall not be coming down at all this weekend. I'll explain later." I rang off.

I looked at the telephone receiver before replacing it. I saw it was glistening with moisture from the palm of my hand. I took out my handkerchief and wiped it before replacing it in position.

I tried to decide how much I was the victim of selfishness and jealousy, and how much I was moved by concern for Kate's welfare. Two voices were disputing inside me.

One was insisting that I was mainly concerned with what was best for Kate. It was telling me that I was really very noble at heart, and that I would gladly sacrifice myself for Kate's happiness if I could be convinced that it was in her interests to surrender her to Prosset. I was worried, said this voice, only because I knew that Prosset would never marry her, that she was not the type of girl whom Prosset would ever marry, and that if she fell in love with him it could only lead to disaster. This was a very loud voice indeed, and almost bellowed at me, doubtless because it knew it had a weak case.

The smaller, feebler voice was hardly more than a whisper, but I knew it could not be shut out because it was the truth, though I did not want the truth at that moment. It was less flattering: I was feeling just as any other man feels when he thinks some other chap may steal his girl. The very thought of it involved possessiveness, hurt pride, wounded vanity, incredulity and helpless fury all rolled into one giant ball of pain; and rendered the worse because with the jealousy there was mingled the feeling, born of old and perpetuated through the years, that in any contest with Prosset I was beaten before I started.

I went back to Harrington Gardens, but I ate no supper. Work was out of the question. I tried to read, but I could not concentrate. I drank a couple of stiff whiskies, which inevitably produced a steady flow of self-pity. It became clear to me that Prosset was not alone to blame; Kate must have encouraged him in some way, otherwise he would not have invited her out. Kate, who had been alone and unloved until I came along, had fallen for the first offer of a flirtation from the first man who made it.

Cynthia Harrison had at least been faithful. I mixed myself a third whisky and soda; stronger than the first two, for I was finding that although the self-pity was stronger, the actual physical pain in my stomach was disappearing. I felt muzzy in the head, but I welcomed that; my thoughts were wandering from Kate and Prosset, and I welcomed that, too. I saw myself back in Palesby telling Cynthia that she was a much nicer girl than Kate. As we talked she was full of understanding about how I had been led astray and full of commiseration for the dirty trick that had been played on me. I was giving her back the golden bracelet she had returned to me; and after that various people appeared and disappeared, including Aunt Edith, Mr. Martin and Ackersley.

I felt a hand shaking my shoulder and found Ethel standing with the usual cup of tea she brought me at 10:30 when I was in.

"Doing no work tonight, Mr. Sibley?"

"I intended to, but I must have fallen asleep," I said.

I looked at the clock. It was nearer a quarter to eleven than 10:30. Kate would be home soon and the evening would be over, and that was that. I drank the cup of tea and had a wash and felt better. But one thing I was determined upon; we were not going down to Ockleton. Certainly not for some time, anyway.

That was now off, whatever Kate might feel about it.

Reaction from the earlier emotions set in and I felt foolish that I should have been so upset. If I put my foot down and saw to it that

Prosset had no further opportunities to make headway with Kate, no harm would have been done. She had naturally accepted the invitation that evening, and I bore her no grudge, but it was not the sort of thing which I wished to happen again. The visits to Ockleton would have to cease. Kate would be disappointed, but she would do as I wished. I felt sure of it. Explaining matters to her would be difficult, though, and I spent a quarter of an hour thinking the problem over.

I decided that the best thing would be to tell her that although Prosset was a nice fellow in many ways, and a good friend of mine, he was a flirt, and the best way to avoid complications which might endanger our friendship was to avoid putting temptation in his way.

"He's an awfully nice chap," I could hear myself saying, "and nobody is fonder of him than I am, but he just cannot help trying to flirt with every girl he meets. It's not his fault," I would add, "he's just made that way. None of us is perfect; all of us have good qualities and weaknesses, and his weakness is women."

I sounded very convincing. I also thought it was rather subtle, since no woman who pretended to love a man would care to receive the odium for breaking up a lifelong friendship. Kate would see my point of view all right. She was a good girl—just a little inexperienced, that was all. She needed a little guidance.

I thought of her at that moment possibly laughing at some joke of his. He would be looking down at her, his handsome, dark face smiling and attentive, the inevitable cigarette between his lips. I felt a return, though in a less violent form, of the earlier wave of jealousy.

I looked at my watch. It was nearly eleven o'clock. Whenever I have decided to do something I am restless until I have started to put it into action. It was too late to start working, and it was too early for bed. I would go round to Kate's room and have a talk with her there and then. I could not telephone her, because the people in the house did not like late calls, but I thought that if she was not at home already she would arrive by the time I had driven across to Manchester Square. I argued that I was just in the right mood of cool disapproval to put the point over with firmness.

I looked up when I arrived and saw that her room was in darkness; I let myself in with the key she had given me to avoid the necessity of ringing the bell on the numerous occasions when I called. I helped myself to a glass of gin and vermouth and sat down to wait, again running over in my mind what I would say.

At a quarter to twelve I decided that she would arrive at any moment; at midnight I began to think that Prosset must have taken her to have a meal somewhere after the racing, and at 12:15 I was sure of it.

But at 12:30 I had reached the stage where I was looking at my watch every five minutes and wandering restlessly about the room. I felt the old sick, jealous feeling gnawing away at my stomach. I told myself that I was being unreasonable; that it was very nice of Prosset to have bothered to give her a meal afterwards; that I hoped she was having a nice, gay evening because she deserved it: she had not had much fun out of life up to now, whereas I had had plenty. Moreover, it was the last time she would be going out alone with him, so it did not matter. Anyone who has suffered from jealousy knows how futile such reasoning is. I knew in my heart that I really hoped she had been bored stiff, and that she certainly had not been. One was amused, interested, entertained, made angry or resentful by Prosset, but never bored by him.

By one o'clock I was half alarmed and half angry and resentful. She had said she would be home in reasonable time and she was not. She had let me down. She had not kept her word. If she had had any understanding, she would have got home in reasonable time and telephoned me, and we could have had a chat. But no, she preferred to stay out and enjoy herself without a thought for me.

But was she enjoying herself? Perhaps they had had an accident. Prosset was not the most careful of drivers. Maybe she was lying in some hospital gravely injured and wanting me to be with her. Perhaps she was dead and could read every mean thought in my mind. I decided to wait until half past one and then drive round to Prosset's place. At least it would be better than doing nothing. I could not telephone him, because I did not know the name of his landlord, and the only number I had in my diary was his office number.

I watched the hands on the little travelling clock by her bed-side creep towards the half hour. At twenty-six minutes past, I was tempted to leave, but with a kind of masochistic determination I forced myself to stay until the time I had decided upon. Then I put out the light and went downstairs and let myself gently out of the front door.

I climbed into my car and lit a cigarette, thinking over what I would say on arrival. It would be better to tell at least part of the truth, and say that I was worried about whether anything had happened. Why not? I guessed that Prosset would look at me in his mocking way and assume that some other reason had brought me there. So what? Let him think what he liked.

I leaned forward and fumbled to find the slot for the ignition key, found it, switched on the current, and reached for the self-starter. But before I could start the engine a taxi drew up in front of me.

Kate got out. She was alone.

The light from a street lamp shone upon her yellow hair. She was wearing her near-white mackintosh. She fumbled in her leather handbag for some money, swayed back a pace, and went and leaned against the lamp standard still groping in her bag.

I opened the car door and scrambled out. I went over to her. Then I asked the taxi driver what the fare was, and paid him. He looked at me questioningly.

I said, "It's all right. I know her. I'll let her in."

"Bit pickled, ain't she?"

"Looks like it. Good night."

"Can you manage, sir?"

"Yes, thank you."

"Righto, sir. Good night." He reached out and slammed the door of the taxi and drove off.

I was left alone in the street with Kate. She was still fumbling in her handbag, oblivious of the fact that the taxi had driven off. I went over and took her by the arm. She raised her head and looked at me unsteadily, opened her mouth as if to say something, but did not speak. She was very white in the face and a strand of hair was hanging over one eye.

I led her up the steps without difficulty, but when she was faced with the staircase in the hall she slumped against me. I placed one of her arms round my neck, put my right arm round her waist, and tried to drag her up the stairs, but failed. So I picked her up bodily and carried her up to her room and laid her on the bed. As I was struggling to get her out of her raincoat, she recovered slightly and assisted me.

"You seem to have enjoyed the dog racing."

She looked at me in a bewildered way. "Dog racing? We didn't go. He didn't want to go."

"I see. What did you do? Or is that an unfortunate question?"

She had sunk back on to the bed with her eyes closed. She groaned and licked her lips.

"I'm dying," she said.

"You're not. You're drunk, that's all."

I sat by her side for a few moments. There was no lipstick left on her lips and no powder on her cheeks. Her head was turned sideways, and I saw some red marks on her neck and throat. I got up to go.

"Well, good night, Katie."

She stirred and moaned. "I feel awful."

"You'll feel worse in the morning."

I felt oddly unemotional. I was tired, cold, but curiously objective, devoid even of anger or resentment now. Something which I had anticipated had happened; rather sooner than I had expected, it is true, but it had happened, and now it was over, it was past history.

Perhaps if she had not worn spectacles, if she had been more beautiful, I should have felt differently. She had dragged off her coloured spectacles and they lay beside her on the pillow. Her face looked thin and pinched and very pale, and childlike, and I guessed that if I placed my hand on her brow I should find it cold and damp.

I felt again that protective instinct I had so often experienced before in regard to Kate and never about Cynthia. I saw that it was all my fault. If I had not been so weak, she would never have been brought into close contact with Prosset. If I had taken a firm stand earlier, she would never have gone out with him.

For two weekends, unaccustomed to much attention from men, she had been subjected to the undoubted fascination of his personality. So far from feeling angry at that moment, I felt a great concern for her. I wondered how far she had fallen for Prosset, if at all.

Later, two days later, she was to tell me the whole story of how he had suggested a light meal in his room before setting out; how he had coaxed her into drinking too much, amused her, flattered her, and finally had taken her into his arms, so that although she knew she was being unfaithful she was unable to resist for long the physical attraction of that handsome and magnetic man. I cannot imagine why I did not feel a great anger towards Kate; possibly it was because I knew Prosset so well from personal experience.

Looking at her as she lay crumpled and ill on the bed, I knew perfectly well that I would forgive her. I picked up her spectacles from off the pillow and laid them on the bedside table, and spread the eiderdown over her and went out of the room and downstairs, and drove back to Harrington Gardens.

But my feelings in regard to Prosset were very different.

I would drive down alone to Ockleton the following day. The idea and the plan whereby I would rid the world of him were growing crystal clear in my mind, and my thoughts caressed the project lovingly as I lay in bed that night.

Yet the whole thing fizzled out. It is typical of all my dealings with Prosset that even when I planned to kill him I failed. I have sometimes wondered whether I lacked the resolution, and whether I seized on his chance remark as an excuse to call the whole thing off. It may be so, but I do not think so. I think I would have gone through with it.

The next morning, Saturday, I slept late. In addition to the Whitsun holiday, I had the Saturday off.

I wrote a short letter to Kate which I slipped through the letter box and told her briefly that I would be out of town that day, but would be returning the following day. I added that she had nothing whatever to worry about and ended on an affectionate note. When I had delivered it, I had a glass of beer and a sandwich and in the early afternoon set off in the car.

I was filled with a great exultation as I contemplated my plan. I never considered the consequences of failure. Few murderers do. I saw the path from the bottom of the garden leading down the steep cliff to the beach, and the broken handrail at a bend in the path. Prosset was walking down in front of me wearing his bathing wrap, and I was following him closely—so closely that to steady myself I placed my hand on his shoulder blade. The bend in the path came nearer. So vivid was the mental picture, that I could hear above the noise of the engine the soft, padding sound of our bathing shoes on the hard ground, and smell the smoke from Prosset's cigarette drifting back to me.

The beach was deserted and on our left we were protected from sight by the cliff face, while on the right we were hidden from the view of the nearest house by a fringe of trees. It was possible that somebody might be watching us from among the trees. Therefore as an added precaution I pretended to stumble and lurch forward at the bend in the path, for nobody can blame a man if his foot catches in something on the ground.

I heard his startled cry above the sounds of the traffic as he hurtled down to the rocks beneath and lay still, his white bathing wrap spread around him like the shattered wings of a mutilated gull. In my ears was the music of the sea at the foot of the cliffs, and through it a voice was shouting that Prosset was dead, dead and gone, and only his empty husk was left behind; and all the mockery and the sneers were wiped out and Sibley by his own action had triumphed over Prosset. Michael Sibley laughed last, and Kate was safe and had her refuge in which she could seek shelter, and the dog it was that died.

Then I thought I saw the white wrap stir and seemed to hear another cry on the sea breeze, and felt myself breaking out in perspiration. But a voice in my ear sneered: "That was only the wind which stirred the wrap, and the cry was the cry of a seabird. Don't lose your nerve, old man. I'm dead. That's what you wanted, isn't it?"

I swung the car to the side of the road, braked and stopped. I lit a cigarette. When I had stopped trembling, I drove on again.

I swung off the road before arriving at the village of Ockleton and took the disused cart track which led to the cottage. When I arrived at about 4:30 p.m., Prosset was out. The weather seemed set fair, the sky blue and cloudless, the sun still warm.

I stood for a few moments enjoying the stillness of the evening after the sound of my engine had died away. I was surprised to find that I felt quite calm. It did not seem natural. I should have been keyed up, tense, apprehensive even, but certainly not calm. I did not even hate Prosset any more. Since he would so soon be lifeless, it seemed pointless to regard him any longer with emotion.

I went to the bottom of the garden, through the side gate, and walked a little way down the path to the beach until I could see clearly the bend and the broken handrail. It was as I had recalled it. I gazed at it for a few moments, then turned and made my way back to the house.

The cottage door was unlocked, and I went into the living room. Almost at once I noticed a slight but peculiar smell, neither pleasant nor unpleasant. It was so faint as to be almost unnoticeable, faintly pungent, yet at the same time sweet.

It was so remote that it made no real impression on me at the time. Indeed, I barely gave it a thought, more particularly because I had hardly gone beyond the threshold of the room before I heard the sound of an engine and guessed that Prosset had returned.

He was backing his Alvis under the trees when I turned the corner of the cottage. He had seen by the presence of my car that I had arrived, and waved to me, switched off his engine, and came towards me.

"Hello," he said cheerfully, "I didn't expect you. Is Kate with you?"

"Sorry to spring on you out of the blue. I changed my mind."

"Glad to see you. Where's Kate?"

"She couldn't come. Her father's not too well. She had to go down there. She doesn't know when she'll be back."

Prosset frowned. "That's damned bad luck. I was looking forward to having her down. I like her."

"You do?"

"Yes; I do. She's got a nice, friendly personality."

"I'm glad you found her friendly. She's rather shy with some people."

Prosset slipped his arm through mine and led me towards the cottage.

"Of course, she's no beauty, is she? But then you're hardly an Adonis yourself, so what the hell? You know, I wish old David Trevelyan was here. It would be like old times. We really must lure him down for a weekend some time."

"I'd like to see him again, I must say. Where've you been this afternoon?"

"Seeing a chap I know along the coast." He looked at his watch and I waited with a curious feeling of detachment for the suggestion which I was convinced was coming.

"What about a dip in the sea? Or is it too late for you?"

"As a matter of fact, I'd rather like one. It was pretty warm in London."

We went upstairs. He told me to put my things in the larger of the two bedrooms, and began to change into his swimming suit. I took rather longer, for I had to unpack one or two things first; while waiting for me, he sat on the edge of the bed talking and smoking. He seemed in good spirits. The calmness which I had felt up to now was beginning to evaporate. I was not frightened, but I was tense and rather nervous, as before a football match or an examination.

I looked at him and found it hard to imagine that that lively and enthusiastic being would in a few minutes be no more, the smooth, suntanned skin broken, the limbs mangled, the voice silent for ever. What shocked me most was that I felt no regret at the thought, nor the smallest urge to change my plans or to allow him to enjoy even for another day the recollections of the previous evening with Kate. He had made no reference to it. Neither had I. By way of making some sort of conversation, I said, "Where are you going for your holidays this year?"

"Ireland," he replied casually, "as usual."

"Do you always go to Ireland?"

He nodded. "Always. It's a hell of a nuisance, really, but there it is."

"Why go, if you don't want to?"

He fidgeted with his bathing wrap.

"Oh, well, the guv'nor looks forward to it, you know. My young brother is out in Canada, and my sister is married to a chap in the Indian Army, so I'm the only one he sees at the moment. He's rather immobile, you know."

"How do you mean—immobile?"

"He had polio a few years ago. Infantile paralysis to you. There was terrific wind-up in case my young brother got it, too. He was only a kid at the time."

I stared at him without speaking. Finally, I said, "Is he completely bedridden?"

"Oh, no. He gets around in a wheelchair a bit, in the garden and so on, like Roosevelt, only he's not quite so active."

"And you go home every year?"

"Yes. As a matter of fact, I'm taking my holiday in a week or two."

"Quite early," I said. Prosset nodded.

"I had a letter yesterday from the Mater." Irritably, I wished Prosset wouldn't stick to these schoolboy terms.

"The news wasn't so hot. The old boy is in a pretty bad way. Heart, or something. He wants me to go over as soon as I can." He hesitated. "I suppose I ought to go. It's not very convenient. Still, one would feel a bit of a swine if anything happened."

What a strange contradiction was his character! So much that was ruthless, so much that was heartless; and here and there, struggling for existence, like garden flowers choked by weeds, were the occasional streaks of sensitivity and the rare flashes of humanity.

I stood staring out of the window, watching the sun sink towards the sea. A gull was perched on the gate at the end of the garden: now and again it placed its beak under a wing, exploring vigorously and ruffling its feathers. Prosset was saying something about sailing, but I was not listening. Why should I worry about Prosset's father? For all I knew, he was like Prosset. What concern was it of mine? Each man had to look to his own affairs in the modern world. I knew that while Prosset lived, wherever he might be in the world, I should not be entirely happy, and the chances were that I should be very miserable. Let Prosset's father face his troubles as best he could. There was Kate, too. Would she agree not to see Prosset again if he were alive? Or would she leave me and hasten with Prosset to a private torment of her own making? In the balance, must the happiness of Kate be jeopardized for an old, dying man?

"Don't stand dreaming all day or we'll never get down," said Prosset.

But I was visualizing an elderly man looking for the letter which should say that his son was arriving soon; and receiving instead a telegram which would drain the blood from his face.

I sighed. I knew that once again in the battle between Sibley and Prosset I had lost. A terrible feeling of depression descended on me as the tension within me relaxed. In this ultimate test I had lacked the necessary resolution, and Prosset had won. Poor old Mike. I had a feeling that I would never again be able to screw myself up to the same murderous decision.

"I think I will change my mind," I said abruptly. "I don't think I'll bathe this evening. It's getting cold."

Prosset laughed delightedly. "I thought as much! This'll amuse Kate. Well, anyway, come down to the beach with me."

"No."

"Why not?"

"Because I don't want to."

"The exercise will do you good. You're getting fat as it is. Come on."

"No. You go alone."

"You always were a lazy swine," said Prosset disapprovingly.

"Yes," I said, and turned away.

In the event, of course, the telegram would still come to the house in Ireland, but at least I was not to be the willing cause of its arrival.

Yet I had my big moment. I tackled him that night just before we went to bed. I am glad I did so. I am pleased that the last time I saw him alive I fought him to a standstill, beginning in my own time and ending when I wished, and leaving him surprised and even, I hope, a little hurt. Malicious? Certainly. I am very malicious about Prosset. Even though he is dead, and thus for some obscure reason entitled with other dead men to have his virtues extolled and his vices forgotten, I still hate him. I will always hate him.

I have tried to portray some of his better points, but not even the fact that he lies in his grave will make me forget his bad points, or how he tried ruthlessly to steal Kate from me for reasons of his own.

"Prosset, I saw Kate last night, when she came home," I said.

He was drinking some beer and reading. He lowered his pewter mug and book and glanced curiously at me. He did not look guilty, but rather amused. He seemed to be more intrigued to see the line I would take than to fear anything I might be going to say.

"Did you? What am I supposed to say?"

"You're not supposed to say anything, if you don't want to. You can listen."

He took a pull at his beer. "It's not my fault that she can't hold her drink properly. She just got a bit pickled. It was hardly my fault."

"Why the hell couldn't you leave her alone?"

"You're not married to her, are you? What's the matter with you tonight?"

I went over and sat on the shabby window seat.

"I suppose you know I am in love with her?"

"What about it?"

"Are you?"

He laughed. He put down his mug and came over and stood in front of me. "Of course I'm not. She's not my type."

"Well, she's mine. And because we were engaged you thought it would be rather fun to see if you could take her away from me."

"You must be off your head, man. Have you been overworking?" He laughed again in his old, hectoring way. "For God's sake pull yourself together man, and talk sense. Have a drink or something?"

"I don't want a drink."

"Well, go to bed and sleep it off. You'll be better in the morning."

"I am perfectly well."

"Well, do you mind if I go to bed?" He moved back to his chair, shaking his head and muttering, "Poor old Mike!"

"That's always been your attitude," I continued doggedly. "Poor old Mike! Poor old Mike! Ever since I've known you, you've despised me. Ever since schooldays. You were more crude at school, of course. You dominated and bullied and sneered and jeered and took from me all you wished."

"Oh, for God's sake, Mike, take an aspirin or go and get your head examined. You make me ill."

"You thought I was amused at your so-called jokes against me. And I let you think that, because it was the easiest way out. You thought I liked you, didn't you?"

"And didn't you?"

"You thought I enjoyed being your tame fool, your court jester, whom you mocked one moment and protected the next. You even thought I was grateful to you for your friendship. Well, you may as well know now that I hated you."

I paused. I had spoken firmly and fast; a voice inside me was saying: You've done it, you're fighting back and you're holding your own at last. For a fraction of a second I had a mental picture of Aunt Nell by the car door telling me to fight and go on fighting.

Prosset got up from his chair and walked across to the fireplace. He said, "Well, well. This is a side of your character which is certainly rather a surprise. I didn't know you were a two-faced hypocrite. Thanks for the information."

"You thought I was sorry when you left school, didn't you? Well, I was never more pleased about anything than when I saw the cab carrying you away from the front door of Buckley's. When you had gone I went into your study and gloated over the fact that you would never come back to it. I revelled in the muck you had left, because it meant I should never see you at school again. That surprises you, doesn't it? I wish I had never seen you since."

"Have you finished, Sibley?"

"No; I haven't. I will now refer to Kate Marsden. Just because she was my fiancée, you thought it would be amusing to flirt with her, and I use the word 'flirt' in its broadest sense."

"What the hell do you mean?"

"What I say. You thought it would be rather amusing to demonstrate to yourself and to me, once again, that I was just dirt in your eyes. You also thought it would be good sport to show Kate that you could even steal my fiancée without a protest from me."

"For heaven's sake stop talking about stealing your fiancée. I am not interested in stealing the bloody girl."

He smiled and looked at me, hands in his trouser pockets.

"Have you finished now, old man?"

"I only want to add that as far as you and I and Kate are concerned, this is the end. Last night was the end. I shall never see you again after tonight. Neither will Kate."

"Oh?"

"Yes. 'Oh.' "

"Perhaps you had better speak for yourself only."

"I am also speaking for Kate."

I got up to go to bed, and picked up the magazine I had been reading.

Prosset said, "Half a minute. Just one thing before you go. You are right in some ways. I did despise you at school. I thought you were a poor sort of fish. So you were. I have had no reason since to change my views. I still think you are, you know. You were quite fun to take a rise out of. David and I used to agree on that. You still are, in many ways. Fundamentally, you are not a bad-natured sort of chap, I suppose. But that's all I can say for you. On the other hand, you are weak and dull. Dreadfully dull, Sibley. You are lacking in all wit, you know. No wonder poor Kate was getting bored. A worthy, plodding lump of suet, that's you."

"At least I didn't stay for years behind a bank counter getting nowhere, and then go into some seedy business in the East End."

"You're just a hack journalist. I see nothing particularly to admire in hack journalists."

Neither of us said anything further. I was quite content that he should have a last word of this kind. I was more than satisfied with my own blows. I had stood up to Prosset at last. I had given rather more than I had taken. I had seen from the look in his eyes that he had been startled and that his vanity had been wounded. Perhaps he was even more deeply hurt than I think. I hope so.

Hate is a terrible thing.

I left early the following morning and never saw him again.

CHAPTER 12

That was the story, then, of Kate, Prosset and me. At first I had been anxious that it should remain unknown, for Kate's sake. Hence my evasions with the police. But now that they knew I had lied, I was particularly anxious that they should believe the story that my dispute with Prosset had been of a political nature rather than anything to do with a woman.

The Inspector knew nothing of the background story, and there was no reason for him to think that Prosset and I were not on the friendliest general terms.

I trusted the Inspector was now satisfied. I had been interviewed on two occasions, and had made a signed statement. I hoped that was that, but I could not disguise the fact that I was nervous about the whole case. However you may try to explain things away, it looks bad, first, to omit to mention having been on the scene a few hours before a murder is committed, and then for it to be discovered that you had had some sort of dispute with the dead man. It is all very fine and dandy to say that an innocent man has nothing to fear, I reflected, but the fact remained that an innocent man can be put to a great deal of harassing inconvenience. Admittedly, Kate could say I was with her at the time of the crime, but I wondered whether the word of a man's fiancée would necessarily cut much ice with the Inspector.

I had naturally given a good deal of thought to the problem of who had killed Prosset. I had one advantage over the Inspector in that I knew I had not done it, whereas the Inspector had still to include me among the possibles. As I finally began to undress after the second visit of the police, on the evening I had made the signed statement, a vague theory was beginning to form in my mind, which was, however, interrupted in an unexpected and unpleasant manner.

My landlord was a bald-headed man in his fifties, a bad-tempered fellow whose thick, bushy black eyebrows contrasted strongly with his thick, greying hair. I have completely forgotten this horrible individual's name, and will refer to him as Thompson.

I had hardly got my pyjamas on when there was a knock at the door. It was Mr. Thompson. He was red in the face, and seemed to be in a furious temper. Without waiting for an invitation, he thrust his way past me and shut the door.

"My wife has just told me the police came again tonight," he said. "This is the second time they have called on you. It won't do."

"I can't help it if police officers call on me. It's their job," I pointed out.

"Yes. Well, it won't do," said Thompson, breathing heavily. "It simply won't do. This is a respectable house. It's the sort of thing which upsets people."

"They wanted to know if I could give them any information about a case they are working on. I can't very well forbid them to call, can I?"

"It simply won't do," repeated Thompson monotonously. "I can't have it. Mr. Sibley, I have been contemplating redecorating this room for some time. I think this is a good time to start. I shall start a week today. No doubt you will have little difficulty in finding alternative accommodation in the meanwhile."

"You mean you are kicking me out? Are you aware that it is every citizen's duty to assist the police?" I am inclined to get pompous when I am annoyed. He turned towards the door.

"I know all about that. But I am afraid I shall require your room next week. I am sorry. Good night."

I thought of several smart replies after the door had closed. For some time my annoyance with Thompson occupied my mind, to the exclusion of the police visit; I kept going over the conversation in my mind, thinking up replies I might have made had I been smart enough. But once in bed the Prosset murder reasserted itself in my mind. I tried to drive it out by reading a humorous novel, but the actions of the characters seemed so unreal as to be stupid, and their words so inane as to be witless. I went over in my mind again the statement I had made. I felt sure there was nothing in it on which they could catch me out. Reviewing the evening visit by the Inspector, the only point that really puzzled me was the inquiry about how many suits I had. I could see no reason for that.

The line of thought I had been following about the murder was tenuous and unsupported by any evidence, but it was better than nothing. I remembered Prosset's meeting with a foreign-looking man called Max in the pub in Chelsea, his references to "import" business, his "friends" on the coast whom he visited, but never introduced to me, and his recently improved financial condition, despite the fact that the firm was not outwardly prospering as well as it could.

Were Prosset and Herbert Day involved in some smuggling racket? Had something gone wrong, some quarrel over profits developed, and because he would not give way and knew too much, had he been liquidated? I recalled that Day's name had been mentioned in what seemed to be a disagreement between Prosset and the man called Max; and I remembered the odd remark that Prosset had made about Day paying him more money or else finding himself "in difficulties." Was Prosset putting the pressure on, trying to extract a larger share of the profits under the threat of exposure?

Theory, all theory and no proof. It got one nowhere. I turned restlessly in bed.

Yet it did not seem impossible to me, as I lay there, alternately fuming about Thompson's rudeness and thinking about Prosset. But the next morning I received a further shock, and Ethel, of all unlikely people, was the one to administer it, when she brought in my breakfast on a tray.

Pointing to a cardboard box standing by the wardrobe, she said, "Your suit came back from the cleaners yesterday, sir."

"Yes," I said, "thank you. I saw it. I shall not be here long, you know. They are throwing me out next week. They don't like me having policemen visiting me."

Ethel sniffed. "Nosey parkers."

"Oh, well, it's their job, you know."

"They upset 'im with their questions last night. That's what did it. I'm sure I'll be sorry when you go, Mr. Sibley."

"Did they question Mr. Thompson?" I asked in surprise.

"And me."

"What on earth about?"

She pointed at the cardboard box. "About that for one thing. 'Did you often have your suits cleaned?' they asked. 'Not more than most,' I said. 'How many had you got?' 'Five,' I said. 'Though what it's got to do with—' "

"But I haven't got five, Ethel," I said quickly. "I've only got four now. I told the police I only had four last night. I gave one away two or three weeks ago."

"Did you sir?" said Ethel indifferently. "Well, I thought you had five. I didn't know you gave one away, sir. I don't suppose it matters much. Four or five, what does it matter? Silly nonsense and waste of time, if you ask me. They told me not to tell you they had spoken to me, but who cares? If you ask me, they'd do better to spend their time catching crooks instead of pestering people about suits."

"In a case like this, they have to enquire into everybody, you know. They're only doing their best," I said in a dull voice, fighting back the wave of apprehension which swept at me. "You can't blame them."

"A case like what, sir?"

"It's a murder case, Ethel. Didn't they tell you?"

"A murder case, sir?"

I nodded. I was aware she was staring at me. Then I heard her go out and shut the door.

I remembered how I had been walking home after an evening with Kate when a figure sitting crouching in the doorway of a house near my digs had whined at me as I went past. I am a mug when it comes to beggars. I always reckon that nine out of ten times they may be rogues, but the tenth time may be a deserving case to whom a shilling may make the difference between life and suicide. I know it is unlikely, but that is the way I think.

Yet that night I did not stop, for once. I went on walking and heard behind me the whining, imploring tones of the beggar. He caught me up as I stood fumbling for my latchkey, and stood at the bottom of the steps in the porch light, a man of about fifty or sixty, dressed in an evil-looking suit, dirty and tattered; he had a muffler round his throat and a dilapidated brown paper parcel under one arm.

"Just a couple of coppers for a cup of tea, sir," he said. I made no reply. "Just a couple of coppers for an old soldier, sir. It's going to be a cold night, sir."

I had found my key and put it in the lock, and the warm hall lighting was revealed when I opened the door.

"Just come out of hospital, sir. Give us a copper, sir. It's the gas that got me, sir. Got me lungs, sir. I've got me papers, sir."

He began to fumble in his inside breast pocket. Oh, well, I thought, why not? I turned round and slipped a shilling into his hand.

"God bless you, guv'nor." He was bald-headed. A wreck, with a thin, unshaven face and dark fawning eyes. He had a long nose and deep lines on each side of a down-turned mouth.

"When did you come out of hospital?"

He wiped his nose with the back of his hand. "This morning, guv—North London. Been in three months."

He began again to fumble for his papers. These people are always anxious to show you their "papers." They cling to their grimy, tattered documents as a drowning man clings to a lifebelt. They have an almost superstitious belief in the magic of their "papers," pointing out things like "excellent conduct" and "discharged after treatment," and their date of joining up and of demobilization. I have often glanced at these documents and never been able to make head or tail of them.

I looked at him and thought how sad it was that a man should have nothing to fall back upon, to recommend him to the compassion and aid of his fellow men, except a few dirty ragged bits of paper, and even those of doubtful authenticity.

He said he was making his way down to Sussex. He hoped to get a job on a farm. The doctor said he should work in the open air.

"Wait a minute," I said.

He was about my size. I had an old suit, a brown pinstripe one which I had bought in Palesby, which had been cluttering up my wardrobe for months. I knew I should never wear it again. It was frayed round the sleeves and the trouser turn-ups, and the seat and elbows shone. I fetched it and gave it to him, together with half a slab of chocolate which was lying on my writing table.

Maybe he didn't want a job at all, and, so far from reaching Sussex, had no intention of going further than the Embankment. You could not tell, any more than you could guess the ultimate, inmost hopes and aspirations of Mary O'Brien, the Palesby prostitute. There is so much in life about which you can make no absolutely certain statement.

Prosset would have classed him unhesitatingly as a good-for-nothing, and sent him about his business, and Prosset would probably have been right. But Prosset, for all his realistic outlook, was dead, and I was alive. I was often bewildered, uncertain and nervous. But I was alive.

I thought now that it was ironic that what might pass as an act of kindness, in so far as intentions went, should end by embedding me deeper in police suspicions. It was easy to see what was in their minds. A violent murder, bloodstains on the suit, and the suit vanishes. Where was it? Had I burnt it? Destroyed it? Perhaps destroyed it that Sunday morning when I returned to London, or even on the way back? You did not need to be a Sherlock Holmes to see the line of reasoning: I had cancelled my visit to Prosset, in case he spoke about it to anybody. Then I had gone down unexpectedly. I picked a quarrel. I killed him. I returned unseen to London. I destroyed or got rid of my bloodstained suit. I did not mention my visit to the police until I had been compelled to. I imagined the Inspector talking:

"But you forgot he kept a diary, didn't you, Mr. Sibley?"

"But he's been my lifelong friend," I'd say.

"That's what you say."

"You can't prove the contrary."

"Not yet. There's still time."

"Miss Marsden can say I was with her when Prosset died."

"Miss Marsden's in love with you, sir."

I felt no inclination for breakfast. I used to eat it in bed, and read the paper and smoke for a while, for we did not have to get to the office until ten o'clock. But that morning, after Ethel had left the tray, I could only face a cup of tea. I could not force the food down. I smoked several cigarettes. I was getting scared. Moreover, the old worry about Palesby had returned. I knew for certain now that something had happened in Palesby which would encourage the police to try and build up still further the evidence against me. I had known it from the first, but what it was eluded me, despite all my attempts to recall it. I tried again, but the unsuccessful effort left me frustrated and depressed.

As I dressed I found myself glancing out of the window when people passed. I was relieved when they were women, or men who had no official air, or children or tradesmen. At the office I felt an uncomfortable fluttering below the belt every time the telephone rang, which disappeared as soon as I learnt that the call was not for me. Another thing which added to my uneasiness, stupid as it seems, was that I had been remembering at intervals the curious dream I had had of the black cockatoos. I would not have minded so much if the central figure in it had not been Kate. I kept hearing the pathetic little cry she had given, and the look of despair she had thrown me as she had turned to pass between the rows of screeching birds. I tried to dismiss the whole thing from my mind, but it kept creeping back.

It was my task that morning to interview Mr. Fawkes, the MP

for Palesby, to get his views on a proposed alteration to a new Rent Restrictions Bill.

Mr. Fawkes was one of the most tiresome MPs imaginable to interview. At the previous election he had narrowly slipped home to represent Palesby. He was uneasily aware of his narrow majority and also, I assume, of his Parliamentary salary. He was like one of those insects which have several eyes distributed around their heads so that they can see in all directions at once. Mr. Fawkes had an eye on the working classes; he had another eye on the middle classes; a third on the upper classes, and on all who might oppose his nomination at a future election; his fourth eye was on the Party Whips; and a fifth and final eye had a sort of roving commission to keep a sharp lookout for any unsuspected danger from any other unmapped quarter whatsoever.

When I saw him he was in rather a quandary because the proposed amendment had been put forward, not by a Conservative or a Socialist, but by an Independent, and Mr. Fawkes was not yet sure of his Party line. Although he knew our group was sympathetic to him, when I cornered him at the House he treated me as though I were a bandit's decoy leading him into an ambush. He at once threw out a light, protective advance guard.

"I do not really care to be quoted in print from an impromptu interview," he said, "but I may be able to help you."

Fearing he might already have said too much, he hastily organized a rearguard to keep open his line of escape: he had not, he said, too much time. Certainly not time to go into any detail. Nevertheless, could he help me? Yes, he could. What did he think of the proposed amendment?

"The proposed amendment," he said firmly. "Yes, the proposed amendment."

"Just a brief statement of your views, if you wouldn't mind."

"It will naturally have to be considered entirely on its merits."

"Quite. I quite see that, Mr. Fawkes."

"Our Party, as you know, had always been conscious of its duty towards the working classes."

"I don't think any reasonable person will dispute that."

"Therefore, in so far as it is likely to safeguard the interests of the lower-income groups, I am in favour of it. I could not be otherwise. Reasonable rents for the masses are essential, quite essential."

"On the whole, therefore, you are in favour?" I asked.

"I think it needs clarification, of course."

"Oh, quite."

"Nothing must be done which would in any way be prejudicial to property owners. God knows," added Mr. Fawkes piously, "they have had enough to put up with as it is. But a limit has been reached. You cannot get blood out of a stone."

"Very true indeed."

"The proposed amendment must therefore be carefully scrutinized from every angle. Providing it tends neither to hamper private enterprise nor open the field to rapacious exploitation of the less well off, then I feel it is worthy of the most careful consideration. You can quote me as saying that."

"I can?"

"Certainly. Yes," added Mr. Fawkes, gaining courage, "quote me as saying that. You can polish it up a bit, of course, if you like. But keep the sense of it. Keep the strict sense of it. Well, there you are, young man. I've told you what I think."

It was then that my memory clicked.

I was reflecting that you couldn't tell what he thought, and that that was exactly what he intended. I was wondering what, in fact, he did think, and what opinion his constituents would have of him if they could see him humming and hawing and dithering because he did not know the Party line. I was telling myself how hard it was to know what people really thought, and then suddenly I was back in Palesby.

I was sitting on the settee in front of the gas fire with Cynthia, and behind us were the little stuffed birds on the upright piano. We were feeling relaxed and friendly, and she was telling me about an office acquaintance who she always thought had liked her, but who had turned against her.

"It isn't as if I wasn't nice to her," Cynthia said. "I went out of my way to be nice to her when she came to the office."

"I'm sure you did," I said. "You're friendly by nature."

"Well, I am. I'll say that for myself. But when old Laurie's secretary left, she thought she ought to get the job. Mind you, she hasn't been in the office six months, and I've been there years—nearly three years, in fact. But because she is older than me, and I got the job, she must have had it in for me. Yet she always acted ever so friendly to me before. I was surprised, I can tell you."

"It's difficult to know what people really think of you," I remarked. "A lot of us would get a shock if we could see into the minds of our so-called friends. I went about with a chap at school who thought I liked him. I not only deceived him, but everybody else as well. I hated him, and everybody thought I liked him. I could have murdered him. I've often felt like killing him. It was odd."

"What was his name?"

"Prosset. John Prosset. That was his name. You are the first person I've ever told about it."

I outlined the story for her, painting Prosset in rather a worse light than he deserved. But she couldn't understand it. It baffled her, as I should have known it would.

"Why didn't you tell him where he got off, and go about with somebody else."

"I couldn't do. I wanted to, but I couldn't."

She said nothing. She couldn't understand it, and in a few seconds she began to talk about something else.

Standing there in the corridor of the House, I could see it all again, hear her voice and the low hiss of the gas fire, and feel her hair against my face as we talked.

I saw Mr. Fawkes, MP, nodding affably, well content with his skilful handling of a tricky interview. I saw him begin to drift off to the House of Commons restaurant. I heard myself thanking him, and I heard Cynthia again, saying, "What was his name?" And my reply, "Prosset. John Prosset. That was his name."

They wanted to telephone the interview to the *Palesby Gazette,* so, because it was getting late, I took a taxi in Parliament Square, but as I was carried back to the office I saw nothing of the streets or the traffic.

I was thinking the Inspector would have a motive if he knew. A pretty vague one, but something to go on all the same. He said it wasn't robbery, because Prosset's money was still on him. He said he would have to look for some other motive. Once you've got a motive, the game's half over. You've got a pointer. As it wasn't robbery, he said, he would have to look for some other motive. A vague motive was better than nothing to a police officer. If the Inspector knew about it, he would be round again, looking at me with his light-brown, pebble eyes. I could see him opening my signed statement, and saying in his slow, unhurried way: "You say here, sir, your association with Mr. Prosset was invariably friendly. Was that quite true, sir?"

I arrived at the office and typed out my interview. It was short enough. I heard Baines say, "Bloody hell. He didn't commit himself much, did he?" And myself replying, "You didn't expect him to, did you? You know what Fawkes is."

For the rest of the day I was busy at the office, and when evening came I wandered across to the Falstaff and had a couple of large whiskies, but the alcohol had little effect on me, except perhaps to increase my depression. I now knew why I had regarded the whole investigation into the Prosset case with uneasiness. At the back of my mind must have been lying dormant this recollection of a few words spoken to Cynthia in front of the gas fire in Palesby. If the police came to know about them, they would indicate, if not a definite motive, at least a frame of mind. They knew already that I had had some sort of disagreement with him. What if they learnt that I had always secretly hated him? I drew in a deep breath to calm myself. I must keep a cool head and not jump to conclusions. There must be no panic. There was no real cause for it yet.

When I had finished my drink I walked down Fleet Street till I came to a telephone booth near the Law Courts. I rang up Kate. I told her I had a late job to do at the House. I did not know if she believed me or not, and I hardly cared. I only knew I felt restless.

A woman's intuitions, particularly if she is in love, are very acute. It is possible that she noticed some timbre in my voice which was not normal. She asked me if everything was all right, and I said it was. She asked if anything was the matter, and I denied it.

I replaced the receiver and walked down the Strand, along

Cockspur Street and up Haymarket, and so into Piccadilly Circus. I did not know where I was going, I merely wished to walk, to keep going. In Piccadilly Circus I again stopped at a public house and had another drink, and then strolled up Shaftesbury Avenue, gazing into shop windows absent-mindedly, or at the faces of passersby. I was not looking for anything and I had no objective in mind. I just knew that I wanted either to drink or keep on the move, one or the other. I could hardly believe that, without doing anything against the law, I could become such a changed person compared to the confident, carefree individual of a few days before.

The question which was nagging at my mind, of course, was whether Cynthia remembered what I had said to her about Prosset. As far as I could recall, she had shown little or no interest. She was a girl who preferred to talk about herself, who was inclined to listen a little impatiently until I had finished saying something, preparatory to talking again herself. To Cynthia nobody was quite as interesting as Cynthia, and nothing was quite as interesting as what Cynthia had to say. But I could not be sure.

At about nine o'clock, having wandered around Soho and down Charing Cross Road, I stopped for a sandwich in Chandos Street. It was one of those places where they have a penny-in-the-slot machine in which metal balls bounce against metal buffers and springs, and scores click merrily up in lights on a scoreboard. I had used up most of my silver on drinks and sandwiches, and apart from some banknotes I had only a few coppers left. I played at the machine idly for a while.

After a few minutes I put my hand in my pocket for another coin, but there was none left. There was only my knuckleduster, my light aluminium knuckleduster, which I had bought so furtively that last whole holiday at school, while Crane was pottering about at the other end of the shop in Avonham.

When my fingers came into contact with it I had a shock.

I remembered that as far as I was aware nobody knew that I carried a knuckleduster. The police did not know, even Kate did not know, for I was frankly a little ashamed of carrying it around. Yet in some way, from being a weapon with which a somewhat immature youth had thought to defend himself, against he knew not what dangers, it had assumed in the course of the years the role of a talisman, and I had never discarded it.

But standing in that public house in Chandos Street, gazing at the electric scoreboard without really seeing it, I at once saw the interpretation which the police would place on it. Surely only a man prepared to use violence, and violence of an unsavoury nature, would carry such a thing round with him? Who would believe me, least of all a police officer, if I said that I carried the thing round largely from habit?

I felt a wave of blood surging into my cheeks, and the palms of my hands grew moist. I had to get rid of it. That was obvious. But how? It is not the kind of thing you can leave on a table or toss on the floor or even into the gutter.

I went to the bar and had another drink, under the impression that it would help me to think, whereas in fact it did the contrary. I found myself unable to concentrate.

I went out into the street and stood uncertainly on the pavement. As I stood there I noticed one of those wire refuse baskets attached to a lamp standard. That was the solution. I would put it into a refuse basket. Not there, in Chandos Street, with people passing, but in some quiet street. Not in Harrington Gardens, because you could not be too careful, but perhaps in Brompton Road, near the Oratory.

I walked along to the Strand to board a bus. On the way I bought an evening paper, for I was going to be very clever about it all.

I got out at Knightsbridge and walked along Brompton Road to where the road forks near the Natural History Museum. I took the left fork, towards South Kensington Station, and saw a litter basket. I had folded the newspaper into four and placed the knuckleduster inside. When I was near the basket I looked behind me, but the pavement was deserted except for an elderly woman who was airing her dog, and even she turned back as I looked round. As I passed the litter basket I tossed the newspaper and knuckleduster into it, as though I was getting rid of a newspaper I had already read.

I felt an immense relief as I walked on to Harrington Gardens, and with the relief came reaction. I realized that I was dog-tired. But I was not destined to get to bed as early as I hoped.

I do not know why later I felt uneasy about the incident of the knuckleduster. There was no reason for it. I had got rid of the thing, and that was that. I had no reason to suppose that I had been followed. Indeed, at this stage of the proceedings it seemed silly to imagine such a thing. I began to worry about it as I turned my bed down before undressing, yet I told myself I was being a fool, and recalled how I had specifically looked around to see if I was being followed. I was overtired. I had rid myself of the knuckleduster, and I had done it skilfully and coolly. It was a neat job. Yet I felt disturbed. There was a question mark in my mind, and I knew I would get no sleep, tired though I was, until I had set my mind absolutely at rest. I decided to do so.

At midnight I switched the light out and lay on my bed fully clothed. At one o'clock I judged that if I was under observation it would be assumed that I had retired to bed for the night. I let myself out of the house at one fifteen, and walked quickly up Harrington Gardens to South Kensington and the litter basket.

When I examined the litter basket and found the knuckleduster no longer on top of the litter, I rummaged hurriedly among the old paper bags, orange peel, and used cardboard cartons. I did not give a thought to the unsavoury nature of the stuff I was turning over with my hands. I felt certain that my knuckleduster must be there somewhere.

I delved right to the bottom of the rubbish, and when I still could not find it I stood looking at the litter basket in despair. I walked home. It was always possible that some tramp had removed the knuckleduster, I told myself. But I knew it was not true. I knew the police found it, and that they had found it because they had been following me.

I was puzzled as well as dismayed. I did not then know that there is more than one way of following a man. When you are being followed, your shadower is not necessarily right behind you on the pavement. He may be ahead of you, anticipating the direction you will take. He may also be on the other side of the road. He may not even be alone. He may have a colleague with him. One of them may be ahead of you and one behind you, but on the opposite side of the road. There are all sorts of combinations.

It is no good just looking behind you, if you think you are being followed. No good at all. But I didn't know it at that time.

CHAPTER **13**

I am no longer surprised when I read that some prisoner in the witness box has made an extraordinary statement describing some wholly improbable act which he says he did in a state of panic. I may feel certain that neither judge nor jury will believe him, but, failing irrefutable evidence to the contrary, I am quite prepared to give him the benefit of the doubt; because I myself now understand how foolishly an innocent man may act when he begins to lose his head.

For instance, there I was the following day at 8:30 a.m. sitting in the train to Palesby. It is almost impossible for anybody who has not been subjected to a similar strain to understand how the action of the mind, in revolving the same thoughts over and over again, can create panic, much as a dynamo creates electricity, and plunge him into action such as that which I was taking.

I knew now that I was under observation by the police. The

case which was being built up against me was straightforward and easy to understand. I had failed to disclose my last visit to Ockleton until the admission was forced out of me, though I had had ample opportunity to do so. There was reason to believe that my fiancée had spent an evening with Prosset, and that Prosset and I had quarrelled. One of my suits had disappeared. I was now known to have had a knuckleduster in my possession. What if it could be shown that, so far from being friendlily disposed towards Prosset, as I had said, I had hated him for years? There was only one person who could tell the police about that. I knew that I would have no rest until I found out, first, whether Cynthia had remembered my words about Prosset, and, second, whether she had been questioned by the police. I also had some scheme in my mind whereby I might make my peace with Cynthia. I thought that, if I could find some delicate opportunity of doing so, I could perhaps make use of the chequebook in my pocket. But that would depend upon various things.

It was, of course, a fantastic and ridiculous, even dangerous undertaking. I should have just sat back and let events take their course. But I didn't, because I couldn't. In the face of what seemed to be a growing menace, it was impossible to remain inactive. I sometimes think the police may well allow a suspect to know that he is under suspicion for the express purpose of trying to panic him into some injudicious act.

I left my lodgings at 6 a.m. I guessed that nobody would be watching at that hour, a guess which subsequently proved to be correct. I left a note in my room, telling Ethel that I had had to go out early on a job for the paper. At St. Pancras I gave a porter a good tip to send off two telegrams: one to Baines at the office saying I would not be in owing to family trouble, and one to Kate saying that I had been sent to the country on a job and would be back the following day. I had thought out my plan of action thoroughly.

It was important that no member of the *Palesby Gazette* staff should see me, because Baines in London knew that I had no relatives in Palesby, and he might well be on the telephone to the *Gazette* office in the course of the day. I had therefore put on a suit which I had bought since coming to London, and was wearing a raincoat. If I kept my hat pulled down over my face and took a taxi at the station, and sat well back in the car with my handkerchief to my face, as though I had toothache, I considered I had a reasonable chance of not being seen as I drove through the streets.

If all went well, I could get Cynthia to keep quiet about my visit, too. Once again, looking back on it all, I am staggered at my optimism. It was inevitable, of course, that I should come to disaster.

The main worry I had as the train drew into Palesby was whether Cynthia would see me at all. I had rehearsed carefully what I should say, and on arrival I hurried into a telephone booth which I remembered was situated in a rather remote corner of the station. I had to look up her telephone number; it was strange that I had forgotten it in so short a time.

It was 2:15 p.m. when I telephoned, and I guessed she would be back from lunch. When the operator answered I said, "May I speak to Miss Harrison, please?"

I adopted a deeper tone of voice than usual, and hoped the operator would not listen to our talk.

"Who wants her?" asked the operator. I recognized her voice. I could even visualize where she was sitting in the office. She was a ginger-haired girl with a rather blotchy complexion who spent most of her time knitting.

"Just say it is a personal call."

I heard her put me through, and Cynthia's hard, brisk little voice came on the line.

"Hello?" she said. I remained quiet.

"Hello?" she repeated. "Cynthia Harrison here."

I purposely allowed her to speak three times, reckoning that if the ginger-haired girl was listening in she would probably interrupt with some remark. But the operator said nothing.

"This is Mike," I said at last.

"Who?" She sounded incredulous.

"Mike. Mike Sibley."

"Well, you've got a nerve, haven't you, ringing me up? You can ring off. I've got nothing to say to you."

"Look, Cynthia, listen just a second. It's important."

"It may be important to you; it isn't to me, I assure you. So you'd better hang up."

I had a feeling she was going to ring off, though I might have known her curiosity would keep her listening.

"Don't go," I said quickly. "I want to see you, and it's important for both of us."

"You want to see me?"

"Yes, as soon as possible. This evening. Directly you leave the office."

"I am not sure that I want to see you. Why should I see you, after the way you've treated me? You've got a nerve, I must say."

"There's something I must say to you and I've got to get back to London tonight. I came up specially to see you. Will you meet me in Central Park at six o'clock? By that bench where I first spoke to you?"

The sentimental touch undoubtedly meant nothing to her, but I knew by then that she would see me, if only out of a desire to tell me face to face what she thought of me. However, she owed it to her dignity still to hesitate.

"As far as I am concerned, you can go back to London again, and this minute, too."

"It's really important."

She paused for some seconds. "All right, then. I'll see you for exactly two minutes. You can say what you have to say in that time or not at all. Then you can clear off." She banged the receiver down.

So far so good. I went into the Station Hotel, said I wanted to have a few hours' sleep, and booked a room. I felt sure I would be unseen in the hotel. I asked them to call me at 5:30 p.m., took off my raincoat and jacket, and lay on the bed under the eiderdown. Although I had had literally no sleep the previous night, I thought I might stay awake brooding and worrying, but nature was too strong. In about ten minutes I was sound asleep.

When they woke me up I felt awful. But I have always found that when you are tired even an hour's sleep works wonders. Although you feel dreadful when you wake up, after a wash you notice the benefit of the rest. I went downstairs, paid the bill, and hired one of the taxis which always wait opposite the hotel. I told the driver to go to the main gates of Central Park.

It was strange passing all the familiar landmarks which I had known so well, and to feel at the same time like a fugitive in the town. I saw one of the office boys coming out of the *Gazette* offices as we drove by, and I remembered helping him with his shorthand outlines a few times; he was an ambitious kid and hoped one day to be a reporter. He waited to cross the road until my taxi had passed and I turned my head away as we drove by. I looked out of the rear window, but he was making his way nonchalantly over the road and had noticed nothing. I envied him his carefree life. I think at that moment I would willingly have exchanged my income for his and started afresh. I would have given it all up, salary, income, and even Kate, too, at that moment. It was a case of Sibley first, last, and all the time; a badly frightened, unheroic man who would have put his foot in the face of anybody swimming around, if it would have helped him to scramble on to some raft.

When we arrived at Central Park I told the driver to wait. I said I might be as long as half an hour or more, and that I would pay him waiting time and generally make it worth his while.

I walked quickly through the park until I came to the bench, but I need not have hurried. She was ten minutes late. As she always left the office precisely at 5:30, and as the park was only a penny-halfpenny tram ride from the office, I assumed she was late on purpose. I watched her walk towards the bench where I sat, and noted she was wearing, by coincidence, the same dark blue coat which she had worn when I first met her. She walked briskly, as usual, a paper carrierbag in one hand and a pair of gloves in the other. She looked what she was, attractive, competent and self-reliant; a very different picture from Kate, who, despite her recent improvements, usually managed to look somewhat disordered, who walked at a slow, easy pace, her eyes often on the ground as though she were deep in thought.

I got up as Cynthia approached and held out my hand.

"Hello," I said. She ignored my hand and sat down on the bench.

"Well, what is it? I'm in a hurry." She did not look in my direction as she spoke, but stared straight ahead.

"You're wearing the same coat and skirt as you wore when I first met you."

"Well, what of it? I'm allowed to, aren't I?"

"Cynthia," I said. "I want to ask you to forgive me for the way I've acted towards you."

She turned towards me and looked me up and down coldly.

"You didn't come all the way up here to tell me that, Michael Sibley. I know you better than that. You haven't got the guts. Nor the decency."

I had steeled myself to receive a reception of this kind.

"I realize now that I've been very silly, and that my stupidity has been the cause of my acting in a very unkind way."

"It's a bit late to discover that."

"You see, you were the first girl who showed any real affection for me."

"What's that got to do with it?"

"A great deal."

"I thought you were what they call a gentleman," she said in a detached kind of voice. "Perhaps you are. Perhaps all you snobs are the same underneath. Selfish, rotten, ruthless. I'm sorry I didn't find it out before, that's all."

For the first time her voice shook slightly. She stopped for two or three seconds, then went on again in the cold, impersonal tones she had used previously.

"I'm not good enough for you, I suppose. But you didn't think that while you were up here, did you? I was good enough to make love to, to go out with, to entertain you at our house, even if it isn't much of a house. So long as it suited your convenience, that is. It wasn't till you got back to London among all the other snobs that you saw it differently."

It was the first time she had referred in any way to the social question. I was surprised, because I had never hitherto imagined that anyone could regard me as snobbish.

"Cynthia dear, that's not true; that's not being fair."

She shook her head impatiently and looked at her wristwatch.

"Isn't it? So what? And don't call me 'dear.'" She got to her feet. "Well, if you've nothing more to say, I'm off."

I put my hand on her arm to pull her down on to the seat again, saying, "Don't go yet, Cynthia," but she shook herself free.

"Anyway," she said, "I should have thought you'd hardly have had the time to come dashing up here to apologize to me. I should have thought you would have been too busy helping the police to find out who killed your great friend, John Prosset. Your great friend!" she added sarcastically. She made as if to move off. I rose quickly to my feet and stood in her way.

"So you read about that?"

She gave a hard little laugh. "Read about it? I'll say I read about it! And I've—Oh, well, what's the use?"

"And you've what?" She made as if to step past me, but I blocked the way. "And you've what?" I asked again. "Listen, Cynthia, I've had you on my conscience so much, I came up here to see whether I could perhaps make some amends to you in some small way. You could have sued me for breach of promise, but you didn't. I appreciate that. I do feel that I would like you to accept—"

"Money?" she asked.

"Well, yes, but I don't want you to regard it in that light. If you accept, say £150, not as compensation, that would be an insult, but if you would regard it as a sort of penance which I am inflicting on myself to ease my—"

"Will you please get out of my way, Michael Sibley?"

She spoke with so much assurance that I would certainly have obeyed her had I not been feeling desperate. I went on standing in her path.

"No; I won't. Anyway, not until you've told me what you were going to say just now."

For the first time she showed real emotion. I saw her mouth tighten, her eyes half close. She looked suddenly much older than I had ever seen her look. Anger made her face shrewish, her voice shrill.

"All right," she replied. "I was going to say—*and* I've been questioned by the police, thanks to you, *and* they came to our house to do it, *and* they drove up in a police car, *and* all the neighbours could see them! *And* the whole neighbourhood is gossiping about us; we, who have never had anything to do with the police in our whole lives! We, who have always been respectable! Right in daylight they drove up, in their damned great police car, with police written all over it, and parked it right opposite the door, so that everybody could see it. They came tramping in, and question, question, question—" Her voice broke. She began to sob with fury. I looked at her miserably.

I was not feeling sorry for her. I was feeling sorry for myself. I think that if I had killed Prosset in reality I might have felt less upset; and that to an imaginative man who is innocent the shadow of the gallows is many times more terrifying than to others, and that the idea that you are comforted because you have a clear conscience is mostly nonsense.

She stepped quickly to one side and passed me. I took one or two steps after her. I knew perfectly well from her earlier remarks that she must have told the police of my early hatred for Prosset, yet somehow I wished to hear it from her own lips. But I was to be denied this.

"Wait a minute!" I called. "Kate!" I suppose I had been saying "Kate" so often in recent months that in my agitation it was the first name that sprang to my lips. She stopped and turned round.

"So that's her bloody name, is it?" she shouted at me. "Well, she's welcome to you—money, police and everything. She can keep you, the bitch!"

That was the end. She walked off, and I let her go. Upon reflection, I think that on the whole she came out of the talk well, even though later she played me what I think was an unnecessarily dirty trick. I have often wondered whether she would have made a different answer to the money offer if I had reached her before the police and gossip had upset her.

To act ruthlessly or cruelly, or to degrade yourself in any way and finally to attain your objective is one thing, and the fruits of such actions may or may not turn to ashes in your mouth, according to your temperament. But to act in some such way, and then to fail, is hard. It is a punishment in itself. During the journey back to London I certainly received a measure of any retribution due to me as a result of the way I had acted towards Cynthia in the past.

The visit to Palesby, conceived in panic and attended with inevitable humiliations, had merely served to confirm my fears. I hated myself because I had lost my head and gone rushing up there with this crazy notion of patching up some sort of friendship with her by means of money. I had learnt that she had not forgotten my remarks about Prosset; that she had almost certainly repeated them to the police; and that no offer I could make her could prevent her from being, in effect, a hostile witness.

Yet the trip had one good result. I found myself physically exhausted and incapable of further emotion, and now in a position where I was compelled to look facts in the face without further self-deception; instead of trying to run away from realities or bolster myself up with false hopes, I had to grapple with things as they were. I remembered Aunt Nell's words again: You're never beaten till you're dead. Never let anything or anybody get you down.

When I remembered her words, and when I had reviewed the facts, a sense of calm came upon me. There was nothing more I could do now except fight in a straightforward manner. There were no twists or turns, no tricks, clever or sordid, which would avail me.

I knew exactly what I would do; I had a plan, the details of which I thought out on the return journey, and, having made up my mind, I no longer felt worried. The strange, dull ache in my stomach disappeared. I felt relaxed and almost at peace. During the last three hours of the journey I slept soundly.

Although I did not get to bed until one o'clock in the morning, I awoke at a quarter to eight feeling refreshed and eager, as usual, to do what I had in mind without delay. After breakfast I telephoned Kate and arranged to see her in the evening. In order to explain at the office my absence on the previous day, I said my aunt had broken her hip and I had had to rush her to hospital and home again with a nurse. Charlie Baines was formally sympathetic. And from an office telephone cubicle I rang Scotland Yard and asked to speak to the Inspector.

He was out, but the Sergeant took the call. He expected the Inspector in about midday. He said that if I wished to see him and explain certain matters, he was quite certain that the Inspector would be glad to arrange to see me during my lunch hour, say at 1:30. This suited me, because I had a loose sort of job in the afternoon which could be done more or less as and when I liked.

I arrived at the Yard at twenty-five minutes past one. The Inspector must have warned the front hall constable that I was expected, for I was shown straight up to his room without even being required to fill in the usual form.

The Inspector greeted me in a jovial manner when I entered his room. Doubtless he felt himself somewhat in the position of a host. He shook hands. He said it was nice to see me again, and what had I been doing lately? This struck me as funny, since he must have had several reports about my movements in his file. Then I realized that he certainly did not have a report about the previous day's journey, so I didn't think it quite so funny after all.

He offered me a cigarette out of an old-fashioned gunmetal case. "Half a mo'. We'll just get the old Sergeant along," he said, and pressed a buzzer. He offered me a light and finally settled back into his chair.

The weather, he thought, looked a bit on the rainy side. Did I not agree? I said it did. However, he pointed out, it would do some good in the country; gardens were dry, very dry. Yes, gardeners would welcome some rain. Did I garden? No; he didn't suppose I did. He supposed I had no opportunity for it. He had a garden himself, not a big one, mind you, but enough for a few vegetables and some flowers for the missus. Out near the Sutton bypass. He remembered the district when it had been quite rural, and look at it now: what a change, goodness me, what a change! And he wasn't at all sure it was for the better. The Sergeant came in while he was inviting me to look at Sutton, and sat down. He had the inevitable notebook.

"Well, never mind about Sutton," said the Inspector. "I believe you've got something to tell us, Mr. Sibley, if what the Sergeant says is correct."

"Yes, I have," I said. "First, I want to correct something I said in my statement."

The Inspector said, "Have a look in that folder, Sergeant. Get Mr. Sibley's statement, will you?"

The Sergeant fetched it off a filing cabinet, and the Inspector glanced through it.

"What is it you wanted to correct, sir?" he asked.

"There's a bit in it where I said my relations with Mr. Prosset were always friendly. In some ways that's true; in others it isn't."

The Inspector had ceased to be the benevolent uncle. He had fallen back into his role of alert police officer and was looking at me with his steady, unblinking eyes.

"It's a simple enough sentence, sir. I should have thought it was either true or it wasn't."

"Well, then I suppose it isn't true. At any rate, it needs elaboration."

"Well, carry on, sir, and we'll see how we can put it."

"The fact is that at school, although I went about with him, I did not really like him. I went around with him and another boy. I liked the other one all right. Mind you, at first I liked Prosset, too, but not towards the end. In fact I disliked him intensely, but nobody knew it."

In telling him this, I was, of course, merely making a virtue of something which I knew he had already learnt from Cynthia. It is a trick which is well known to the police, but I was unaware of that.

"But you went on seeing him after you left school, sir?"

"He was a difficult man to say no to; that's why."

"All the advances came from his side?"

"That's right."

"I see, sir." It was quite clear he did not see at all.

"Did you still dislike him when you met him recently? I am just asking so that we can think of some way of putting it nice and neatly in the statement."

"Yes. At heart, I think I still rather disliked him."

The Inspector nodded. "But not quite as much as at school?"

"On the whole, no."

"Why on the whole?"

"Sometimes I thought he was trying to flirt with Miss Marsden. Then I disliked him as much as ever, if not more. Naturally. I am being quite frank."

"Yes, sir. Saves a lot of trouble, as I think I mentioned last time."

"In fact, I had already decided to break off relations with him."

"Because Miss Marsden spent some time in his room, sir? You remember the entry about 'K' in his diary, of course, sir?"

"I told you at the time that that almost certainly means nothing. There are thousands of people in London whose names begin with K."

"Did the quarrel you had with him the last time you saw him finally decide you, sir?"

"It wasn't a quarrel. It was a political argument. We both got a bit heated, that's all."

"Anyway, you decided before he was killed that you didn't want to go on seeing him. You decided to break things off. And then," said the Inspector with a faint smile, "the job was done for you, so to speak. Not that one wants to joke about things like that, of course. Well, now, I wonder why you made that statement about invariably being friendly with him. You signed at the bottom that—"

"That it was true," I interrupted. "I know that. In a way, it was true. I never had an open row with him. You can't call a political disagreement in which you both get a bit excited a real row, can you? So to all intents and purposes my relations with him were friendly."

The Inspector said nothing. He leaned forward and carefully removed some ash from his cigarette into an ashtray on his desk.

The Sergeant said with his soft Welsh intonation, "No, sir. Your relations with him were not friendly, sir. They only appeared to be. That's rather different, isn't it, sir?"

"That's right," said the Inspector. He nodded his head.

"Your relations with him only appeared to be friendly, so the statement was not true, sir. Now then," he went on cheerfully, "let's see how we can phrase your correction."

"There's one more thing you might as well know, Inspector. Up to the day before yesterday, I used to carry a knuckleduster around."

I glanced at them both. The Sergeant was staring down at his notebook. His face was expressionless. In fact, it was too expressionless. It would have been more natural for him to glance up and show some interest. The Inspector did better. He raised his eyebrows in simulated surprise.

"A knuckleduster? That's a nasty sort of thing to have. May I ask you why you had it, sir?"

I told him how I had bought the thing one school holiday. It all sounded so unlikely that I felt embarrassed by the silence which greeted my words. The Sergeant was looking at me thoughtfully, his dark, intelligent eyes on my face. He put his pencil down and leaned back and said, "So you've had it for about thirteen years, sir?"

"About that."

"It must have amused your friends."

"My friends didn't know. Nobody knew I had it. I thought it was rather silly and I didn't tell anybody. When I grew older I went on carrying it. It became a sort of habit, a kind of talisman, in a way. You know how it is when you get used to something?"

"What was the name of the chap who was with you when you bought it?" asked the Inspector.

"Crane. I think his Christian name was Philip."

"Where does he live?" asked the Sergeant.

"I don't know where he is now."

"What did he say? I mean when you bought it?" The Sergeant was looking down at his notebook again. He appeared to have ceased taking notes and was doodling.

"He didn't say anything. He didn't know. I've told you, nobody knew I'd bought it. I've told you that already," I repeated irritably.

"There's no need to get huffy, sir," said the Inspector.

"I wasn't getting huffy."

"All right, sir, you weren't. Now, where were we? Well, what shop did you buy it in?"

"A kind of field-sports shop in the main street, where you could buy fishing tackle and nets for ferreting and things like that."

"And you bought this to defend yourself against a ghost?" The Sergeant looked up with a faint smile on his sallow face.

"I was hardly more than a boy. You needn't tell me it sounds silly, because I know that."

"I was not about to make any comment at all, sir. But nobody knew you had it, not even Miss Marsden?"

"Or Miss Cynthia Harrison?" added the Inspector. Perhaps he thought the revelation that they knew about her would jolt me.

"Not even Miss Marsden or Miss Harrison," I said carefully. Neither of them said anything for about half a minute. The Sergeant resumed his doodling in his notebook. The Inspector had stubbed out his cigarette and was filling his pipe out of a well-worn rubber pouch. He teased some tobacco into the bowl and prodded it down with his square, pink fingers, then dragged some more out and prodded that down. He examined it critically, fumbled for his matches and lit it.

"All right," he said at length. "Let's leave it at that. Where is it now, this knuckleduster?"

"I threw it into a refuse basket the night before last."

"Why did you throw it away after all these years?" asked the Sergeant.

"Because I suddenly realized what implications could be attached to it, what anybody might think, what you people might think, if it comes to that, of a person who carries a thing like that around and gets mixed up in something like Prosset's death. I'm still being frank, you notice."

"Well, well," the Sergeant said smoothly. "I see what you mean, sir."

"It's a curious story," said the Inspector. There was a long pause. Outside I heard the traffic going along the Embankment, the clang of a bell on a tram, a car changing gear and then accelerating, and the sound of a taxi's horn.

"Well, sir, shall we see what we can do about a statement?" said the Inspector at last.

"You don't need to make another one if you don't want to," the Sergeant pointed out.

"I've obviously got to."

"No; you haven't. If you do, it will be voluntary."

I smiled. I no longer felt nervous in the presence of these two men. I had had my nervous crisis about the case, and now it was over. For the moment, anyway, I felt cool and vigilant. I watched the Inspector take a sheet of foolscap paper from the centre of his desk, and unscrew the top of his fountain pen. He said, "Shall I write it down, like before, or will you?"

"We got on all right last time. You can write it. Before we start, can I ask you whether you have considered a possible smuggling angle to this case? I understand Prosset was interested in imports as well as business in this country."

"How do you know?"

"He told me so. Also he took a cottage on the coast, and he knew people along the coast to whom, for some reason, he never introduced me. And you remember me mentioning a foreign-looking man he met in a pub in Chelsea? Well, Prosset and he seemed to be in disagreement about something. The other man was called Max, I now remember. And the name of Herbert Day cropped up in their talk."

The Inspector glanced at the Sergeant. Their faces were expressionless.

"Why do you only mention this now?" asked the Sergeant.

"Yes; why only now, sir?" repeated the Inspector.

"The significance of it did not strike me at the time."

"I've no doubt it didn't, sir," said the Inspector gently.

"When did all this happen?" asked the Sergeant.

"About last November."

"This man called Max, sir. What did he look like?"

"He was rather tall and broad, olive-skinned, with dark hair and a moustache."

"What was the colour of his eyes?"

"I don't know."

"How was he dressed?"

"He had a fawn raincoat on. That's all I remember."

"Did he wear a hat, sir?"

"I don't know. Not in the bar. He may have carried one."

"And you don't know his other name, or anything else about him?"

"No."

The Inspector leaned back in his chair. He looked at me for a while without speaking. Then he said, "Where were you standing in relationship to them, sir?"

"I was at one end of the bar, and they were at the other."

"What time was it?"

"I don't remember exactly. Early evening, though."

"You admit, of course, that most bars are pretty crowded at that time, sir, and that there is a good deal of conversation going on?"

"Yes, but I could tell from the expressions on their faces, and their movements, that there was some disagreement."

The Inspector thrust his head forward slightly, and tapped the desk with his forefinger. He said, "And in spite of the hubbub in the bar, you heard them mention Mr. Day's name, sir?"

"Yes," I replied flatly. "I did."

"You've got good ears, sir?"

"Just ordinary. But there was one of those sudden brief silences you sometimes get in a bar."

"A bar's one of the few places in which you hardly ever get a silence, sir."

I made no comment, but pressed on doggedly with my final point. "And that same evening, Prosset told me that soon Day would be paying him more money, or he would find himself in difficulties, as he put it. It sounded almost a threat."

They said nothing for a few seconds, and remained still, staring at me. Finally, to break the silence, I said, "It's only a theory, of course."

The Inspector glanced at the Sergeant. "Well, we'll certainly bear it in mind, sir. Now, about this statement."

We went briefly over the ground again, and finally produced my second signed statement. This was as follows:

I, Michael Sibley, now wish to make a further voluntary statement. I have been warned and realize that it may be used in evidence.

I wish to correct something which I said in my previous statement. Although I never quarrelled openly with John Prosset, my feelings towards him were not as friendly as my previous statement may have suggested. I found him selfish and overbearing, and, since leaving school, only continued to see him from time to time because I did not wish to offend him by refusing.

Last November I saw Prosset in a public house in Chelsea with a foreign-looking man whose name Prosset told me was Max. They seemed to be in disagreement. I heard Mr. Day's name mentioned.

Later Prosset told me that Mr. Day would be paying him, Prosset, more money, or he would find himself in difficulties. It seemed to me to be a threat.

I further wish to state that while I was at school I purchased a knuckleduster. I have never used it. I carried it largely from habit. It was in my possession until about two days prior to the date of this further statement. I threw it into a refuse container. I frankly admit I did this, which today I voluntarily reported to the police, because I realized from my connection with the Prosset case that possession of such a weapon might lead to unjust inferences.

All the other facts contained in my previous statement are correct. I have read this further statement over, and it is true.

Michael Sibley

It was witnessed, as before, by the Inspector.

CHAPTER 14

When I left the Yard, I went into a telephone booth and rang up Prosset's business address. Somebody lifted the receiver and for a second or two I heard the sound of Herbert Day's nasal voice talking to somebody else in the room. Then he spoke to me.

"Hello, who is that?"

"This is Michael Sibley. Is that Mr. Herbert Day? I don't know if you remember me. I met you one evening with John Prosset many years ago."

There was a short pause. Then, "Yes. I remember you. Well?"

"How are you keeping?"

"All right," said Day in his muffled kind of voice.

"I would like to see you for a few minutes if you can spare the time."

There was another pause. Then Day said, "All right. When?"

"Now. I can be with you in about a quarter of an hour."

"All right, then. I'll expect you. Don't make it later. I've got to go out."

I took a taxi through the City to Middlesex Street and paid it off at Prosset's former office. This proved to be on the third floor of a tall, smoke-begrimed building occupied by a number of different firms. In the narrow, dirty entrance a dilapidated board showed the name of Prosset and Day, Ltd. I went up the uncarpeted stairs. On the first floor one of the doors was open; two men in shirtsleeves, cigarettes hanging from their lips, were engaged in moving some cardboard boxes from a large stack occupying three-quarters of the room. On the second floor, behind doors badly in need of a new coat of paint, a Mr. Mackintosh, credit bookmaker, carried on his business. The premises of Prosset and Day looked no smarter. The little landing was littered with dust, a scrap or two of paper, and two or three cigarette ends; it was covered with a square of brown linoleum, rotting and torn round the edges. On one of the badly fitting doors was a piece of cardboard on which, written in ink, was the word "Inquiries."

I went in, and on the other side of the door at once found myself in what I took to be the main office, if you could call it such. It was a small room, the bare boards of which were partly covered with a rectangle of cheap carpet. The walls had once been yellow, but were now blotchy and dirty. In winter the room appeared to be heated by a small gas fire.

There was a communicating door which led to what seemed to be a larger room, and through the doorway I caught sight of piles of wooden boxes, cardboard cartons, paper packages, bales of cloth, and other material. Under the little window in the office were two tables and chairs, face to face, apparently used as desks. Merchandise from the adjoining room had overflowed into the office, and here too were a few cardboard cartons, stacked against the walls or thrown carelessly into a corner.

One of the desks had doubtless been occupied by Prosset. It seemed strange that he had chosen to come to this dump from the cleanliness and order and assured future of a great bank. But then perhaps he had not realized it would be like this. Perhaps he thought, listening to Herbert Day's proposal, that they would take a smart office in the West End, all chromium plate and thick carpeting and smart secretaries; probably that is what Prosset, the optimistic fellow, would have visualized.

I had a swift mental picture of him leaving old Buckley's house to play for the college: immaculately dressed in white rugger shorts, red and black jersey, black blazer with the school crest on the pocket, white silk scarf, and the black, red and gold tasselled cap of the First Fifteen on his head. Whatever I felt about him on other occasions I had been glad to walk up to the rugger field with him then, linked arm in arm after the college custom: Prosset, David and I. People envied David and me on those occasions.

Herbert Day looked up from his desk. He rose to his feet. He seemed to have changed little since I last saw him, except that he looked a little seedier, a little dustier. He still wore a black pinstripe suit and suede shoes, and when he took his cigarette from his mouth I noticed how his fingers were stained dark yellow with nicotine.

I noticed something else, too, something that sent the blood rushing to my head with excitement, and set the pulse throbbing in my throat so forcibly that I could hardly speak.

It was the smell in the office.

The same half-pungent, half-sweet smell of Day's Cyprus cigarettes, the smell that had finally made me sick at the party with Prosset, Margaret Dawson, and the others; the smell which I had caught, so faintly that I did not recognize it, at Prosset's cottage while I was awaiting his return.

"What can I do for you?" Day stood in front of the gas fire, leaning on the mantelpiece.

"I suppose you can guess why I've called."

"No. Why should I?"

"It's about Prosset's death," I said.

He ran his tongue over his lips with the quick little snake-like movement I remembered.

"Oh, yes. What about it?" he said. As if realizing he ought to say something more, he added, "It was a bad business. Very bad business."

"The police have been in touch with me about it, of course. I suppose they have been here, too?"

"Naturally."

"They asked me whether I could suggest any line of inquiry."

"And could you?"

"Nothing very firm. But I have been thinking about something. Perhaps you can help me."

"And what have you been thinking?"

"I remembered a foreigner—I think Prosset said his name was Max—whom he met in a pub in Chelsea; and that he had mentioned one or two people near Ockleton who he said were interested in the import side of your business. I suppose you told the police about them? I wondered if it were possible that Prosset had fallen out with one or other of these people."

Day took a packet of cigarettes out of his pocket, and lit another one without offering me one. He said nothing.

"I'll be frank with you," I went on. "For reasons which I won't take up your time with, I have been rather closely questioned by the police. Perhaps more closely than most people in this matter."

Day walked over to the window and looked through the grimy little pane.

"There is no import side to this business," he said flatly.

I stared at him. I could not believe I had heard correctly.

"What do you mean?"

"What I say. We don't touch foreign stuff. There is no import side to this business."

For a moment I felt a return of the old panic I had experienced during my trip to Palesby. Then it was gone. The implications of his attitude were beginning to take shape in my mind when I heard him add, "Such being the case, I have rather naturally not been able to help the police in that connection."

"Do you mean to say you have never heard of Max, or of anybody with whom Prosset was friendly at Ockleton?"

Day turned from the window.

"I have heard of nobody called Max. John Prosset may well have had friends near Ockleton. Why not, indeed? I have no idea who they are. It is possible, too," he continued, beginning to walk up and down the room, "that he may have engaged in some sort of import business. I know nothing of it."

"But damn it, you were his partner."

"That does not preclude Mr. Prosset from having had some other sideline, of which I knew nothing. Does it?" He stopped and looked at me.

"Possibly not. But—"

"There is no but about it. I don't mind telling you that the books of this firm have been examined by the police for reasons best known to themselves. They found no mention of import goods, of course. Is there any other way in which I can help you?"

"You must have noticed that things had looked up for him lately. He bought a better car, rented a cottage. Do you know why?"

"The personal, financial affairs of Mr. Prosset were hardly my concern, Mr. Sibley."

Now, the normal man faced with such questions about imports would have shown bewilderment: if he had already been questioned by the police on the subject, he might well have mentioned it; if he did not know anything about such imports he would have said how puzzling it all was, and how surprised he was that Prosset had not confided in him. He would have been prepared to discuss the subject at some length, to offer theories or explanations of his own.

I knew from Day's cold, formal answers that he was lying.

I felt sure now that there was something in my theory; that there had, in fact, been an illicit side to the business, that it probably took the form of smuggling—"importing"—and that something had gone wrong inside the organization.

I walked to the door. I had yet to play my strongest card.

"Is that all you will say, then?"

"Unless there is anything else you want."

"There is no other point of importance. Prosset wasn't lying to me. He did do import business."

Day was back again at the window, his back half turned to me. He made no movement. He went on staring out of the grimy pane at a blank wall opposite. He repeated in the same snuffly voice, "There is no import side to this business."

"What were you doing at Ockleton on the Saturday before Prosset was killed? Have you told the police you were there?"

Herbert Day turned round slowly and stared at me.

"I beg your pardon?"

"You heard. You were in the house shortly before I arrived, and you left behind you the smell of those Cyprus cigarettes you smoke."

He looked at me for ten seconds without replying. Then he passed his tongue over his lips and turned back to the window.

"Unfortunately, Mr. Prosset had a habit of borrowing cigarettes off me."

"Prosset hated your cigarettes. He often told me so."

"Unfortunately," repeated Herbert Day in a dull, monotonous tone, "Prosset had a habit of borrowing cigarettes off me."

⁓

Even a rogue can have a twinge of conscience if he thinks another person may suffer for his crime. Possibly Herbert Day, gazing out of the dirty window, was steeling himself to continue to act ruthlessly and thus to save himself. I was hardly in a position to point an accusing finger. It was only a matter of degree. During my period of panic, I had been willing to abandon my position, my income, even poor little Kate, if I could have attained the physical security of the office boy I had seen crossing the street in Palesby. I had been willing to push anybody back into the water provided only that Michael Sibley could climb on to the raft. When a man is in peril, the danger can bring out the best or the worst. It is a toss up which it will be, and nobody can prophesy for certain how the coin would fall in his own particular case.

⁓

I did not know if I was still being followed.

After the happy results which had rewarded the police on the evening they had found my knuckleduster, I thought they would certainly feel sufficiently encouraged to continue with it. I therefore assumed that I was. But it did not worry me.

I knew they had not followed me to Palesby, and for the rest it simply did not matter. Once or twice I glanced round, or paused and looked into shop windows in a rather amateurish attempt to see if anybody was on the job; but I had no success. It is probably different in the country, or even in the suburbs, but in the busy thoroughfares of central London it is almost hopeless trying to spot a shadower. I could not see anybody who looked conspicuously like a detective, but for all I knew they might have put a woman on the job. After a while, I simply got used to the idea, and hardly gave the matter a thought.

At 6:30 I telephoned Kate and arranged to meet her at the Criterion for dinner, and at 7:15 I saw her coming into the lounge.

A drizzle of rain had begun to fall, and she was wearing her pale, almost white mackintosh over a simple red dress. She wore no hat and walked in with her usual long, boyish gait; she was carrying a short, dark blue umbrella under one arm, and with one hand her bag, while the other hand was in her mackintosh pocket. Her fair hair fell straight down from her face and only curled a little at the point where it touched her shoulders. She adjusted her spectacles with one hand and began to glance diffidently about the lounge. I felt a wrench at the heart when I thought of what she might have to go through if this case took an unfortunate turn. But I was glad I had gone to the Yard that day. I was pretty well in the open now, resolved to take things as they came, to fight back as and when necessary. I was going to let them come at me with what ammunition they had, but unless they faked some evidence, which I was certain they wouldn't do, I felt that all in all there was little further they could go. They had enough against me to make them highly suspicious, but not enough to bring a charge. I felt sure they couldn't bring a charge against me, and I was more than hopeful that they would switch their attentions to Herbert Day.

"Hello, darling," I said, and kissed her. We sat down and she looked at me, her wide, generous mouth parted in a smile. She said it was ages since she had seen me.

"Two evenings and three days," I answered, and beckoned a waiter for some drinks.

"What were you doing up in Palesby?" she asked.

I had decided how to deal with this question. There was going to be no more subterfuge between Kate and me. We drank three cocktails while I told her the story of my association with Cynthia in Palesby; and of the "understanding" I had had with her until I met Kate again, and of what Cynthia knew of my true feelings for Prosset. The acid test came when I had to describe the story of Prosset and myself, for I knew in what a curious light that story showed me. I knew that if she could understand the strange effect the man had had on me she could understand anything.

We were sitting side by side on a couch against the wall, and when I had finished I said, "Well, that's all. It's quite enough, isn't it, Kate?"

I sat unhappily staring at the opposite side of the room. As I have indicated before, I am not a fluent talker, and it had sounded a horrible, sordid little story.

She put her hand on my knee and I knew by the gentle pressure that I need not have worried about Kate.

"Poor old Mike. You have been through a time, haven't you?"

"Will you forgive me?" I said, though I could hardly get the words out.

"I was a mug once, too, Mike. So it only makes it even. But you're a fool, you know."

"Of course I am."

"Promise me you'll always tell me your worries in future?"

"I promise. You'll get them all in future. The whole lot. Poor Katie!"

"Well, start now."

"What do you mean by that?"

"Tell me exactly what you feel, darling, about this case. How bad is it? How good is it?" I turned round and faced her. I could see the shadow of anxiety in her eyes. I put it to her fairly and squarely.

"They know I disliked Prosset, and that I disliked him making advances to you, and that I had a knuckleduster, and that I was with him the day before he was killed. They *think* you may have been with Prosset the evening when, in fact, you were; and that I may have quarrelled with him about you. There are grounds for suspicion, but with your evidence that I was with you around midnight when he was killed, they would not dare bring a charge. There are several things they *think*, you see, but which they can't *prove*. How fortunate that you never told them about that evening with Prosset. If they brought a charge, any counsel would knock the bottom out of it in five minutes. Why, it wouldn't get beyond the Magistrate's Court. It wouldn't even get to the Assizes."

She asked me how they came to think she was with Prosset, and why they thought Prosset and I had quarrelled. I had promised to keep nothing from her. This was the first test: I told her about the diary which Prosset kept. She sat upright. When I looked at her I saw that her face was pale; it looked strained and rigid, the skin stretched taut over the cheekbones.

"I see," she said.

"He recorded your visit, giving your name simply as 'K.' I told the Inspector there were thousands of people in London whose names begin with K. Has he tackled you about it?"

"Not yet," she replied briefly.

"He will."

"I'll go on denying I was there. He can't prove anything."

So that she should know everything, I even told her about the suit I had given away.

"Are you afraid, Mike?"

I looked into her eyes for a moment. I saw no reason why I should conceal anything any more.

"Well, I was, Katie. I was scared stiff. But I'm not now. They know most things. I don't think they'll do anything now. There's no real motive which they can definitely prove."

"Is that truly what you think?"

"I promise you that is what I truly think."

She remained thoughtful for a few moments, playing with the cocktail stick in her glass. At length she said, "Supposing they find some more evidence?"

"They won't. They can't. They'll have to make what they can

with what they've got. They've been on the wrong trail, and now they'll have to try another line. But it's a bit late."

"Mike, who do you really think did it? Have you any ideas at all?"

I told her of my smuggling theory, of the Cyprus cigarettes, and of my visit to Herbert Day and his strange, laconic attitude. It is doubtful if she was listening.

Suddenly she said, "Mike, I couldn't stand it if anything happened to you, darling. Not now. I've been so lonely all these years, Mike. There seemed to be nothing in the future for me at all. And then you came into my life, and it was like suddenly lighting a fire in a cold room which had not been lived in for a long time."

"Nothing will happen to me, sweetheart." But a voice in my brain seemed to be whispering: What if it did? How do you know nothing will happen? And a second voice was whispering: Don't be a fool. If they were going to do any thing, they would have done it by now, and you wouldn't be here. You'd be in Brixton.

"If they were going to do anything they'd have done it by now," I said aloud, "and I wouldn't be here. I'd be in Brixton."

"Mike, don't say that, even in joking."

"All right, I won't say it, even in joking."

Dinner passed quickly enough. Both Kate and I regained our good spirits. It seemed she had found in Chelsea a furnished flat which would fall vacant in early September. She had found it some weeks before, she said, but had been unwilling to talk about it because, first, it was so modern, so light, so cheap, that beside it all other flats seemed dull and expensive; and, second, because not until now was she certain that it would be available. We arranged to visit it together the following Saturday, and if I found it as wonderful as she did we would take it forthwith.

At 9:30 I took her home.

It was early, but I could hardly keep my eyes open for fatigue. She asked me if I would care to come up for a few minutes, but I said I needed my bed.

So we said good night in the hall, under the dreary yellow light where, I suppose, I had really fallen in love with her in the first place. She kissed me and said, "I love you, Mike."

"And I love you, Katie. Don't worry. Don't worry about anything at all. Everything is going to be all right."

She nodded and smiled, and went up the stairs. At the turn in the staircase she looked round and waved.

⁓

After a long period of exhaustion, the body either breaks down or takes its own steps to put itself once more in order. I overslept the following morning. I believe Ethel made some attempt to wake me, but I took no notice.

When I woke up at 9:30 I did not in the least regret the lateness of the hour. I would be late for the office, but I did not regret that either. There is a certain elasticity of hours in many newspaper offices, based upon the principle that if you expect reporters to work overtime now and again, you should try to exact a kind of automatic clocking-in system.

I did not hurry. I felt fit and refreshed. I took my time dressing, and even stopped at a café on the way to Fleet Street to have a scone and a cup of coffee. It was a glorious day, cloudless and warm, yet periodically cooled by a little wind from the north; so that, although you longed to be in the country or fishing by the side of some quiet stream or cutting through the sparkling water in a yacht, you still did not mind so very much being in London, because it was almost impossible to be depressed in such weather.

Charlie Baines was merely sarcastic when I arrived. He said it was a shame he had had to ask me to break my holiday in such lovely weather. Then, although he had not asked me much about the Prosset case until now, he said, "What's happening in that bloody case of yours? Dickson says they think it is murder."

"Quite a lot is happening," I said, "and most of it in the wrong direction. They questioned me myself like mad, two or three times. I began to feel myself figuring in one of those paragraphs which say it is understood that a man had made a statement to the police; or even, 'Mr. Sibley, who is assisting the police in their inquiries, was still at the police station at a late hour last night.' "

"What other lines are they working on, apart from you?"

"They don't exactly take me into their confidence. But if you want to know whether an arrest is likely, I should say the answer is 'No.' As far as I can see, they are lashing out in various directions hoping they'll hit on something. Personally, I think Prosset was engaged in a smuggling fiddle of some kind with his partner, but one can't write it, of course."

"Do the police suspect that?"

"I just don't know, Charlie."

Nor did I know. Despite their apparently abortive talk with Herbert Day, I did not rule out the possibility that they had received a tip from some source or other to indicate illegal activities.

As a kind of penalty for arriving late, I had to prepare for syndication to our provincial papers an article on "The Modern Holiday." Charlie Baines said they were whipping up a page on advertisements about holiday resorts and wanted something to go in the middle of the page.

"Nobody will read it," he remarked by way of encouragement.

It required a certain amount of minor research into facts and figures, and the preparation for it took the remainder of the morning and a good part of the afternoon.

At lunchtime I strolled across to the Falstaff for a pint of beer and a snack. Charlie came, too. He asked me whether I had been worried about the case.

"It's not been a question of worrying," I said. "It's simply been such a waste of time."

I saw no reason why Charlie Baines should know the truth, because, if Charlie Baines knew it, all Fleet Street would know it in twenty-four hours.

"Who's on the job, Mike? I used to know one or two of the coppers at the Yard."

When I told him, Charlie said he didn't know them.

"Well, you haven't missed much," I said ruefully.

Back at the office I began writing the article in the late afternoon. It was to be about fifteen hundred words, and once I had the facts it didn't take too long to knock it out. Still, I had started the job late in the day, and it was getting on for seven when I stepped out of the office.

I was due to be at Kate's for a meal round about 7:30. I walked towards Temple Bar, glad to be in the fresh evening air. I looked up at the sky and saw that it was still cloudless.

The previous day or two, appropriately enough, had been cloudy. But now it seemed to me that I was through the worst; and the evening sky was in tune with my mood.

I stooped to light a cigarette by the kerb. As I did so, I was conscious of a car pulling up by my side. I looked up in time to see the Sergeant open the door.

"Good evening, sir," he said. "Could you spare the time to come along to the office?"

I must have looked doubtful, for he added, "It may not take too long, sir."

"I've got an appointment," I temporized.

"With Miss Marsden?"

I nodded. "You could telephone her from the Yard, sir. I am sure she will understand."

He appeared to be in no doubt about my decision, for he leaned back and opened the rear door of the car. I stepped in. I pulled the door shut after me. The driver, a uniformed man, let the clutch in and we moved off, weaving our way through the traffic in the direction of the Embankment and the Yard.

CHAPTER 15

I sensed a different atmosphere before I had been half a minute in the Inspector's room.

He was seated at his desk in his shirtsleeves; although the window was wide open, there was a blue haze of smoke in the room which smelt unpleasant after the air outside.

His desk was covered with papers and files; his own particular ashtray was filled with matchends, and another, on the corner of the desk, had a large number of cigarette ends in it. So much I noticed, and guessed there had been some sort of conference. A man in plain clothes was seated at a small table in a corner of the room looking through a shorthand notebook. There was a chair on the opposite side of the desk to the Inspector, and another at the side of the desk.

"Good evening," I said when I came in.

He looked up and murmured, "Good evening. Sit down."

He pointed to the chair opposite him. The Sergeant, having put his hat and gloves on top of one of the filing cabinets, sat down in the chair at the side of the desk.

"I'm rather glad you sent for me," I began airily, "because I've some news for you."

Neither the Inspector nor the Sergeant said anything.

"You remember my smuggling theory?"

"What of it?" said the Inspector.

"Well, when I went down on the Saturday—I forgot to tell you this—and while I was waiting for Prosset, I noticed a smell of Cyprus cigarettes in the cottage. Herbert Day smokes Cyprus cigarettes."

"Does he?" said the Inspector.

"My theory is that Day, either alone or with somebody else, saw me arrive and walk about the garden. They could have slipped out of the back door. Perhaps they left their car some distance away. Perhaps they came back on the Sunday."

My voice died away.

"Perhaps," said the Inspector; he stared at me a moment, and began to read a file on his desk. The Sergeant said nothing at all. For a moment I felt angry at their indifference. Then the anger vanished. I felt tensed and alert. I thought: so it wasn't the end, after all. This is it, one way or another. This is the final clash. My happiness, Kate's happiness, depend on this. Two ordinary, rather insignificant people. I must keep my head. For our sakes, I must keep my head. This is England, and I have nothing to be afraid of. I will take my time. I will think out every answer. I will not be ruffled. I felt the dreadful premonition of defeat creeping upon me, but fought it back. I could not afford to go under, because Kate was involved, too. Kate, Kate, Kate, a voice inside me kept saying.

The Inspector continued to read the file for a few seconds. Once he glanced up and stared at me with his hard, merciless eyes. I stared back at him, and he dropped his eyes to the file again, frowned, and went on reading.

I saw him then for what he was, a hard-bitten career police officer; a man who had started from humble beginnings and fought his way to his present position against competition, against envy and even malice from others who were similarly struggling to the top; a man who had fought free of the rut, who was going to hold his position come what might, and even improve it. I read it in his observant, unfeeling eyes.

I could understand what I represented to him. I wasn't Michael Sibley at all. I was a threat to his reputation or another rung in the ladder to promotion; one or the other, according to whether he succeeded on this job or failed.

I was a name in the file on the Prosset case. It was a step to improved pay, a chance to win a better pension, to consolidate his position in the suburbs, perhaps to a better house, better education for his children, better clothes for his wife, and a more assured social position in general. I was of great importance to the Inspector. And one day somebody would sit in the chair I was occupying who would be of equal importance to the Sergeant; but the Sergeant could only expect reflected glory or second-hand failure from the present case.

When the Inspector spoke, he was not a patient, tolerant, good-humoured inspector with a half-wheedling, polite voice; he was only indirectly an inspector trying to fight crime for the protection of the community.

He was much more dangerous. He was fighting for himself and for his family. Primeval. Out to win the meat.

His words came suddenly and without warning, in a hard aggressive voice which he had never used before with me.

"Well, Sibley, what about stopping this boxing and coxing?"

"What do you mean?" I said. "What boxing and coxing?"

"You know bloody well what I mean. What about the truth for a change?"

"I've told you the truth, as far as I know it."

"Have you? Have you? You've told the truth as far as you know it, have you? What do I gather from that, eh? Don't you know the truth when it is the truth, eh? Eh?"

I said nothing. I wasn't going to fall for that one, to get tied up in a useless argument about the meaning of truth. I thought again: this is it; take your time; there's a chap taking it all down in shorthand in the corner of the room. Take it easy, don't be bustled.

"Let's go right back to the beginning, shall we, Sibley?"

There were no "sirs" now; it wasn't even "Mister" Sibley.

"If you like," I said indifferently. "It doesn't matter to me one way or another."

"I don't want you giving me any sauce, either, see?"

"I wasn't giving you sauce. I merely said—"

He tapped the table impatiently with his pencil. "All right, all right. Skip it. Listen to me. You and me have got to understand each other right, see? I am going to ask you some questions. How's your memory?"

"It's all right."

"I'm glad to hear it. Some people have bad memories in here, and it doesn't help, see?"

He was speaking in short, quick little bursts, his eyes fixed on my face, watching for any emotions.

"Now listen here. I'm going to ask some questions, like I told you, and if you know what's good for you you'll give the right answers at once. No more bloody dodging. The truth. It's your last chance, see?"

"What do you mean by that? That sounds like a—"

"You're here to answer questions, Sibley, not ask 'em. I'm doing the asking. You're doing the answering. Got it? All right."

He leaned back in his chair, glanced at the file, and went on in a calmer voice.

"Do you remember the first time we called on you?"

"Of course I do."

"I'm going to ask you a question about that. I want a straight answer, mind. Do you remember telling me that Miss Marsden knows no more about Prosset than you—in fact, much less?"

"Yes; I remember."

"How do you know she doesn't, eh? Were you always present when she was with him, eh? Or was she ever alone with him—say for an evening? I'm asking you that straight, and I want a straight answer, and don't forget Prosset's diary. Well?"

I had told myself I would take my time. But that wouldn't apply to this question. Once again, in my dealings with the police, the reply, to be convincing, had to come out quickly and smoothly.

"No; she was never alone with him for an evening."

The Inspector appeared to be examining his right thumbnail closely. "All right. Now tell me what you did immediately after we left you that first evening. Go on. I suppose you can remember that, can't you?"

I hesitated. I recalled that Kate had told them, on my instructions, that it was a friend at her office who had telephoned.

After a pause the Inspector said, "Memory failed you, has it? Want me to help you? All right. I'll help you. We're always anxious to help, aren't we, Sergeant? You rang up Miss Marsden."

"No, I didn't," I said quickly.

"You didn't? Make a note of that, Sergeant. In that case, I expect you'll have no objection to making a voluntary signed statement to that effect. Will you, eh?"

"Must I make a signed statement about everything I say?"

The Inspector ignored the question. He was lighting his pipe. When he had finished he leaned back and said in a mild voice to the Sergeant, "You know, Sergeant, I don't think we're being quite fair to the gentleman, do you?"

The Sergeant looked up from his interminable doodling. "Perhaps not, sir. No, perhaps we aren't, sir."

"Shall we let him into a little secret, Sergeant?"

"It might be fairer, sir."

"All right, Sibley, just to show you we're all square and above board and not pulling any quick ones, I'll tell you. We saw Miss Marsden at her place of work this afternoon."

So I was suddenly brought face to face with it, the one tremendous advantage which the police have in any interrogation: you cannot tell how much they know, and how much is bluff. And your instinct, bearing in mind all the resources they have, is inclined to credit them with knowing more than they may do.

"Tell him what Miss Marsden said, Sergeant. Tell him what she said when you asked her for the name of the office friend she said had telephoned her that evening."

"All right," I broke in, "all right, all right. I did telephone her. Why shouldn't I?"

The Inspector put on an act of exaggerated surprise. "I never said you shouldn't, did I? Did I say he shouldn't have telephoned her, Sergeant? Of course I didn't. She's your fiancée, isn't she? What's more natural?"

I waited for the next shot. It came from the Sergeant.

"Why did you lie about it? It wasn't necessary, was it?"

"The Inspector said he wanted me to keep the interview with him to myself. That's all. That's the reason. I knew he would assume I had spoken about the interview, if she told him who it was on the phone, so soon after his visit to me. I thought he might be annoyed."

"That sounds a bit complicated: was that the only reason?"

"Yes," I said. "That was the only reason."

"So you told her to tell us it was an office friend ringing her up, is that it?"

"Yes."

"What else did you tell her?" The Sergeant looked up and gazed at me thoughtfully as he spoke, his dark, Celtic eyes watching mine. "Try and remember what else you spoke about."

"Nothing much else. Just ordinary things, you know. Anyway, if you've learned so much from her, no doubt she told you that, too."

The Sergeant looked down and began doodling again. He said, "Look, it won't really pay you to make smart-alec replies, you know. The Inspector here doesn't like it."

The Inspector had been listening, rocking backwards and forwards on his chair, and now he broke in with some of his heavy, sarcastic, let's-all-be-fair stuff.

"Now, now, Sergeant, we mustn't try to catch him out, you know. Tell him what Mr. Reynolds and Mrs. White told us."

"I think you've got their statements in that folder there, sir, on your desk."

"Have I? Dear me, so I have. Here is a Mr. Reynolds, Sibley. Do you know who he is? I see you don't. He lives above Mr. Prosset's flat. He remembers the Friday before Whitsun very well. That was Mr. Prosset's last night in London, before going down and getting bumped off at Ockleton, if you'll excuse my slang. He remembers the date well, because it was his birthday, and although it was his birthday he wasn't feeling very well, and Mr. Prosset was playing his radio so loud that he thought of going down and complaining. But he didn't. Let's see what he says, shall we, Sibley?"

"If you wish."

" 'Just after one o'clock in the early morning, I still could not sleep,' says Mr. Reynolds, 'though the radio had stopped. It was very warm. I went to the window to open it wider at the bottom. I heard Mr. Prosset's door close, and looked out. I saw a girl in what appeared to be a white mackintosh walk away. She walked unsteadily. I formed the impression she had had too much to drink.' That's what Mr. Reynolds says, Sibley. Miss Marsden has a whiteish mac, hasn't she? Odd, ain't it?"

"Lots of women have white mackintoshes," I said stolidly.

"And women whose names begin with 'K'?"

"My opinion will make no difference to you."

"Doesn't he take a lot of convincing?" said the Inspector, still in his exaggeratedly mild voice. "Well, now, here's Mrs. White. I should have thought he would have known Mrs. White, wouldn't you, Sergeant, seeing he was such a good, close friend of Mr. Prosset's? Mrs. White was Mr. Prosset's charwoman, Sibley. Do you know what she found in Mr. Prosset's flat the morning after Mr. Reynolds had had such a disturbed night? Why, a lady's handkerchief. Like to hear what she says? 'I remember the name on the handkerchief was K. Marsden. I remember the name because I thought, that is a new one, meaning a new girlfriend. I put the handkerchief on the mantelpiece.' And Mr. Prosset put it in his drawer, see? And that's where we found it. He might have given it back to her, if he had lived to meet her again, mightn't he, Sibley? Anyway, he put a nice bit in his diary about a girl called K., didn't he?"

I said nothing. I sat still, staring at the reports on the Inspector's desk. I was trying to reorientate things, to think clearly and to see what was jeopardized or compromised by this new evidence.

"We wondered why Miss Marsden said in her signed statement that she had never been alone for any length of time with Mr. Prosset," said the Sergeant. "So we saw her this afternoon, like the Inspector said, see? Bearing that in mind, can you remember now what else you spoke about on the phone when you rang her up after our first visit?"

It was hopeless. It was always hopeless when two people who are trying to keep up a fabricated story are questioned separately by the police. I did not know what she had admitted or what she had not admitted. I thought that possibly they had even bluffed her into thinking that I had admitted things which I had not. I tried to think quickly but it was no good. The Inspector's voice broke in harshly on my thinking:

"Why don't you tell the truth, Sibley? Why don't you admit you told her to hush up her visit to Prosset? Eh?"

"Must I answer all these questions, or can I have legal advice?" I asked suddenly. For a second they looked at me in surprise.

"Stop boxing and coxing," shouted the Inspector, but the Sergeant interrupted him.

"Of course you need not answer these questions, if you don't wish to. But when you think of the various errors in your statement and Miss Marsden's it might make an unfortunate impression if you won't assist us to clear them up, don't you think? What do you think? But of course, you needn't answer. Of course not, if you don't want to."

"An unfortunate impression on whom?" I enquired.

"On a jury," replied the Sergeant calmly.

"On a jury? A jury?" I repeated the words stupidly.

"You heard what the Sergeant said," put in the Inspector. "On a jury. I suppose you know what a jury is, don't you? Or have you forgotten that, too?"

So I gave in on that point.

"All right. I told Miss Marsden on the phone that it would be just as well not to mention her visit to Prosset, because she might be called as a witness at the inquest."

"What's wrong with that?" said the Inspector. "Why not? It's a citizen's duty to give evidence when required."

"She is very sensitive and shy."

He looked at his wristwatch. "Do you realize it's taken us half an hour to get a couple of straight answers out of you, eh?"

I did not answer.

"Is the rest of it going to be like this?"

"Like what?" I asked patiently.

"Lies and shuttlecocking about the place. See here, Sibley, take my advice. Stop all this dodging. It's doing you no good. How many suits have you got?" he asked suddenly. I knew what he was getting at.

"Four—and two or three pairs of grey flannels and a sports jacket."

"I'm not interested in your flannels or your damned sports jacket. My question was how many suits have you got?"

"Well, four, then. As I said."

"How many had you a week ago?"

"A week ago?"

"You heard the question, didn't you? A week ago. Come on."

"Well, four. The same. Four. Why?"

The Inspector looked at the Sergeant and shrugged his shoulders with an air of hopelessness. He said, "See what I mean? Fiddling and twisting all the time. What did I say?" He turned back to me, and said in the manner of one trying to restrain his anger:

"Just think again, Sibley, will you?"

"A week ago, I had four suits," I said dully.

"Suppose I tell you that the maid at Harrington Gardens says that a week ago you had five suits and now you've only four? Where's the fifth? Or have you forgotten that, too?"

I said angrily, "I gave that suit away. I gave that fifth suit away three weeks ago, or more."

"Gave it away, did you?"

"Generous, wasn't it?" said the Sergeant.

"Must be a rich man, giving suits away, eh, Sergeant? Who did you give it to, eh? The Lord Mayor of London?"

"I gave it to a chap who asked for some money. A down and out chap."

"Did you give him anything else? Some money? Overcoat?"

"Pair of pyjamas?" said the Sergeant. "What else did you give him? What else did you give him? Why did you give it to him?"

"Or have you forgotten?" said the Inspector.

"That was all I gave him," I replied sullenly. "That and a bob and a bit of chocolate. I was sorry for him. That's why I gave it to him. It was an old suit. All worn out."

The Inspector was looking me up and down like a naturalist might gaze at a specimen in a glass case.

"Wasn't there any other reason?" asked the Inspector. "Were there any stains on it, for instance? Which you couldn't get out? Which even a cleaner couldn't be relied on to get out completely. If you did give it to him, that is."

"What do you mean, stains?" I said it to gain time.

"Bloodstains," said the Sergeant briefly. "Bloodstains. That's what the Inspector means."

I was aware that everybody in the room was sitting very still and quiet, waiting for me to say something. The Inspector had his hard, probing eyes on my face; they moved up and down, quickly and speculatively. His mouth was set in the straight, cruel lines I had noted when I first met him. I found that my brain was growing dazed. It was registering impressions, but it was not functioning logically. I heard my heart thumping in my head, felt it throbbing in my breast, my hands, even my fingers. The man at the desk in the corner shifted ever so slightly. I knew I had to say something, but I was not thinking of what to say, but rather wondering what my voice would sound like when I spoke, because I knew my throat was constricted. I was wondering what I looked like, too. All the inferiority complex of my youth returned, all the toughness acquired after years of knocking around as a reporter disappeared. I felt ugly, bespectacled, and insignificant, an ordinary pasty-faced little man surrounded by big self-confident men who did not believe anything I said.

"Bloodstains?" I asked feebly.

The tension in the room broke, and with it my own fatal concern with the impression I was making. I began to think again.

"Yes, bloodstains," snapped the Inspector. "You heard. Or didn't you? Or has something gone wonky with your hearing now?"

"That's silly. There were no bloodstains on that suit."

The Inspector leaned forward in his chair.

"Don't start telling me what's silly and what isn't, Sibley."

"Well, it is silly, because—"

He would not let me finish. He banged the desk with his fist. "Don't you tell me I'm silly!"

He pushed his chair back and came round and perched himself on the corner of the desk, and thrust his red, cleanly shaved face down into mine, so that I could see little beads of perspiration standing out on the side of his nose.

"Remember what I said when I started? About you and me understanding each other? Well, listen. I don't want any of your lip, see?"

"I wasn't giving you lip."

"Listen, I'll judge what's lip and what isn't, see? If I think you're giving me lip I may lose my temper. I'm a hot-tempered man, aren't I, Sergeant? It won't be anything official, mind you. Just something between you and me, see? Kind of man to man. If you're saucy, that is."

He put his right forefinger under my chin and tilted my face up so that he could force me to look into his eyes at close range. He stared at me angrily for about five seconds. It says much for the intimidating effect of his personality and of the surroundings that I did not knock his hand away. He said, "You wouldn't like that, would you? You wouldn't like me to smack you around, would you? Eh?"

He heaved himself off the desk and went back to his chair. I tried to reassert myself.

"I suppose you know I'll put in a report about you if you get rough. They may take some notice, as I'm a reporter."

He laughed out loud. It was the first time I had ever heard him laugh aloud.

"I've a damn good mind to bash you for that, Sibley—just man to man, of course." He laughed again. "There's two other people here, besides me, who'll say you were treated with every consideration. That's so, isn't it, Sergeant? Sibley here has been treated politely and considerately, hasn't he? He always will be, won't he? You know that."

The Sergeant looked at him, and smiled faintly.

"The prisoner was calm and composed throughout the interview, sir."

"Of course he was," said the Inspector, and looked across the room at the man in the corner.

The man in the corner said, "That's right, Inspector. He was calm and composed throughout the interview. Of course, he might bruise himself a bit if he slips up going downstairs, so to speak, sir."

The Inspector laughed a third time. "That's right, Sid. He might bruise himself a bit, if he doesn't watch out. Going downstairs, of course."

The other two joined in the laughter.

I saw myself as a small boy of about nine, pinned in a corner by three or four boys older than myself. One of these boys pulled my hair, and when I turned on him another crept up and kicked me. And now, when I rounded on him in turn, a third pulled my tie round my neck. The recreation yard was bathed in sunshine and the ten minutes' break was drawing to a close. A master came up and asked what we were doing. "Just playing, sir," they replied, and when he looked at me I repeated, "Just playing, sir."

"Do you know the Sunshine Dry Cleaners?" asked the Inspector abruptly.

"Yes, I do. In Gloucester Road. I take my things there."

"Of course you take your things there. I know that. That's not information. Do you remember going there on May 31st?"

"I don't remember the particular date."

"You ought to. It was two days after Prosset was killed. Your friend, you remember."

"Yes. I remember now. I went about some ties."

"Never mind about the ties." He leaned forward and said slowly and deliberately, "Do you remember asking them if dry-cleaning would remove bloodstains from clothes?"

"What? What did you say?" I looked at him aghast.

The Inspector turned to the Sergeant. "Am I speaking plainly, Sergeant, or is he really getting deaf?"

But I remembered then. I had gone to collect some ties which had been cleaned. I had been glancing at the evening paper while I awaited my turn to be served. I had been reading about the Hudson trunk murder. I had asked the girl, whom I knew quite well, whether bloodstains could be removed from clothes by dry-cleaners. It was perfectly true.

"Yes," I said at last.

My mouth felt dry, and the word as I spoke it had a funny cracked sound. "Yes, I remember asking them," I went on. "I had taken some ties there and was collecting them, and had been reading about the Hudson case. That's why I asked. That's the reason. The only reason."

Perhaps the Inspector did not expect such an outright admission. He looked at me rather oddly for a moment. Surprisingly, he did not pursue the point. Instead he turned over one or two pages of the dossier in front of him.

"Did you and Prosset quarrel about Miss Marsden at the cottage on your last visit?"

"No, we didn't. I've told you that."

"Well, tell us again," said the Sergeant.

"We had a political discussion."

The Inspector banged the table. "Come off it, Sibley. I wasn't born yesterday."

"Nobody would think you were," I said bitterly.

"Keep your damned impertinence to yourself. What did you quarrel about?"

"We didn't quarrel. We had a discussion."

"What about?" said the Sergeant. "Go on. Tell us about it."

It is not easy suddenly to invent a political discussion that never took place.

"Surely, you're not interested in our political discussion?"

"The Sergeant wouldn't ask you if we weren't," said the Inspector. I thought quickly.

"Well, he said there was a lot to be said for a dictatorship in certain circumstances. I disagreed. He said a dictator could get things done. I said the price one had to pay in freedom wasn't worth it. We argued about it for a good while, and got a bit heated, but it was all quite friendly in reality."

"Prosset said in his diary you quarrelled."

"I can't help that. We didn't."

The Inspector said quietly, "You bashed him, didn't you?"

"First with your knuckleduster, then with something heavier, didn't you?" said the Sergeant.

The Inspector said, "Then you spread some petrol around, and dragged a few drink bottles in to make it look as though he had got tight, and set fire to the place."

"I didn't bash him," I said heatedly. "I didn't do it. I never touched him."

"Perhaps you were provoked," suggested the Inspector.

"A jury can be very sympathetic in cases like that, especially if you quarrelled about your fiancée," said the Sergeant.

"I'm not falling for that line of talk," I said stolidly. "You can talk till the cows come home. I didn't bash him, and nobody will make me say I did."

I looked at the Inspector. His eyes were blazing.

"You're a dam' liar!"

"Thank you."

"I'll prove you're a liar, if it's the last thing I do, Sibley." He tapped the dossier. "See here, in your first statement you say you were with your fiancée between 9:30 and about one o'clock, or so, on the night Prosset was killed. Right?"

"That's right."

"I shouldn't count on that too much, you know."

"My fiancée can vouch for it."

"Yes. And I should think it may be true."

For the first time since the interrogation began I felt a slight feeling of relief. Here was something that he accepted without quibble. He believed it to be true. He had said so.

"The only thing is, Sibley, you told me at our first interview that Prosset was killed around midnight."

I looked at him in bewilderment. "So he was."

"No, he wasn't," said the Inspector.

"It said so in the papers," I said quickly. "It said so!"

"I dare say it did; but he was killed around four o'clock in the morning. For some reason the first newspaper report mentioned midnight, and the others repeated the mistake. It's not a bad idea to let a mistake like that go unaltered, see? In case somebody is preparing an alibi, as it were. See? A lot of people think I'm a bloody fool, but I'm not. Not always."

After a while, during which I said nothing for I had nothing to say, he threw his pencil on the desk.

"Well, Sibley, want to make another statement?"

"You needn't, if you don't want to," said the Sergeant, "but if you do, it can be used in evidence."

My third and final statement ran as follows:

I now wish to make a third statement, to add certain facts, and to correct errors in previous statements.

In my first statement I said I stayed with my fiancée until about one o'clock in the morning, but this was not true. I said this to avoid damaging her reputation. I really stayed with her until I left for the office the following morning.

It was at my suggestion that Miss Marsden said in her statement that I had only stayed until one o'clock. I also suggested to her that she should deny any acquaintanceship with Prosset other than she had cultivated in my presence. I did this to save her being called as a witness at the inquest.

Some three weeks prior to the date of this statement I gave an old brown suit to a down-and-out man who asked me for money. It was a pinstripe suit, frayed at the cuffs and trouser turnups. I have not seen this man since. He was about fifty, bald, dressed in dilapidated clothes, and said he had been in hospital and was an ex-service man. I do not know any more about him.

It is true that I asked a girl at the Sunshine Cleaners, Gloucester Road, whether bloodstains could be got out of clothes. I did this because I had been reading about a recent murder case in which this point occurred. I did not quarrel with Prosset the night before he was killed. We had a lively political discussion. It was really quite friendly.

I have read the above statement over, and it is true.

Michael Sibley.

⁓

At ten minutes past eleven that night I recalled the kind of words I had spoken to Charlie Baines at lunchtime that day: "Mr. Sibley, who has been assisting the police in their investigations into the murder of Mr. John Prosset at Ockleton, accompanied police officers to Scotland Yard last night, and was still there at a late hour."

Something like that; the old, old stuff. I had written it often enough about other people.

The Inspector had taken my statement out of the room an hour before. Maybe two hours. I cannot remember exactly.

When he came back, accompanied by others whom he left at the door, he said, in almost a friendly voice, "Michael Sibley, I now charge you with the murder of John Prosset at Ockleton in the early hours of May 29th, and I warn you that anything you say may be taken down and may be used in evidence."

I said, "Yes."

He turned to a uniformed sergeant who came in. "See he gets a cup of tea and some sandwiches or something."

The Inspector was no longer fighting for himself. He was no longer dangerous and ruthless. He had won. He had solved another case, at least to the satisfaction of his superior officers. He was a step nearer promotion, a better pension, a better house. It had all been very satisfactory. He could afford to relax until the next job, when the tooth-and-claw battle for better things would be resumed.

But for the moment the Inspector could permit himself to think not only of the Inspector, but even of Sibley: let Sibley be brought a cup of tea and some sandwiches! The Inspector wasn't wicked. He was merely unimaginative, insensitive, and ambitious.

CHAPTER 16

A criminal trial is in at least one respect like a war in that the aggressors, the prosecution, never begin one unless they think they have a more than reasonable chance of victory.

The accused, waiting in another part of the building for the jury's verdict, inevitably going over in his mind the points which his counsel has made for the defence, is apt to forget this.

He may feel that the judge has been unfair in his summing up. He may, and frequently does, think that his own counsel could have done better, but he consoles himself with the hope that the jury will note all the weighty points which are in his favour and which are so palpably clear to him. If he is innocent, as I was, it seems almost impossible to him that the jury could come to any other decision than the one which is correct from the standpoint of justice.

He has a fervent belief in justice, of course, and is certain that right will triumph. He sees himself being set free by the judge, possibly with a few comforting words to the effect that on the evidence no other verdict could have been arrived at; he pictures himself the centre of a circle of congratulatory friends and relations, imagines the warders, gruff but kindly, bidding him the best of luck, and his own counsel declaring how admirably he gave evidence in the box.

If it is a quick verdict, these rosy dreams may last right through the period of waiting. In my case they lasted about twenty minutes. But if the jury are slow in coming to a decision he begins to have doubts.

He becomes increasingly disquieted and petulant at the errors he thinks were made by counsel for the defence; and, reviewing once again the summing up, he acquires the beginnings of a nice sense of grievance at the unfairness of the whole thing. I remember thinking very bitterly that the judge had not stressed nearly strongly enough the fact that almost the entire evidence was circumstantial and consisted, when you examined it, of a series of unfortunate incidents aggravated by my own admitted foolishness. He should surely have pointed this out, not once, as he did, but several times. Certainly, as a judge, he knew the dangers of circumstantial evidence. He must also have known that even perfectly normal actions could be worked up by astute police officers and a clever prosecution so as to look damning.

I had had plenty of time for thinking, during the period of remands, of police court evidence, and of waiting for the next session at the Central Criminal Courts. In addition to the evidence, I had gone over in my mind the parts which everybody had played in the case, and I saw nothing to astonish me. Each had acted primarily in the ways which accorded with his own interests or feelings, regardless of other people. It had been, over and over again, a case of "Pull up the raft, Jack. I'm all right."

I was tempted to the conclusion that in ninety-nine cases out of a hundred people do react in this way if the matter is important, but eventually I modified the view. It was too sweeping and too harsh. Many people were quite prepared to keep the raft available provided that they themselves were on it; they might even extend a

helping hand to a fellow swimmer on the condition that they themselves were not only on the raft but also secured, and in no danger
of falling off it.

I had tried to save Kate from publicity. But when I saw myself
in danger I had thrown all considerations for her reputation aside
and without the slightest hesitation had stated things which could
not but be a veritable gift to scandalmongers. When Sibley was in
danger, it was Sibley who came first, last, and all the time, and it
didn't matter about Kate.

The Inspector had been less concerned with justice than with
his career and his pension. He had selected the most likely suspect,
and he had built up his case slowly, methodically, and with all the
considerable skill at his command.

I think the Inspector must have had, at the very least, certain
doubts about whether I was the guilty man. There is something
about an innocent man, as compared to a guilty man, under interrogation which an officer of his experience would have learnt to
detect. I recalled the curious look he had given me when I had so
readily admitted asking the cleaners about the bloodstains.

I do not think he was worried about justice, or the community,
or crime; he would have found it difficult to put himself emotionally in my position, and it would never have occurred to him to try
to do so. When he was, in his own way, in peril, that is to say when
his reputation was at stake, he built up a case against me using the
available evidence and all his experience to do so.

If he thought about the matter ethically, which is highly
doubtful, he no doubt considered it was his duty to act as he did. It
was not for him to decide whether I was guilty or not. That was for
the jury. All he had to do was to collect the evidence, weave it to fit
a prosecution, and convince his superior officers that he had solved
the Prosset case. Why should the Inspector worry what happened
to Sibley so long as the Inspector was on the raft?

It was not as if Sibley was a kid. Sibley was a grown man, able
to take care of himself. It was the Inspector against Sibley, man
against man, as it always had been in the fight to get on in the
world; and if Sibley went down, and if the charge was a capital
one, well, that was just too bad for Sibley, wasn't it?

Cynthia, too, had acted in her own interests. She thought she had found a man who would marry her and raise her higher in the world. It didn't matter to her if it was fair to marry for mercenary reasons. When he let her down, quite apart from any feelings of spite, she was not going to get involved in any way by hushing anything up. In fact, as I learnt during the trial, she had gone out of her way to keep the record straight: she had communicated with the police and told them all about my sudden visit to her.

Herbert Day, of course, had acted purely and simply to save his own skin, if my theory was correct. As far as he was concerned, he was quite prepared to see a man hang if only his own activities remained hidden. How far, if at all, he was involved in Prosset's death was a matter for speculation.

Only Kate had come out of it all without a blemish. There is no doubt that but for my suggestions to her she would have told the truth the whole time. She had struck at nobody, hurt nobody, had been loyal all the way along. But then Kate had not been in any particular peril. How would she have acted if she had been? Although I disliked myself for doing so, I could not help wondering.

It was strange that, as I sat there in the cells thinking of Kate, there should come to my mind the dream of the black cockatoos. I also thought, probably through an association of ideas about dark birds, of the black carrion crow or raven I had shot in a wood, and of the curious feeling I had had that I had done something forbidden by age-old lore.

I shook these thoughts off.

The jury had been out an hour now, and the strain was beginning to tell heavily. There was a circle of cigarette ends at my feet. Even the warders had given up any attempts at conversation, either between themselves or with me. Outside in the stone corridor there came the occasional tramp of feet passing by. Each time I thought it was the summons to go up into the dock once more.

Mr. John Aldwick, KC, my counsel, had done quite well, but I was now in grave doubts as to whether he had done well enough. The prosecution was in the hands of Christopher Smerton, not at that time one of the most eminent KCs, but a youngish man who was making a name for himself. I recalled with some misgivings points from his final speech to the jury.

"Let us imagine for a moment," he had said in his quiet, reasoning tones, "the state of mind of the accused man when he was first interviewed by the police. I think it is permissible to assume—and you, members of the jury, may agree with me—that even though, as I submit the evidence shows, he had on his conscience the murder of his schooltime acquaintance, his state of mind was composed. He may even have been happy and confident. The police visit would be no surprise to him, of course. On the contrary, he would have been daily, hourly, expecting it. His story was complete. He knew exactly what he was going to say. No wonder he was composed and confident!

"Remember this, ladies and gentlemen of the jury, this is no clumsy killer whom you see in the dock, no rough individual of low mentality who has blundered into the crime of murder more by ill-luck than design. You have before you an intelligent man, a reporter by profession, a man trained by his calling to be analytical and careful; a man, moreover, with more than a nodding acquaintanceship with at least the rudiments of police methods.

"I have drawn your attention to this aspect of the case, members of the jury, because in his very able address to you my friend the counsel for the defence has laid considerable stress upon the circumstantial nature of the evidence. Goodness me! What other evidence, against a man of this kind, did he expect us to produce?

"Does he seriously think that a prisoner of this man's mental calibre would leave fingerprints on chair legs for the benefit of the police? Does my friend think that the accused, after carrying out a carefully planned if somewhat crude murder, would retain bloodstained clothing in his possession? That he would allow himself to be seen, shall we say, in the neighbourhood of the crime, or that, in case somebody may have seen him, he would fail to provide himself with a suitable alibi in order that that evidence might be contested? An alibi, I may add, which he has not hesitated to produce at the expense of the reputation of the unfortunate Miss Marsden. However, in view of that position in which he found himself, why should a man guilty of murder, as the Crown submits that he is, shy at a little thing like that?

"Or maybe," said Mr. Smerton, KC, "my learned friend thought we could produce incriminating letters as in the case of the stupid Bywaters and the neurotic Mrs. Thompson? Or something of an equally convenient nature, such as an entry in the prisoner's own diary, which could be used against him? There was, indeed, an entry or two in a diary, ladies and gentlemen of the jury, but hardly of the kind which the accused could expect!"

He looked round, hitched his gown a little higher, and contin-ued, "I have said that the accused was in all probability in a happy frame of mind that memorable evening when, did he but know it, the police were already on his trail. Why not, indeed?

"The man he had, by his own confession to the witness, Miss Harrison, so cordially detested all his life, a detestation he had cun-ningly and hypocritically hidden—this man was dead. Prosset, whom he envied as a youth because Prosset was a better man than he; whom he had, I submit, grown to hate even more strongly in manhood because Prosset threatened to win from him the affections of the woman, Kate Marsden—this man was dead! He was no more. Sibley had had his revenge. It had been a long time coming, but it was complete. It was about as complete, ladies and gentlemen of the jury, as any revenge could be."

He paused for a moment to allow his words to sink in, his head bent in thought. He gave the impression that he was visualizing Prosset lying battered and lifeless. He was a master of timing, and, after just the appropriate pause, his voice rang out loudly with a note of triumph in it. "Unfortunately for the accused, as in so many horrible cases of this kind, he made one or two mistakes for which we must be grateful. He forgot that Prosset kept a diary. He tried to be too clever in concealing his visit to Ockleton on the Saturday. He tried to rid himself of a knuckleduster in a particularly stupid manner. He asked a very foolish question at the dry-cleaners. Be-lieving from a newspaper account that the murder had taken place around midnight, he arranged his first alibi, unfortunately for him-self, at that hour.

"Little knowing that evidence would be forthcoming to prove

its falsity, he advised the unfortunate Miss Marsden to make a statement denying any exclusive association with Prosset. How convenient it would have been for him if this evidence, this pointer to his jealousy, could have remained unknown! Is it difficult to imagine this reasonably intelligent prisoner saying to himself: 'They need not know about it, and they must not know about it. Without this there is no motive!'?

"What is his attitude now, when all is discovered? How, if it comes to that, did he pose to Miss Marsden? Why, as the chivalrous knight, disinterestedly advising her to lie to the police in her own interests to avoid being called as a witness at an inquest! How convenient indeed that his chivalry coincided so admirably with his own interests."

I remember looking at the jury while he made this point and noting with uneasiness a faint smile on a juryman's face.

He went on, "But let us see, members of the jury, how this pose of knightly virtue compares with the other actions of this gentleman, for by doing so we may assess what worth to place on his protestations that he acted, at least partly, in Miss Marsden's defence. What, to our utter astonishment, do we find?

"We find that although, in his alleged anxiety to save his fiancée the necessity of answering a few simple questions at an inquest, he is prepared to advise her to lie to the police, he is not averse to her declaring that he was with her until a late hour on the night of the murder—and when that alibi proves useless, he has no scruples in attempting to provide evidence that he stayed all night! A fine Sir Lancelot, indeed!

"What else do we find this very parfit gentil knight doing? We find him engaged to Miss Cynthia Harrison. You have seen Miss Harrison in the box. You have formed your own opinion of her. Perhaps your opinion coincided with mine. To me she seemed, and I say this without offence, a simple, trusting, provincial girl, who had placed her future, as she mistakenly thought, in the hands of the prisoner, Sibley. Poor, foolish child!

"Scarcely has he come to London than he renews his friendship with Miss Marsden. He finds now that he does not love Miss Harrison after all. With hardly a thought for her, he abandons her and calmly announces to her that he made a mistake. He does not love her after all. It is Miss Marsden whom he really loves all the time!"

Mr. Smerton stopped, looked at the jury, and tightened his lips.

"But now follow me closely, please. We can all make mistakes; most of us, indeed, have made grievous ones of one kind and another. Let us not blame Sibley for honestly avowing his change of heart, callous though we may think it. But what do we find? Suddenly, for some reason which may be clear to him, and which may, unfortunately for him, also be clear to you, we find him rushing up to Palesby a few days after the murder.

"Why? You have heard his explanation in the box, and an incoherent and curious story it is, of a kind of mounting remorse for which he wished to make amends. Do you believe it? Is it not more reasonable to suppose that, knowing the kind of evidence which Miss Harrison could give, he went up there, armed with his chequebook, in a desperate attempt to buy her forgiveness and possibly even her friendship? You know the high-spirited reply he justly received from her."

The accused, said Mr. Smerton, had tried to build up a picture of panic, of an innocent man filled with fear, striking blindly in all directions as he saw the net undeservedly closing around him. Was that picture in keeping with the intellectual level of the prisoner, of his past experiences, of one who had had enough dealings with the police in the course of his work not to be in awe of them? Why should he panic if he was innocent and why all the evasiveness at the beginning? But if he was guilty, as the Crown submitted, then indeed there was a reason to lose his head.

Sitting in the cells below the court, I thought: first, it is the Inspector v Sibley, and then it is Smerton v Sibley.

Smerton was only interested in my conviction because it would enhance his reputation, lead to more briefs, more publicity, a fatter income. It was not a case of Rex v Sibley. It was Smerton v Sibley, man to man, but while Smerton was only fighting for greater glory, Sibley was fighting for his life. But that would not matter to Smerton. Like the Inspector, he could throw off any doubts in his own mind, and place the whole ultimate responsibility in the hands of the jury.

As for Smerton, so for Aldwick, my counsel. I did not know how he felt about the case. I had only seen him once. Perhaps he thought me guilty; that did not matter. Even if he thought me guilty, but could have me proved innocent, he would be pleased enough. On the other hand, if he thought me innocent and they found me guilty, well, it couldn't be helped. Unlucky, but they might still say: "Aldwick put up a magnificent fight."

It was only Sibley who would really care. Sibley and Kate.

I did not like the prosecution's aspersions on Kate. Smerton accused her, in effect, of perjury, but his method was heartless.

"And now we come to the chief witness for the defence, the young woman, Kate Marsden. Her, too, you have seen in the witness box. I say seen advisedly, because it is somewhat important that you should not only have heard her, but have had an opportunity of observing her. It is important because you must decide how much weight you propose to give her evidence."

He paused and shuffled momentarily with his papers.

"I do not wish to seem unkind to a girl who has already had a great deal to go through, but I would ask you to put yourselves in her place for a moment. She is not, you may think, a glamorous type of young woman. She was not very happy at home. She was living alone. At the moment when, as it may have seemed to her, life was passing her by, the prisoner first paid serious court to her, then offered her marriage. Would it not be natural if this unfortunate young woman were prepared to do anything to defend the man for whom she may genuinely feel some affection, and whom she may well see as the one man likely to provide that fuller life to which every girl legitimately aspires?

"How much weight, I ask you again, should we attach to her evidence? How much weight to the alibi upon which the prisoner relies as the main prop of his defence?

"Much as we may wish to do more, how much reliability dare we place on that evidence if justice is to be done? She made, you will remember, two separate and somewhat different statements. In the first, she said she had never been alone for any length of time with Prosset. And that Sibley had been with her up to one o'clock on the night of the murder. In her second, however, faced with the prisoner's own third and final statement, in which he tells an entirely different story, what does she do? 'Oh,' she says, in effect, 'that is quite right. It is just as the prisoner says. My previous statement was all a mistake! I now wish to make a statement to fit in with his!' The Crown submission concerning the written and verbal evidence of this young woman is that it would be wiser to disregard it—let me put it no stronger than that—and in coming to your verdict consider as more pertinent those other aspects of the case to which I have drawn your attention. If, however, you feel that some consideration is called for, then I submit that her first statement, in which she describes Sibley as leaving her flat around one o'clock in the morning, is the one which merits your attention. He would, you will observe, members of the jury, have had time to spare to journey down to Ockleton by four o'clock, and, having established, as he hoped, his presence in London, to go about his carefully premeditated crime."

Mr. Smerton was, of course, sardonically scathing about the three separate statements which I had signed. His speech bristled with such phrases as "for reasons which we can well guess at," and "realizing the truth could no longer be concealed," and "correcting the results of a very conveniently bad memory."

Were there any reasons to believe, he asked, that the third statement which the accused had made was in essence any more truthful than the first two? Was not the whole thing a tissue of lies, and could any reliance be placed upon anything which he said in the box, on trial for his life, when he had so manifestly told a packet of lies and indulged in concealments and evasions even when he was in no immediate danger?

The jury had heard medical evidence to show that at least one of the wounds on Prosset's temple could—in fairness, he would put it no higher than that—could have been caused by a knuckleduster. Why had Sibley so hastily discarded what he would have them believe had become a cherished talisman? Let them not be astonished at the absence of blood on the knuckleduster; aluminium was the easiest thing in the world to wash clean. What had happened to that brown suit? Who was the mysterious outcast to whom the accused alleged he had given it? Did he even exist? The jury had heard of the strenuous efforts made by the police to trace the man, in work-houses, hospitals, dockland, Labour Exchanges, even in ships at sea and in highways and byways. He must repeat: did the man exist? The jury might well doubt it. They might consider this yet another of the lies with which this case was cluttered, and that in all proba-bility the incriminating and, they might think, bloodstained suit had been disposed of in a way which they might never now discover.

I thought sadly that on the films an excited old tramp would be seen, at this point, pushing his way through the crowds around the court room, muttering that he must get through; it was a matter of life and death. At first they would hold him back, but in the end he would burst in; and he would be wearing my suit. The prosecu-tion would collapse and I would be discharged without a stain on my character.

But it didn't happen like that in real life.

Actually, the old man might not be able to read properly, or if he could perhaps he only read the racing results. He might be on some remote farm helping with the crops, or he might have sold the suit for a few coppers, or he might be dead. He might even turn up later; when I was dead myself. I recalled Mr. Martin's views on cap-ital punishment. It is funny how your views change with your own position. I thought of Kate, who would have nothing to look for-ward to, not even in twenty years' time, for if I was found guilty I did not visualize a reprieve.

When I died, Kate would die, too, in a way, as Mr. Martin had said.

I had long since decided that if the verdict went against me I should consider it the end. I would brook no suspense in my heart. I would prepare my mind, so that when the final act came it would be carried through with dignity. Oddly enough, the analytical side of my mind had long since come to the conclusion that, from the point of view of pure justice, I could hardly complain if the jury found against me. I had killed Prosset in my heart and in my imagi-nation. Only a chance phrase or two had saved me from killing him in practice.

I looked at my watch. The warders stirred restlessly. It was unusual for a jury to be out so long. I could imagine the early evening
papers coming out with a bit in the Stop Press: "Sibley: jury still
out after 1 hr 40 mns."

John Aldwick had done his best. The trouble was that, due to
the strain, my early optimism had given place to pessimism. That
was why I remembered more of Smerton's points, towards the end
of the long wait, than my own man's. But my counsel had scored
some highly successful points. As I recalled them, my optimism returned slightly.

It turned out, for instance, that one person did know about the
knuckleduster: Ethel the maid. She said that one morning the post-
man had demanded some money for a letter, and I, half asleep, had
told her to take it from my trouser pocket. She had come across the
knuckleduster, but did not know what it was. The significance of
this had escaped her at the Magistrate's Court—until indeed, she
had heard, that very day, the prosecution put forward the view
that I had acquired it specially for the murder.

Her evidence went to corroborate, at least partly, my own evidence that I had had the thing a long time. More important, it
was psychologically useful as a surprise refutation of prosecution
theory.

My counsel made a good deal of smuggling, "imports," the
mysterious Max, and Prosset's unknown "friends" on the coast.
But he would not touch the Cyprus cigarette angle.

"Juries don't like us to smear a man's character who is not in
the dock," he said, shaking his head. "Makes a bad impression—
very bad impression. Judges don't like it, either. No proof, Mr. Sibley. No proof, see? All theory."

Of course, so many of the facts had been admitted that all he
could do was to try to strip them of their sinister import, and to explain them away as natural, normal things which could have happened to anybody. But some witnesses he had challenged outright;
notably Ethel, concerning when she had last seen my brown suit,
and the girl in the cleaners.

It is terrifying how significant can sound a phrase like: "Is it
possible to get bloodstains out of clothing by dry-cleaning?" I had

asked it in a normal, casual sort of voice. But nothing could remove the sinister implications when it was repeated in the cold, clinical silence of the court.

"You have said," John Aldwick, KC, asked the girl from the cleaners, "that the accused had no newspaper in his hand when he spoke to you, and that therefore his evidence was false when he ascribed his question about bloodstains to something he had just read in the paper?"

"Yes, sir."

"Yes, what? Yes, he had a paper, or yes, he hadn't?"

"He hadn't, sir."

"How long afterwards was it that the police questioned you?"

"About two or three days, sir, I think."

"You think? You can't remember that, but you do remember for certain that the accused, only one of many customers, had no newspaper in his hand?"

"Yes."

"You have a curiously selective memory, have you not?"

"I don't know what that is."

"All right. We'll leave that. Do you still wish to say that you know for absolute certain that the accused had no newspaper, or will you say, perhaps, that as far as you recall he had none?"

"No, he hadn't one, I'm sure."

"You have heard him say that he was carrying one?"

"Yes. Well, he wasn't."

"You realize the importance of the point? He says that he only asked you about bloodstains because he had been reading of a murder case in his newspaper."

"Well, he hadn't one."

"What sort of voice did he ask the question in?"

"Just an ordinary sort of voice."

"Just an ordinary sort of voice? Did he seem anxious or nervous?"

"No, sir. I don't think he did."

"Did he look pale or overwrought? Did he look like a killer with a bloodstained suit at home?"

"No, sir."

"In fact, he looked like a normal person might who had just called to collect some ties and had been reading about a murder case in which bloodstained clothes had been involved; and who might well have been asking a very natural question—considering he was in a dry-cleaners? Do you agree with all that?"

"Well, yes, I suppose he did, really. He might have done."

"What do you mean, you suppose he did, he might have done? Surely he either did or didn't? Did he look a normal person asking a normal casual question, or didn't he?"

"Well, all right—he did, if you like."

Mr. Aldwick, KC, sighed patiently.

"It's not a question of what I like, madam. A man's life is at stake."

"He looked ordinary, sir."

"But you still maintain he had no newspaper in his hand?"

"Yes, sir."

"I am going to ask you one last question. When I rose to cross-examine you, was I holding some papers in my hand or not?"

It was a clever question because the significance of it was at once apparent to the witness. Therefore very naturally she hesitated some seconds before answering.

Even had she given the correct reply, he would have pointed out how long she took to answer. As it was, she gave the wrong one.

Aldwick, of course, was on her like a ton of bricks.

"And yet you expect the jury to believe you, when you say you can remember today, many weeks after it happened, an exactly similar detail, but one of infinitely more importance?"

He did not wait for the answer, which he knew would not be forthcoming, before sitting down.

⌐

When the footsteps approached the door again, I expected them to go past, as they had so often done before, but they did not do so. We went up to the dock. I remember dropping my cigarette end at the foot of the steps and pausing a second to crush it with my shoe. Then we mounted the steps.

I stared at the various counsel with their juniors, and the counsel from other courts who had crowded in to hear the final stages of the trial, each dressed in his black gown and wig; grouped together or chattering in pairs; black gowns rustling, now whispering, occasionally smiling, nodding their heads, their noses like beaks under their wigs.

Sometimes they adjusted their gowns as a rook will flutter its feathers. Now and again they moved, black feathers twitching, beaks opening and shutting.

It was clear to me that they were not men; they were dark birds, possibly ravens. I looked in vain for the dark raven I had shot in the windy copse on the hilltop; or maybe they were rooks or carnivorous crows; or simply black cockatoos. I felt that if I banged the front of the dock they would take fright, fluttering up into the air. But I did not do so, because they would come down to earth again in two long rows, screeching and mocking and jeering, and I did not want to see Kate running the gauntlet between them.

"You all right?"

I felt one of the warders put his hand on my arm. I nodded. I tried to tell myself that it was just that I had eaten little or no lunch, but I felt certain now what the verdict would be. I had seen the dark birds again.

It was almost a relief to see the red robes of the judge.

I felt so certain of the verdict that I did not understand—indeed, I thought I had misheard—when the foreman said: "Not guilty."

Then I realized that I had heard aright. All the dark birds in the court fluttered their wings, with a great flapping of feathers, and rose in the air, beaks opening and shutting, cawing and protesting at the verdict. Flapping and flapping. A voice shouted, "Order! Silence!" But they swirled round and round, higher and higher, up into the roof of the court, flapping, dying away, growing fainter, till they disappeared.

"Take it easy."

I felt an arm at my back, supporting me. It was damned silly. Prosset would not have nearly fainted.

Just before I stepped from the dock to freedom I caught sight of Herbert Day standing near, among the spectators, waiting his turn to file out. His face above the black, dusty-looking suit was green. I saw him glance towards me. He wiped his forehead with a handkerchief. His tongue quivered along his lips in the old, snake-like movement that was characteristic of him.

I did not know if he was green with relief that an innocent man had not been hanged, or with apprehension in case the hunt should still be on. But I did know, in that second, that he killed John Prosset, either alone or with somebody else. I knew it for certain.

He need not have worried. Once the police have shot their bolt, it is the end. Nobody was ever hanged for the murder of John Prosset on May 29th at Ockleton.

~~~⁓~~~

Kate and I were married by special licence a couple of weeks after the trial, and I resigned from my office. Happily, I had always written my fiction stories under another name. I had even carried on correspondence with editors under this name, and received cheques made out for that name. Thus, there was no question of this side of my career being affected by the trial.

I decided to gamble on making a living out of fiction; and I succeeded. I bought my present cottage, up in the Cotswolds, just months before war broke out, and in fairness to Kate I changed my name. In theory, if you leave a court after a murder charge a free man, you do so without a stain on your character. In practice, some mud always sticks. Some people are always inclined to think that the jury may have been wrong. So Michael Sibley had to die, so to speak, after all, but it has proved a pleasant enough death. I may add, in passing, that from what I heard later, one reason why I was acquitted was because I am a bad talker. It seems that I made such a faltering, tongue-tied, nervous impression in the witness box that the jury thought it unlikely that a calculating murderer would have been so lacking in coolness and self-possession.

When considering whether to change my name, I also had to

bear in mind the probability that Kate and I would have children; I did not wish them to go through life known as the offspring of a man who had once been tried for murder. I am glad now that I acted as I did.

We have a fair-haired little daughter called Margaret, aged four, and a boy of nine called Francis, who is dark, like myself, but better looking than I ever was. He was born early in 1940, while I was stationed with the Royal Engineers at Aldershot, before I was posted to the Middle East. Poor Kate, the war was perhaps more trying for her than for most other wives. Having nearly lost me once, she seemed in peril of doing so again, and I think she was convinced I would not survive the hostilities.

As I write, with my typewriter in the garden, it is a glorious spring day. There is a fine view across the Cotswolds, and the sky is cloudless. At the bottom of the garden there is a little wood and a stream, and I can hear a pair of jays scolding each other. The trees are bright with that clean, crisp, green foliage peculiar to this time of year. Kate has gone down to the village on her bicycle to buy some groceries, and I am supposed to be "keeping an eye on the children," whatever that means.

The short-story market is not what it was before the war, of course, owing to the paper shortage, but I was wise enough—or perhaps I should say I was sufficiently hard-up—to maintain my connections during the war years, and I cannot complain. I have also written a couple of books, one of which may be filmed.

So I am really extraordinarily lucky.

The dark days of the past, the inferiority feelings of school days and youth, have gone; I wonder now how I ever felt as I did about Prosset. The trial, too, has receded in my mind, and the war years are fading.

The village is only ten minutes' walk away, and when Kate comes back I shall probably stroll down myself. I can see from my garden the little church steeple; opposite the church is the Crossed Keys tavern, where the beer is very reasonable, all things considered, and you can usually get a game of darts around midday or in the evenings.

I usually have a game with George Farrow, if he is about. He is a heavily built man, with a large moustache and dark, ox-like eyes. Thanks to him, I live a blameless life: my gun licence is always in order, my radio and car licences are renewed on the exact dates required of me, I have a dog licence for the spaniel, and I never under any circumstances whatever ride a bicycle "without a red rear light or reflector"; for, as PC Farrow says, once you've got a conviction, you're a marked man for the rest of your life. You've got a police record.

"Of course, if you're convicted of murder," I once said to him, "I suppose the rest of your life hardly matters."

He turned his heavy eyes on me in astonishment. "Murder, sir? Nobody's ever been accused of murder around these parts."

"They haven't?"

"Not since I've been here, they haven't. Nor ever will be, I hope."

"Nor ever will be, I hope," I repeated fervently.

"They're friendly, steady folks around here. They'd no more think of doing a murder than you would, sir."

"They wouldn't?"

"No, sir."

"No more than I would?"

"No, sir, they wouldn't. That's a fact."

I looked round the bar, at the friendly faces, at all the evidence of good fellowship and good humour, of countryside self-reliance and tolerance.

PC George Farrow was classing me with all that. I felt a curious upsurge of spirits, almost of exultation, as of one who had somehow made good.

"Let's have another round," I said suddenly.

"Celebrating something, sir?"

I nodded. "Emancipation." I laughed at the puzzled look on his face. But I could hardly explain, since I hardly knew myself what I meant. I only knew that it was somehow very important to me.

Also by John Bingham
With a new introduction by his protégé, John le Carré

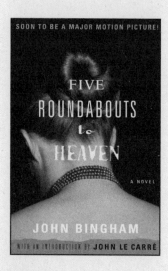

When Peter Harding and Philip Bartels meet up again in the French countryside of their youth, the history—and the dark secrets it holds—is still there. The two share more than a friendship: stuck in a disenchanted marriage to his distant wife, Philip meets and falls in love with the graceful Lorna Dickson. Philip decides to poison his wife; however, unbeknownst to him, Peter and Lorna have fallen in love with each other. A chilling psychological study of how murder can so easily enter the minds of ordinary people.

When gentle old Lucy Dawson was murdered on holiday in Italy, criminologist James Compton began to ask questions. As his investigation into the lady's former residence unfolds, Compton finds a sinister net closing in around him: curious phone calls, frightening invasions of privacy and threats, as the hunter slowly becomes the hunted. . . .

Available wherever books are sold or at www.simonsays.com